Praise for
Kristin von Kreisler

Earnest

"*Earnest* lives up to his name. He is a dog who earnestly desires only one thing, to keep his family intact. Kristin von Kreisler deftly spins a tale of human failings and canine devotion that will have the reader reaching for the tissues."
—**Susan Wilson,** *New York Times* Bestselling Author of
One Good Dog and *The Dog Who Saved Me*

"Kristin von Kreisler captures the emotional intelligence of Earnest, a dog who provides much needed guidance to a human couple spiraling into catastrophe. When Anna and Jeff both feel the depth of betrayal, only the steady loyalty and un-wavering love of Earnest can save them."
—**Jacqueline Sheehan,** *New York Times* Bestselling Author
of *The Center of the World, Lost & Found,* and *Now & Then*

"Be prepared to fall in love with Earnest, a yellow Labrador re-triever adopted from a shelter who teaches his humans a thing or two about resilience, loyalty, and forgiveness. Von Kreisler goes beyond depicting Earnest as a catalyst and instead deftly portrays him as an actual character with a point of view and feelings. A truly charming story sure to please dog lovers everywhere."
—**Amy Hill Hearth,** *New York Times* Bestselling Author of
Miss Dreamsville and the Lost Heiress of Collier County
and *Having Our Say*

"If you've ever wondered whether animals were smarter than humans, Kristin von Kreisler's *Earnest* is the book for you. This charming tale (pun intended!) leads us through the kind of conflict real families face and shows us, through the wisdom of a dog, what matters most in life."
—**Nancy Thayer,** *New York Times* Bestselling Author
of *The Guest Cottage*

"Kristin von Kreisler's deep understanding of both people and dogs shines through in her compelling new novel, *Earnest*. Animal lovers will fall for the yellow Lab who saves his favorite humans from heartbreak. I had tears in my eyes less than half an hour into it! But the good kind of tears!"

—Jeffrey Moussaieff Masson, *New York Times* Bestselling Author of *Beasts: What Animals Can Teach Us About the Origins of Good and Evil*

An Unexpected Grace

"Kristin von Kreisler is an acute observer of dogs and a fine novelist. Her novel about the healing powers of dogs is enchanting. I was captivated from page one and I learned a great deal from this heartwarming, thrilling book."

—Jeffrey Moussaieff Masson

"Kristin von Kreisler weaves a modern tale that seems at first to be a relentless search to understand a workplace shooting. But wait; von Kreisler takes us deeper into the powerful connections between humans and animals who are wounded by the incomprehensible and bound together by love."

—Jacqueline Sheehan

"In *An Unexpected Grace,* Kristin von Kreisler deftly tackles the age-old question of how to make sense of tragedy. When Lila's world falls apart, she learns that hope can come from unexpected places. With vivid descriptions and true-to-life characters, von Kreisler proves it's possible to heal, trust again and love deeper than before. A heartwarming story on the healing power of dogs."

—Susy Flory, *New York Times* best-selling author of *Thunder Dog*

"Kristin Von Kreisler understands the unique bond between survivors of trauma in this captivating novel of a woman and a dog learning to trust each other in a threatening world. You have to root for them as the damaged heroines of *An Unexpected Grace,* woman and dog, find the healing power of trust and love in each other."

—Susan Wilson

"A sweet and charming story of the tender, patient, and forgiving nature of our canine friends, Kristin von Kreisler's *An Unexpected Grace* will warm the heart of anyone who has ever loved a dog."

—Amy Hill Hearth

"A heartwarming and beautifully written tale about trust and compassion. Grace provides the story with a wonderful balance of humor as her heroine, Lila, poignantly brings the reader into her frame of mind. Dog lovers will be particularly enthralled with the novel."

—*RT Book Reviews,* 4 Stars

"A terrific, uplifting novel . . . Von Kreisler deftly shows how the love between a dog and a person can prove transformative."

—*Modern Dog Magazine*

"Lively narrative, detailed descriptions and engaging scenarios . . . A soulful dog serves as a sobering inspiration and comfort pillow—and a poignant relief valve for the reader."

—*Seattle Kennel Club*

"*An Unexpected Grace* is a poignant contemporary novel . . . Readers will appreciate Lila and Grace helping each other heal."

—*Midwest Book Reviews*

"Devoted dog parents will read *An Unexpected Grace* and relate to the deep bond and heartfelt connection that can develop between the human and canine species. Von Kreisler's passion for dogs is the underlying theme throughout the book and easily relatable by dog lovers wanting a happy ending. For that reason you will enjoy the book."

—*Seattle P. I.*

"A heartstrings-tugging novel with many a heart-stopping incident, the story of a beautiful dog in search of a loving home. Basically, it's a love story. Read it, if you can, in the sunshine."

—*Hudson Valley News*

"In Kristin von Kreisler's heartfelt novel *An Unexpected Grace,* a woman and a dog rescue each other from violent pasts. This is a story that underlines the irrevocable bond between dog and man—or, in this case, between dog and woman."

—*WV Gazette*

EARNEST

EARNEST

KRISTIN VON KREISLER

KENSINGTON BOOKS
www.kensingtonbooks.com

KENSINGTON BOOKS are published by

Kensington Publishing Corp.
119 West 40th Street
New York, NY 10018

All Kensington titles, imprints, and distributed lines are available at special quantity discounts for bulk purchases for sales promotion, premiums, fund-raising, educational, or institutional use.

Special book excerpts or customized printings can also be created to fit specific needs. For details, write or phone the office of the Kensington Sales Manager: Kensington Publishing Corp., 119 West 40th Street, New York, NY 10018. Attn. Sales Department. Phone: 1-800-221-2647.

Kensington and the K logo Reg. U.S. Pat. & TM Off.

eISBN-13: 978-1-4967-0044-5
eISBN-10: 1-4967-0044-9
First Kensington Electronic Edition: February 2016

ISBN-13: 978-1-4967-0043-8
ISBN-10: 1-4967-0043-0
First Kensington Trade Paperback Printing: February 2016

10 9 8 7 6 5 4 3 2 1

Printed in the United States of America

In memory of Hosea and Nellie Warren.
And for their daughter Sue Warren Todd.
They have all been very dear to me.

PROLOGUE

⌾

Seattle's Second Chance Shelter smelled of damp fur and dog breath. Frantic barks and whines pierced the air and assaulted Anna's ears. She shrank back from the desperation that hung in the air like mist. All the sad eyes begging for a home. The furry foreheads rumpled with anxiety. Anna's tender heart slid to her feet.

"We shouldn't have come here," she shouted to her boyfriend, Jeff.

"You wanted to check out the dogs," he said.

Anna was clutching the Second Chance flyer she'd found that morning on Jeff's windshield. Coming here had seemed the best way to goad themselves into action after weeks of talk about adopting a dog. But now, engulfed by the dogs' distress, Anna wasn't so sure.

"We could have looked for a dog on Petfinder," she said. In their rented condo, they could have studied photos on the computer screen.

"You can tell a lot more if you see a dog in person," Jeff said.

"Yes, but I want to take all these dogs home."

"We can only afford to care for one."

"Why do you have to be so practical?" Anna smiled, revealing lovely teeth.

She was the pretty flower child, the impulsive one. If she had her way, by evening their condo would be an orphanage for these homeless dogs—somehow she and Jeff would manage their upkeep. But he was innately cautious and responsible. He'd adopt only if he could provide the best vet care and premium kibble.

Not that being reliable was bad. Actually, Anna liked that quality in Jeff. After living with him the last two years, she'd concluded it would make him a good father—and that was partly why she'd suggested getting a dog. Jeff wanted a buddy, but Anna secretly wanted a trial run at parenting. Maybe a dog would nudge Jeff closer to marriage, which they'd discussed but always as something in their vague and rosy future. Now they were both almost thirty-five, and it was time.

In enclosures lined up along the aisle, most of the dogs were making their case for adoption. Some ran to their gate and pleaded their cause with eager yips. Others stood back, polite, and demonstrated good behavior. Or they looked adorable, as did two matching Chihuahuas, whose whimpers urged, clear as crystal, *Take us home with you! See how lovable we are!*

"I'd be afraid of stepping on them." Jeff steered Anna to the next run, which housed a Great Dane mutt the size of an adolescent moose. On massive hind legs, he leapt up and pressed his huge paws on the gate. Jeff shook his head. "Not a condo dog."

He and Anna looked at a dog of unknown lineage with a bald tail and fur the color of a napkin that had wiped one too many mouths. When she curled her lip, she informed them of her resentment at being confined.

"What if no one adopts her?" Anna asked.

"Don't worry. It's a no-kill shelter." Jeff reached for Anna's hand and pulled her to the last gate. "Look at him!"

A Labrador retriever bounded toward them, wagging his tail so hard that he wagged his whole back end. He weighed about eighty pounds, and his personal infinitive might have been "to galumph," but he didn't seem to be the type of dog who'd stomp through flower beds or knock over lamps with his tail. He looked up at Anna and Jeff with big brown eyes, which politely asked, *Please, will you take me home and love me?* He pressed his side against the gate to get as close as he could to them, and his body begged, *Pet me! Oh, please!*

"Whatcha doing, boy?" When Jeff reached through the gate's bars, the dog nuzzled his hand. He'd cornered the market on wholesome. He could have been a Cub Scout mascot or costarred in movies with a freckle-faced kid.

Anna's eyes brightened. "He's a love bug."

"He's a purebred Lab. The real deal. Why would someone give him up?"

A laminated sign on the dog's gate explained that he'd been tied to the shelter's doorknob with a note under his collar. He was a healthy three-year-old, and his name was Moonbeam, of all the preposterous things. His slightly wavy fur looked like it intended to curl but never got around to it, and it was the color of wheat in candlelight, though his ears had a touch of biscuit beige. His nose looked like a licorice gumdrop, his muzzle was softly rounded, and his ears were upside-down isosceles triangles. When Moonbeam blinked, any woman in her right mind would have envied his thick, dark lashes.

His confident eyes were what grabbed Anna. Anyone could see that behind them lived a wise old soul. At the same time, though, his eyes were tinged with sadness, probably because he'd just lost his home and family. Anna wanted to bake him gourmet peanut butter cookies, buy him squeaky toys, and mother him. "Let's adopt him!" she said.

"He wouldn't be too big for our condo?" It was only nine hundred square feet, and their barbecue grill and potted tomato plants crowded the small deck. A large dog could cross the backyard in ten steps.

"It's not like he'd be locked up at home all the time. He could come to work with me every day." Anna imagined him napping under her flower shop's counter, surrounded by buckets of mums.

"What if he scares your customers?" Jeff asked.

"How could they not love him?"

Through the bars, Jeff held out his hand to Moonbeam. "Can you shake?"

A wheat-colored paw plopped onto Jeff's palm.

"Sit?"

With impeccable cooperation, Moonbeam sank down on his haunches and gazed up at Jeff with adoring eyes that said as plainly as anyone ever said anything, *I will be exemplary. I want to be your dog.*

"He's trying to do the right thing. He's so earnest," Jeff said.

"'Earnest' would be a good name. Far better than 'Moonbeam.'"

Jeff squatted down, eye to eye with Earnest. "Maybe we should think about him for a day or two before we decide."

"Someone else would adopt him," Anna said.

Jeff stroked Earnest's soft ears. "You're too good to pass up, aren't you?"

Absolutely! agreed Earnest's tail wags.

Anna walked Earnest outside while Jeff filled out the adoption form. Owner: *Jeff Egan.* Occupation: *Architect.* Address: *1735-B Wood Avenue, Gamble Island, Washington.* If you rent, name of landlord: *David Gray.* Who will be responsible for vet bills? *I will.* Jeff checked "yes" that Earnest would have a fenced yard and sleep inside at night. Finally, Jeff paid the fee with his credit card and hurried to find Anna and Earnest.

In the backseat of Jeff's Honda, Earnest stared out the window at Seattle's skyline. He gazed at the Space Needle and seemed to note with interest Safeco and CenturyLink Fields. Looking angelic, he did not smudge the window with his nose, and he did not paw or drool on the upholstery. On the half-hour ferry to his new home, he curled into a trusting ball and slept as if the Honda had been his bed forever.

Anna and Jeff joked that his glomming onto them might be a sign he was part barnacle, and they discussed people's tendency to adopt dogs that looked like themselves. Jeff pointed out that Earnest's fur wasn't so different from Anna's ash-blonde hair, which was cut between a shag and a pixie. She said that behind Jeff's horn-rimmed glasses, his expressive brown eyes were like Earnest's, and Jeff's short hair, though dark and slightly thin on top, had Earnest's hint of waves.

Anna pictured Earnest sprawled on their deck among the tomato plants, a paw over his eyes to shade them from the sun. Or leaping into gold maple leaves piled along the sidewalk in the fall and crunching them with his paws. She and Jeff would take him on hikes in the Hoh Rain Forest and teach him to fetch a Frisbee. They'd bathe him in their tub and invite him to sleep on their bed.

"We'll be a pack of three," Anna said. *A family.*

CHAPTER 1

Anna Sullivan pulled up in front of her beloved Victorian house. Well, it wasn't really hers. She rented it with two other business owners, and they were saving up to buy it, but in her heart she owned it. As on every Monday morning, her ancient van was loaded with wholesale flowers and plants from Seattle, and Anna would have to lug them into Plant Parenthood, her shop on the first floor. Earnest leapt to the street, happy that he'd had a ferry ride, as Anna lifted two buckets of roses.

"Good morning, dear house," she whispered as she and Earnest started down the sidewalk.

Good morning, dear Anna, she imagined the house whisper back. In Anna's mind the house winked for good measure and added, *Enjoy this beautiful autumn day!* A crow flew across the house's half-acre front lawn and landed on the white porch railing.

In a historic town of old clapboard buildings, the house stood on the main street like a dignified dowager. Built by Gamble's first attorney, she had two stories and lots of gingerbread. Her fourth owner had been Anna's grandmother, with whom Anna had lived as a child until Grammy died and the house was sold. When Anna talked with the house, she always responded as Anna imagined Grammy might have. In Anna's mind, Grammy and the house were one and the same.

Grammy's spirit lingered in the turret, redbrick chimney, old wavy-glass bay windows, and flower boxes of lobelia and geraniums. She was in the sky-blue paint and the white curlicue brackets adjoining posts along the front porch. Her humor showed in the lion's puzzled face embossed on the front doorknob, and in the doorbell, which was the round black tongue of a small brass bear. Grammy's love of football remained in the porch's beadboard ceiling hook, from which she'd hung a giant Huskies banner on University of Washington game days.

Though willowy, Anna was strong, but even so, carrying buckets of sloshing water into the house took effort. She set them down to give her hands a break before hoisting the roses up the porch steps. As her loyal protector, Earnest plopped down by her red ballet flats while she flexed her fingers and smoothed down the little tufts that sometimes appeared in her hair whether she liked them or not. As she picked up the buckets again, she heard from across Rainier Avenue, "Hey, Anna! Wait up!"

Waving to her were Lauren, who owned the beauty salon and used bookstore on the house's second floor, and Joy, whose gift shop was on the first floor at the back. Though old friends, the two women were opposites. Six foot two, brunette, and ruler thin, Lauren was like a shy giraffe, but put a pair of styling scissors in her hand, and she became a confident lion. Joy was five feet tall, bleached blonde, plump, and feisty. When business was slow, she worked on *Wild Savage Love,* a bodice-ripper novel featuring her ex-husband as the villain.

Joy stopped to look at pastries in the Sweet Time Bakery's window, but Lauren dodged a cab speeding to the ferry and jaywalked across the street. At the end of the sidewalk, she slipped copies of her September poem into a Plexiglas box attached to a metal pole, which she called her community poetry post. As she reached Anna, Earnest got up and gave her a proper sniff.

"I wish I could help you unload, but I've got a full foil in ten minutes," Lauren said.

"No problem. I'll manage," Anna said.

"I'm desperate for coffee. Want a cup?"

"Sure."

Overhearing them, Joy followed, her face flushed, a giant canvas tote bag in her arms. "Be careful with our Mr. Coffee. He's started rebelling. You have to smack him on the lid to get him to turn on his light."

"I guess we need a new one." Lauren knitted her eyebrows.

"I'll check out New to You this afternoon," Anna offered.

"I don't want to use some stranger's nasty old used Mr. Coffee," Joy said.

"We have to save every penny for the house," Anna said.

"If Anna can't find a nice one, I'll go to Macy's. Deal?" Lauren asked Joy.

"Okay," Joy said.

But Anna was reluctant. The sooner they saved money, the sooner the house might be theirs.

At their monthly finance meetings, they combed their bank accounts like misers and plotted how to approach their landlady, Mrs. Blackmore, whom they called Mrs. Scroogemore. She should be glad for them to take the house off her hands since she couldn't bother with repairs. In the kitchen, the lights flickered, and you had to be an expert at wielding a plumber's friend to coax the sink to drain. But once Mrs. Scroogemore learned of the women's interest in the house, she'd milk them for every cent they had.

"I've got to rush. See you at lunch." Lauren ran up the porch steps on her size-eleven feet, her feather boa streaming behind her long vintage skirt. She disappeared into the house.

"Let me help you," Joy offered.

"Thanks, but you're carrying enough." Anna grabbed the handles of her buckets and hauled them through the front door.

Joy turned left and went to her gift shop. Anna turned right, passed the oak newel post, and walked down the hall. As Earnest followed, the stained glass windows cast red and gold rectangles on his fur. Anna wiped her feet on her straw welcome mat and opened Plant Parenthood's door—and the fresh smell of flowers and plants hit her like a gentle breeze. In one breath, her morning changed from fall to spring.

When Earnest stepped inside, he changed too—from a dog to the guardian of Anna's magic kingdom. She liked to think that gnomes, wood nymphs, sprites, and trolls would be at home in her shop. With love and care, she'd transformed what had been Grammy's adjoining dining room and parlor into a fantasy forest of plants and flowers. You could imagine a unicorn disappearing into the greenery, or Tinker Bell flying through the air and landing on a rose bud.

In the center of the rooms were old tables and chests that Anna had rescued from the New to You Shop and she and Jeff had painted Chinese red, Prussian blue, and emerald green. On the wood surfaces, she'd set Buddhas, folk-art angels, carved animals, and brightly glazed pots of orchids and African violets. Around the bay windows were her larger plants: *Ficus benjaminas,* schefferas, philodendrons, tree ferns, and palms.

Edgar, her rubber plant, who was not for sale, stood like a sentinel in the corner next to Constance, her favorite feathery fern, who resided on her own oak pedestal. Anna had filled the windowsills with colored glass vases of flowers, jars of Earnest's dog biscuits, and pots of small carnivorous plants, such as bladderworts and Venus flytraps, which Tommy, a neighborhood kid, stopped by to check for captured insects.

Anna set the roses in her refrigerator, and she and Earnest went back for more flowers and plants. Eight trips later, the lilies, freesia, and carnations were cooling with the roses, and the heartier mums and sunflowers were in buckets on the floor. With orange-handled scissors, Anna snipped the rubber bands around each bunch of blossoms and spread them out to give them breathing room.

His escort duty over, Earnest settled down to nap on his round green pillow, which looked like a giant lily pad. Soon he was on his back, snoring, with his paws in the air. If someone set a slab of wood on them, he could have been a bridge table.

At her workspace behind the counter, Anna started on voice-mail orders that customers had left yesterday. Monday morning was her busiest time. She placed hydrangeas and irises in a vase for Mr. Holloway because they were his wife's favorites and she was having surgery. To boost Mrs. Holloway's spirit, Anna added four free irises, though Jeff, who'd said her shop was not a charity, might disapprove.

As she was tying purple ribbon around the vase, Earnest got up and paced the room. "What's the matter, Sweetie?" Anna asked as a man came in, wearing sunglasses, tasseled loafers, and a polo shirt with a tiny alligator on his well-toned pec.

"I meant 'Sweetie' as my dog, not you," she said, smiling.

The man didn't look at her. He shuffled to her counter, his gaze downcast, and fingered his house and Porsche keys like worry beads. As Earnest came over and checked him out, the man said, "Er . . ."

Finally, he managed, "I want something special for my wife. Um . . . she just got on our neighborhood watch committee."

So. Your neighborhood watch committee! Not exactly the pinnacle of every woman's dreams. Anna read the signals. She'd dealt with so many guilty husbands that she'd designed the Virtue Special, a bouquet for them to give their wives to mend their marital fence.

"How about some beautiful lilies? Women love them," she said.

"Um . . . sure. That sounds okay."

"Here. I'll show you." As Earnest returned to pacing, Anna went to the refrigerator and pulled out her bucket of lilies, which radiated innocence. "I like to mix these with baby's breath." She pointed out the clouds of equally innocent tiny white flowers in their bucket on the floor. "If you'd like to wait, I can have the arrangement ready in a few minutes."

"Good." He walked to the window and looked out at the sunny day. "Do you smell smoke?"

Anna sniffed. "It's Mr. Webster down the block. He refuses to pay for garbage pickup so he's always burning trash. We've gotten used to it."

She counted out a dozen lilies, snipped their stems, and worked puffs of baby's breath out of a clump. *Thank goodness Jeff would never need a Virtue Special. He'd never betray me,* she thought.

"Do you want a gold or silver ribbon?" she asked the man. When he didn't answer, she looked up. He must have sneaked off to call his girlfriend.

Anna was filling a glass vase with water when Earnest walked out of the shop and crossed the hall to the kitchen door. He sniffed the crack below it as if someone were sautéing sirloin on the stove.

That's odd. Earnest sticks to me like lint. "It's too soon for lunch, sweet boy," Anna called. He could be a promiscuous glutton.

Ignoring her, he sat in front of the door and stared at the knob. His gaze seemed to will it to turn and let him inside.

"Earnest, you had a big breakfast. Come back." Anna put a lily into the vase.

Earnest didn't budge.

"Maybe he needs an obedience class." The man walked back into the shop.

No, Earnest was thinking something, and he seemed to be

getting worked up. He whimpered and insisted in no uncertain terms, *I want in the kitchen.*

"Just a minute, Earnest. Let me finish this first."

He whined again, louder and more forcefully. *This is important! I want in the kitchen! NOW!*

Earnest scratched the door, his first-ever destructive act and so out of character that Anna became alarmed. She set a lily on the counter and told the man, "I'll be back in a second."

As she hurried into the hall, she demanded, "So what's the *matter,* Earnest?!"

His barks were almost loud enough to shake the window-panes. *HURRY! HURRY! NOW!* He clawed deep, sweeping scratches into the door.

When Anna opened it, black smoke billowed in her face. She coughed like she'd never breathe again. Her eyes watered so she could hardly see, but she made out flames crackling across the kitchen. The red-checked café curtains were burning. So was the cabinet that held the fire extinguisher.

As Anna blinked against the smoke, she screamed, "Joy! Lauren! Fire! Fire! Everybody get out of the house." She slammed the kitchen door and herded Earnest to her shop. The man was gone. She grabbed her purse and slammed her own door. As she groped down the hall, all she could see was smoke.

Earnest took her wrist in his mouth and led her, slow and steady, toward the porch. Choking, she shielded her face with her hand. Her eyes stung, and tears streamed down her cheeks. Again she called to Lauren and Joy. *What happened to the guilty husband?*

Anna was the first to reach the front door. When Earnest got her to the porch, she gulped fresh air and coughed. Her hands shook as she grabbed her phone and punched 911. "Good boy, Earnest!" she managed.

She leaned down to thank him for getting her out, but he was gone. She turned around. Earnest was running back toward the front door.

Anna lunged to grab him, but he wriggled away and disappeared into the house, surely to find Lauren and Joy. "Oh, no! Earnest! Earnest, come back!"

"Nisqually County 911. What emergency are you reporting?" asked the dispatcher.

Earnest vanished in undulating waves of thick black smoke.

CHAPTER 2

Jeff looked around the meeting room of Gamble's city hall. The room shouted "institution." It could have been a prison cafeteria. The walls were pea-soup green; the linoleum, speckled gray; the ceiling's acoustical tiles, sickly off-white. Sunlight worked its way around the edges of the closed venetian blinds that covered the only window.

Worse than the cheerless surroundings was the palpable tension left over from earlier meetings. It seemed to hang around like a bad-tempered ghost. *You could almost serve up the tension on a platter,* Jeff thought. He didn't like stress, but who in this world could escape it?

Though he considered himself as strong and tough as most men, he also wasn't wild about unpredictable situations that were crucial to his career. This morning's meeting with the Gamble city planner assigned to Jeff's new project, Cedar Place, could lead to success, but it could also end in failure and spin his work out of control—*though no one has much control over anything.* No matter who you were, control was an illusion.

Especially when dealing with Gamble's staff, who were notorious for being erratic. The planner assigned to Jeff's project could be a bastard or an angel, and he'd never know which till the meeting started and he faced a gantlet or a marshmallow.

And the planner had all the power over whether or not Jeff got his permits. That was the hardest part for him to take. He'd worked hard on the architectural drawings, tried to anticipate objections to the project, and put his creative ducks in a row. Though he was as prepared as possible, anything could come out of left field and derail his effort. Today was uncertain.

Jeff brushed Earnest's fur off his gray Dockers. He'd run the sticky roller over them this morning, but Earnest had an endless supply. *Small price to pay for the world's greatest dog,* Jeff thought as he opened his briefcase next to the stacks of papers he'd set down on the table.

As required for a building proposal, he'd brought seven copies of all drawings and supporting documents, including the demolition and building permit applications and the plans for the site, landscape, construction, engineering, and storm drainage. He pulled sets of elevation drawings out of cardboard tubes and wrestled with the papers' curling edges, which were the bane of an architect's existence.

Jeff glanced at his elevation drawing of the building's front. Cedar Place was meant for commercial use. He'd had a hell of a time dissuading his client from the hard-edged box she'd wanted to rent to Shell Inc. for a chain drugstore, which Gamble's citizens would have hated. Now instead of the box, Cedar Place would have two stories with alcoves, decks, and dormers. The roof would have interesting angles, and classic cedar shingles would cover the exterior walls. There would be as many skylights and multi-paned windows as the city's code allowed. Though the building would be new, its Pacific Northwest architectural style would blend in with historic structures around it.

Jeff had put his heart and soul into the design, and he hoped the building would become a destination spot. Its nine spaces would go to small restaurants and shops that would draw in tourists, for a needed boost to Gamble's economy. Then there was the large space that Jeff and his client had invited the island's Kids Discovery Museum to move into at a highly discounted rent, and as of now the board was ecstatic about it. Jeff's design would improve many lives.

Including his. He smiled to himself. For months he'd wanted to marry Anna and start a family. The raise he expected to get from carrying out the project would make him financially stable enough to propose.

As Jeff straightened his papers into orderly piles, two fire engines and a medic unit rumbled down the street with sirens blaring. Surely old Mr. Webster was beating back flames at his fire pit in his baggy pants and undershirt again. Last spring he'd burned six months of *Gamble Criers* at once, and ashes had fluttered over his head like bats and brought the neighbors running—for the umpteenth time.

The sirens added to Jeff's tension. He mopped his neck with the Valentine's Day handkerchief Anna had embroidered with hearts and their initials. As he took off his glasses and cleaned the lenses, anxiety nibbled his stomach.

Here we go.

Bristling with self-importance, the man Jeff assumed was the planner assigned to Cedar Place strode into the meeting room. He was maybe forty, dark haired with a broad flat nose. He wore rings on all his stubby fingers, and hair sprouted from his knuckles. The word "gorilla" came to mind. His beard was a jungle of hair that a flea would need a machete to hack through. His eyebrows looked like the clumps of moss that Earnest liked to bite.

"Randy Grabowski." He extended a clammy hand.

"Jeff Egan."

"I've been looking at your preliminary plans. You're ready to submit a formal application?"

"As you can see." Jeff gestured toward his papers. If you spread them out in a single layer, they'd cover half a basketball court.

Metal chair legs scraped on linoleum. Grabowski sat across the table from Jeff and sniffed with what seemed like disdain. Jeff prepared himself not to like him. Condescension was no way to start a meeting.

Grabowski said, "I'm sure you realize we can't guarantee permits."

"Every architect knows that." Jeff's smile shone at about three watts.

"We'll study your application and go from there. As you also know, our concern is that your building complies with the city's master plan."

"The property's zoned for commercial development. That's exactly what we're trying to do," Jeff said.

Grabowski smoothed his hand over his beard—it had to be infested at least with lice, but roaches could be hiding there. "You're planning nine small units and one large one, right?"

"Yes."

"Anybody lined up for them yet?"

"Not specifically for the small, though we've got some ideas. We'd like for Cedar Place to draw people to galleries, nice shops, places to eat," Jeff said.

"What about the big space?"

"My client agreed to let a nonprofit have it for below market rent. We're talking with people at the KiDiMu. If that falls through, we'll ask the senior center."

Jeff had expected this revelation to sweeten Grabowski's attitude, because planners were supposed to love community support. But all he got was, "So the KiDiMu's not a done deal?"

"The plan's in the pipeline. Nothing's signed yet."

"Let us know when you've got a firm commitment," Grabowski said with the animation of concrete.

He picked up the elevation drawing of the building's front and barely looked at it. "You'll have to run this project by the planning commission. They don't support everything that comes in."

How well I know.

"Most people have a preliminary talk off the record with them first. Have you done that?" Grabowski asked.

"No. But I'll be glad to meet with them." Jeff sounded willing, though he was gritting his teeth.

Grabowski shrugged and held out the drawing at arm's length, as if plague were nesting in the paper. He tossed it to the table. "If the commission doesn't like your project, whatever you say to them won't make a lot of difference."

Was Grabowski trying to antagonize him? Or taunt him? For Cedar Place's sake, Jeff smoothed down his raised hackles. *No point alienating the jerk from the get-go.*

Grabowski leaned forward, his fists palm down on the table, his rings in a brass-knuckle line. "Let me tell you my main concern."

Whoa. Jeff braced himself.

"You're aware that you want to tear down a historic house," Grabowski said.

"It's in bad condition. Nothing's up to code. It wouldn't make financial sense to renovate it."

"I'm not sure the historical society would agree with that."

"We have engineers to vouch for what the termites have done," Jeff said. "Making the house first class again would cost a fortune."

"Sometimes money's not the only point." Grabowski arched a mossy eyebrow. "You should expect some opposition. It's not going to be an easy ride."

Jeff mopped his neck again. "How long do you think the permits are going to take?"

"Remember, no guarantees." *Taunt, taunt.*

"So *if* we get permits," Jeff backtracked, "how long for them to go through?" *Gamble's planners are known to work at the speed of narcoleptic snails,* he'd have liked to have pointed out.

"Sometimes the process is fast, but I just signed a bulkhead permit that took four years."

Three years and nine months too long.

Grabowski got up and raised the venetian blinds, and dust motes flew through shafts of sunlight. "You know, Cedar Place seems worthy enough."

Jeff grabbed on to "worthy's" glimmer of hope.

"I wouldn't mind some new stores downtown. We've been stagnant for a long time. We could use some new blood," Grabowski said.

"That's nice to hear." *Very nice.*

"Yeah, but you need to get ready. Lots of folks want things to stay the way they are."

Jeff couldn't fool himself. Opposition was coming, and, unlike a leopard, Grabowski could change his spots tomorrow and decree that Cedar Place would be a blight on downtown. Nothing was sure. Nothing would be settled for months. To get a permit, a long road lay ahead, and Jeff would be dodging plenty of potholes.

CHAPTER 3

In Vincent, as Anna had named her van, she screeched to a stop in front of Dr. Lars Nilsen's veterinary clinic, which, thank goodness, was only five blocks from the house. Earnest was lying in a dismal heap on the backseat, his beautiful wheat-in-candlelight fur now a sickly ash color, his eyes closed as if he were an inch from giving up. Usually, his fur had the fresh, clean smell of a forest, but now all Anna could smell of him was smoke. As she yanked her key from the ignition, her hands were icy with fear for him—and for her shop and the house, which, for all she knew, were burning to the ground.

"Stay here, Sweetie," she said, but then she thought with a pang that Earnest couldn't get up on his own, much less go anywhere. She reached back, quickly stroked his head, and tried to seem calm.

When she pushed open the door and jumped to her feet, she saw smoke rising downhill in the distance. The town's old clapboard houses would burn in a minute if the fire spread. The thought was too unbearable to contemplate. She ran toward the clinic's front door.

Her cell phone rang. Breathless, she pulled it out of her purse.

"Did you get Earnest there okay?" In the confusion on the house's front lawn, Lauren was yelling.

"I just got here. I need help to get him inside. Is the fire out?"

"I can't tell. You wouldn't believe the water."

Yes, Anna would believe it. A river flowing into her shop. The hardwood floors buckling and dark stains of moisture spreading over the walls, which would need to be replastered. She pressed her fingertips against her temple as if they could push these thoughts from her mind. "Lauren, I have to call you back. I've got to take care of Earnest right now."

Anna ran through the clinic's door to the receptionists' counter. Behind it, Mary and Yvonne, who always fussed over Earnest, were sitting side by side in dog-print scrub suits.

"Get a gurney. I need help," Anna shouted. "Earnest's been in a fire. I can't get him in here by myself."

The alarm on Yvonne's and Mary's faces told her that she must sound hysterical, but how could she not? She felt the eyes of all the clients in the waiting room bore into her.

Yvonne threw down her phone's headset and ran to the back of the clinic, where the gurney was kept. Mary hurried around the counter to Anna.

"I heard sirens a while ago," Mary said.

"Our house. On Rainier. You've got to help me with Earnest. I'm terrified for him. He's in my van."

Anna rushed back through the front door with Mary. Just as they reached Vincent, Yvonne appeared at the clinic's side door. She hurried toward them with the gurney as its wheels rattled on the parking lot's gravel.

Anna's phone rang again. *Damn.* She whipped it out of her purse.

"Anna? Doug Holloway here. Can I pick up Jane's flowers before I go to the hospital this afternoon?"

"Mr. Holloway, our house is on fire. I'm with Earnest at the vet's. He's hurt."

"Oh, my. What happened? Can I help?"

"I can't think straight right now. I don't know about your flowers. I'll have to get back to you." Anna realized she was shouting.

Mary and Yvonne stooped down and stepped through Vincent's sliding door. They positioned themselves next to Earnest, picked him up, and set him on the gurney as gently as they'd have set down a spiderweb's gossamer thread. Though he did not protest being moved, a shiver undulated down his body from his shoulders to his haunches. *From pain? Fear? Oh, my beloved dog.*

Anna felt like an elephant was standing on her heart.

As Mary and Yvonne rolled Earnest down the clinic's dark back hall, Anna followed. She clicked on her phone's "Favorites" list and pressed "My Honey" at the top. Jeff was her favorite of favorites, chiseled into the highest peak of her personal Mount Rushmore—and now she longed to reach him more than she ever had since they'd met. She needed him to share the worry. She wanted to tell him about the fire and beg him to leave his Seattle office and come home *now*.

But with each ring, Anna's heart beat faster. Jeff wasn't there. *Of all the times. Where is he?* His cell's voice mail recording finished just as Yvonne and Mary pushed Earnest into an exam room. "Call me," Anna said and hung up.

Dr. Nilsen was waiting, his arms crossed over his white lab coat, a grim expression on his face. A blue-eyed, blond Norwegian, he usually seemed hardy, the kind of man who'd rise out of a sauna every morning, beat his chest, and charge, naked, into snow. But today his eyes had a tentative cast, which suggested he was unsure he could save Anna and Jeff's dog. His expression said more clearly than words that he didn't like emergencies that might not end well.

"Please, please help Earnest," Anna shouted.

"Yvonne said he'd been in a fire?" Dr. Nilsen asked.

"In the old house where my shop is. After Earnest led me out-side, he ran back in and rescued the women who rent with me."

"I'd expect no less. Such a good dog." Dr. Nilsen patted Earnest's shoulder—but, far away in the distant land of suffer-ing, Earnest didn't seem to notice.

Anna rubbed her hands together to warm them. Dr. Nilsen's exam room smelled of bleach. There were no windows, and the too-bright overhead fluorescent lights made the room feel harsh. They glared on the edges of the steel gurney, where Earnest was lying on his side and laboring to breathe.

His eyes were opened just to slits, and his dear, sweet face made clear that he was traumatized. On former visits, he'd greeted Dr. Nilsen with squeaks and tail wags and waited for biscuits to emerge from his lab coat's pockets. But today Earnest only twitched his tail, as if he wanted to wag it but didn't have the strength.

When Anna saw that, the tears she'd been holding back on the drive here leaked out. She quickly wiped them away with the back of her hand and coughed to keep Earnest from seeing her distress. He always seemed to feel that comforting her was his personal duty, and he would want to nuzzle and soothe her—when he couldn't lift his head.

"Will Earnest be okay?" For his sake, Anna tried to tamp down her voice's urgency.

"Let's have a look."

When Anna's phone rang again, she prayed Jeff was on the line. She checked the caller ID. Joy. Anna let out a small invol-untary cry of frustration. "I have to take this call." She stepped into the corner of the room.

"I'm afraid I've lost everything," Joy wailed.

"The fire's spread beyond the kitchen?"

"I don't know. We can't go inside yet."

"Well, is the fire *out?*"

"Mostly. I think."

"So that's good news."

"What about our shops? What are we going to do?"

Images of her shop, a heap of ashes, flashed through Anna's mind. Her Buddhas and angels now charcoal. Her entire inventory gone. The possible loss made her head spin. It was too much to consider, when Earnest could be fading.

"Joy, we have to talk about this later. I'm here with Earnest. I have to think about him now."

Anna hung up and turned off her phone. She'd have to wait for Jeff.

Dr. Nilsen lifted a side of Earnest's mouth and examined his gums, which looked pale.

"Will he be okay?" she asked again.

"I hope so."

Hope isn't enough. I want guarantees.

"At least he hasn't gone into shock," Dr. Nilsen said.

"Could he *still?*"

"I'm sorry to say that anything's possible."

Anna closed her eyes and prayed so hard that she felt she might crack open.

On the back of her eyelids appeared an image of the brawny fireman, rivulets of sweat streaking his face as he carried Earnest toward her across the lawn. In the man's arms, he was cradled like a baby, and with each step, his paws had flopped. Anna's first thought had been that he was dead, and a black fishing net of grief ensnared her soul and dragged her to the ocean's depth so she could scarcely breathe.

"I found your dog upstairs. Quick, get him to a vet," the fireman said.

So Earnest was alive! Relief bore Anna up through suffocating fear to air again. *But, then, he could still die,* she'd thought.

Now Dr. Nilsen worked his stethoscope's buds into his ears and gently pressed its chestpiece against Earnest's heart.

"Is it beating okay?" Anna asked.

"A little fast, but that's not surprising." Dr. Nilsen removed the ear buds. As he quickly checked Earnest's body, he pointed out a flinch-inducing burned paw.

"Okay. I know you want answers, but they're going to take some time. Here's the plan," he said. "We put Earnest in an ICU cage with oxygen and IV fluids for a while. We examine him more thoroughly and check his airway. Then we decide where to go from there."

"Where do you mean?"

"We might x-ray his lungs for fluid and damage. Do blood work and a urine analysis to see if he's got carbon monoxide poisoning."

"You think he *does?*"

"It can happen with smoke inhalation. I wish it weren't so."

The color drained from Anna's face. Dr. Nilsen looked at her as though he thought he should offer her a glass of water and a Valium. She could tell he didn't like to see any dog fight for his life—and especially Earnest, who, he'd once said, was a favorite patient.

"Try not to worry, Anna. Tell Jeff that too," he said. "Why don't you go back to work?"

Where can I work if my shop has burned?

"I promise we'll do everything we can. I'll call you the minute I have news."

Though desperate to get back to the house, Anna dragged through Dr. Nilsen's waiting room with lead weighing down her shoes. Every footstep away from Earnest took effort when she was leaving him and had no guarantee he'd survive. She could not get out of her mind his whimper as she'd reached down, kissed his forehead, and told him she loved him and she would be back soon.

What if he goes into shock? What if he dies? What if I never see him again? Waiting to hear from Dr. Nilsen was going to be wrenching. Anna needed the reassurance of Jeff's voice. *If only he were here.*

She glanced at Dr. Nilsen's aquarium, which divided the waiting room into dog and cat sections and was supposed to keep everyone calm. But the angelfish and kissing gouramis swimming languidly through aerator bubbles did not soothe her nerves, and the orange clown fish with their white wimple markings looked too cheerful. As Anna made her way outside, she turned on her phone. She was starved to talk with Jeff. More than anyone, he'd understand how hard it had been to see Earnest hurt and Grammy's house burn. He'd know how catastrophic it would be if Anna lost her shop.

In her van, Anna clicked on "My Honey" again. This time she tried Jeff at his office. After three rings, for the second time she was losing hope of reaching him until Kimberly, his assistant, answered with a casual "hi."

"Kim, I need to talk with Jeff."

"He's not here right now."

"Where is he? It's urgent."

"Oh, he's at city hall," she drawled, as if "urgent" carried the significance of a dust mite's antenna.

"Where? In Seattle?"

"In Gamble."

"He's *here?!*"

"As far as I know."

"Why?"

"He's filing for permits for a commercial building he designed."

Jeff and I share everything. Why hasn't he told me? "What building? Where?"

"It's called Cedar Place. Downtown. On your main street. It's going to replace some old Victorian house."

Like Earnest, Anna struggled to breathe.

There was only one Victorian house on Gamble's main street and only one in the whole town with enough land for a commercial building. Kim was talking about Grammy's house.

Anna clicked off the phone. She pressed her eyes closed and rested her forehead on Vincent's steering wheel. *Today can't be happening. It just can't.* She sank into a mental swamp of brackish water.

CHAPTER 4

⁓

As Jeff walked out into the sunshine, he smelled smoke. He couldn't see its source over the buildings on the street's uphill side, but the smoke seemed to be coming from Mr. Webster's direction. For years people had unsuccessfully lobbied the city for a law against burning trash in town. *The Gamble city planners should write an ordinance for that instead of harassing architects about their projects,* he thought.

Jeff turned on his phone. On the wallpaper, Earnest and Anna appeared in a photo that always cheered him. They were cuddling on the sofa in a patchwork quilt, their faces close together, tilted up toward the camera. Anna's smile and her gorgeous blue-gray eyes, which, in his opinion, could conquer nations, beamed light and love straight at him.

She had an unshakable sincerity about her. It made her look vulnerable, and it made him want to protect her. Not that she needed it. Anna could be stubborn and strong, but he liked that. She was his equal. She could take care of herself.

Jeff clicked on the e-mail icon to check for messages, but there was nothing that couldn't wait, including one from his father, whom Jeff called Brad, now living in New Jersey, two thousand miles from his mother, in Arizona. An Olympic champion flake, Brad was surely asking to borrow money that he'd spend on Jim Beam whiskey and never repay—again. Jeff would get back to him later. Much later. After Jeff's innate sense of responsibility began to nag him.

He called his voice mail. A client asked about an appointment next week, and Anna said her quick "call me." Jeff would phone her from the twelve-twenty ferry to his office, when they could talk in peace. Right now, he needed a minute to decompress from Randy Grabowski.

Sitting in city hall's damned meeting room with every muscle on high alert had made Jeff tense. Also troubling him was the corner he'd backed himself into. Ever since he'd taken on the project, he'd been mulling how to explain it to Anna. But he'd kept putting it off because many things could hijack a project before anyone lifted a hammer and nails—and why borrow trouble? Now, however, he'd filed for permits, and the train had left the station—the time had come. He couldn't delay telling her about Cedar Place any longer.

In the beginning, Anna might resist the idea because she was so attached to her grandmother's house and she would not want to see it torn down. Anna never seemed bothered by its warped floors, peeling paint, and dry rot. If Jeff brought up the hazards of uneven stairs and faulty wiring, she waved them off, unconcerned. She said, "It doesn't matter to me if half the windows are painted closed. If the chimney flashing leaks, it can be repaired."

Jeff supposed that was true, but he shook his head with wonder at Anna's free spirit—and at her denial that the house needed work to make it safe. The house also needed money for repairs. But Anna was no financial star. Managing her business challenged her, and she often needed shoring up. She could be impractical, the opposite of Jeff.

In the end, he believed he could bring Anna around to approving his project. She'd understand the boost Cedar Place would give the town, and the benefit of getting rid of the old to make way for the new. He'd tell her about the three spaces he'd designed for her, Lauren, and Joy to set up shop in the new building. And about the warehouse he'd found for them in Gamble's industrial park, where they could keep their businesses going while Cedar Place was built. He'd tried to think of everything to make her happy.

But, then, he wasn't sure she'd *be* happy. That was the problem. The uncertainty about her reaction worried him more than the uncertainty about Grabowski's support.

He put on his sunglasses and started along Madison, which was three blocks downhill from Rainier. A shopper carrying a bright blue eco-friendly bag came out the back door of Pegasus, a kitchen store. Aging hippies in Birkenstocks walked by, licking ice cream cones. In Waterfront Park, the town fixture, Lloyd McGregor, was wearing kilts and playing "Amazing Grace" on bagpipes. A man with dreadlocks to his waist was sitting on a bench, writing a postcard. Bicyclists pedaled by in a swarm.

The enticing smell of cinnamon rolls wafted from the Latte Da Coffee Shop and reminded Jeff how hungry he was. He'd get a slice of pizza to take on the ferry. He walked by Puget Sound Bank, where Earnest always dragged him because his favorite teller gave him Milk-Bones, and the library, where Anna loaned Earnest to encourage kids to read out loud each Monday afternoon. Jeff avoided Rainier—and Plant Parenthood—where he'd risk running into Anna and have to explain what he was doing on the island in the middle of the day. He had to prepare himself before talking with her about Cedar Place.

Should I do it tonight? Jeff nodded to himself, resolved.

He'd take Anna to Sawyer's. They'd sit at a quiet table in a corner with a candle flickering between them and lighting up her creamy skin. They'd drink a glass of wine, and he'd reach over and smooth her hair, a gesture that always made her close her eyes. Then he'd tell her about his project and explain that it wasn't about him. It was about them. And the community they loved. And the raise he'd get so they could marry.

Yes. That was the honest way to go.

On Madison, a block from the ferry terminal, was Say Cheese. Jeff often came here for pizza so he could share a bite with Earnest. It was Earnest's favorite place on earth because it had a permanent Parmesan reek. He would sell his soul into slavery for any kind of cheese—the more fat in it the better, but Parmesan was his favorite. How he knew what it tasted like was a mystery, because he gulped it down—no chewing, one swallow, and that was it.

Say Cheese was located in a small white bungalow, built in 1915, according to a framed sign beside the door. On the front porch was a cougar-sized sculpture of a housecat, next to three tables, where Earnest liked to put on his starving desperado act. He planted himself at a customer's feet, gazed up at a pizza bite about to be taken, and conveyed with anguished eyes his one small step from malnutrition. It worked every time.

Inside, Jeff joined the lunch crowd waiting at the counter for pizza slices to go. On this warm day the darkened room and overhead fan did little to cool the oven's heat. A vague smell of sweat joined the cheese, salami, and garlic.

"Hey, Tony," Jeff said to the owner, who had a buzz cut and wore a gold stud in one ear. "You have a pesto chicken slice?"

"Sure." Tony took Jeff's five-dollar bill and started counting out change from an ancient cash register. "How's it going up at Anna's shop?"

"What do you mean?"

"The fire department was there this morning."

Fire department?! Jeff froze. A jolt of fight-or-flight coursed through him. His heart pounded.

"I thought you'd come back from Seattle to help," Tony said.

"I didn't know. Is anybody hurt?"

Tony shrugged. "I couldn't leave here to find out."

A bead of sweat trickled down Jeff's spine. He had to get over there. "Forget the pizza." With long, hurried strides, he headed toward the front door.

"Wait. Go through there." Tony pointed to a ten-foot hallway leading to a screen door in the back. "From the parking lot, there's a shortcut to Rainier."

Jeff turned and rushed down the hall.

"Your money!" Tony shouted.

"Later." Money was the last thing on Jeff's mind if the person and dog he loved most in the world could be hurt.

As the screen door slammed behind him, bright sun, smoke, and dust from the unpaved lot stung his eyes. He blinked and wiped them with the back of his hand. Behind a row of parked cars, he saw a narrow path through menacing eight-foot-tall blackberry bushes. *So what do a few thorn scratches matter?* He tucked his briefcase under his arm and ran.

CHAPTER 5

Anna hurried down the hall to Plant Parenthood, her heart an anxious fist inside her chest. The house reeked of smoke. When she stepped into what had been her magic kingdom, her breath caught in her throat. The white walls were a dingy gray, and footprints of ash covered the oak floor. Those things could be fixed, but not her beautiful plants, which had collapsed in the fire's heat. Some resembled wilted lettuce. Others looked like the devil himself had sprayed an herbicide on their stems and leaves.

Anna rushed to Edgar, her loyal old friend. Though green floral tape still held his stem to a supporting stake, his leaves flopped down like dark flags of a vanquished country. Constance had fallen off her pedestal, and her pot had broken when she'd hit the floor. Her once-graceful fronds had withered. If she had lungs, she'd be fighting for breath.

Anna's scheffleras and *Ficus benjaminas* had drooped. Her carnivorous plants seemed to have melted—including Fang, the Venus flytrap that Anna's youngest customer, Tommy, visited after school. Smoke and heat had also ruined all of Anna's flowers, except those behind her refrigerator's now-gray glass door. Though many of her animal and angel sculptures could be cleaned, some had toppled over and broken when firemen had dragged the tables away from the walls.

Anna looked around and sighed. Everything in Plant Parenthood seemed to have turned a shade of gray—charcoal, battleship, slate, gunmetal, carbon, iron. Part of her wanted to weep into her hands, but the other more determined part—which Grammy had instilled in her—pointed out that tears now would be useless. Anna would find a way to keep going. She would not let fire or shock at Jeff defeat her.

"Anna! I didn't know you were back." Joy plowed through the mess of dying plants and hugged her.

"I wanted to see if I still had a shop," Anna said.

"You do, but I don't. The wall between the kitchen and me is pretty much gone, along with everything else. It's a nightmare." Tears crept down the mascara trails already on Joy's cheeks. "The audacity of those damned flames. How could they *do* such a thing?"

Anna rested a hand on Joy's shoulder. "We've got to clean up and keep going. We can work together."

"I can't. The heat even killed my computer. At least my printed chapters of *Wild Savage Love* are at home."

"What about Lauren? Is she okay?"

"Her sofa and books are ruined, but her equipment's fine. She fared better than I did." Joy glanced down at Earnest's lily-pad bed, now a cheerless charcoal gray. "How's our guy?"

"The vet's checking him out. He's hurt, but nobody knows yet how badly."

Joy shook her head with obvious concern. "He *has* to be all right."

Anna blinked back tears. She would *not* cry. "What's the kitchen like?"

Once Joy led her across the hall, Anna wished she hadn't asked. The main counter and the wall behind it were rubble, so

Anna could look directly into what had been Joy's shop. The cabinets, maple table, and three mismatched chairs were burned beyond recognition. Smoke grayed the stove, refrigerator, and porcelain sink. The firemen had nailed plywood over what had been the back door.

Lauren was gathering up broken dishes and glasses. She put her arm around Anna, but that was not enough to cushion her dismay. "Is Earnest all right?"

"We don't know yet."

"Hey, Anna." Ted Carcionni, the fire marshal, left the ashes he was combing through and stood up to greet her.

He was Gamble's Rotary Club president and Citizen of 2013. Anna had donated plants to his annual auction and tossed Hershey's Kisses from his red 1957 Chevy in the last July Fourth parade.

"It doesn't look like much is left here," she said.

"Could have been a lot worse. We'll salvage everything we can." Against his grimy face, Ted's teeth looked as white as a fastidious elephant's tusks. "You were lucky. In an old house like this, fire can travel straight up to the attic through the walls. We had to rip out one wall upstairs and make sure that hadn't happened."

Anna pictured another mess, of torn-up laths and plaster. More to clean up.

"We found a time capsule someone sealed up there between the walls in a Mason jar. I put it on the front porch," Ted said.

"Thanks," Anna said.

He pointed at what had been the counter, where the toaster oven and Mr. Coffee had resided. "The fire probably started there. Did any of you ladies see it happen?"

"None of us knew about it till my dog warned us," Anna said.

"Any lights flickering around here lately?"

"All the time," Lauren said.

"What about overloaded circuits?"

"We had appliances and computers in our shops," Joy said.

"Any appliances going in the kitchen when the fire started?"

"The refrigerator," Lauren said. "And our Mr. Coffee. I made a pot this morning."

"Is this its base and warming plate?" Ted stooped down and picked up a clump of barely recognizable plastic.

"That's it," Joy said. "It was old, but it worked."

"Our investigators will look it over. They'll be here to figure out what caused the fire."

What if it was our Mr. Coffee? Anna wondered with a shiver.

"What happens once you know why the fire started?" Lauren asked.

"We send our report to your landlady's insurance company. After their own investigators come here, the cleanup crew takes over."

"Do we have to move out?" Anna asked.

"That's not for me to say. Gamble's building official should be here this afternoon. He'll decide if this place needs to be condemned," Ted said.

"But we have to keep our shops going. The kitchen's the only part that's really wrecked," Anna argued.

"You've got renter's insurance, don't you," he said, implying it was an established fact.

Anna, Joy, and Lauren looked at each other.

"No," Anna said, glum as rain. They'd canceled their insurance in order to save money for the house.

"Renter's insurance would have replaced everything you've lost. It would have paid for you to set up somewhere else." Ted gazed at the floor. He might have felt too sorry for the women to look directly at them. "That's too bad. A damned shame."

★   ★   ★

While waiting for the insurance company's cleanup crew, Anna, Lauren, and Joy got on their hands and knees and mopped the entry with smoky towels so no one would slip in the puddles. Lauren's boa feathers, which had been white and fluffy that morning, now looked like they'd been plucked from an exhausted turkey vulture. Anna's denim skirt was drenched and streaked with grime.

"If our Mr. Coffee started the fire, you think Mrs. Scroogemore could sue us for negligence?" she asked.

"It was an accident. No way could she claim we set out to burn down the house," Joy said.

"But we knew he wasn't working well. We could be liable. I'm worried. Mrs. Scroogemore could come after us with lawyers," Anna said.

Lauren wiped ashes off a baseboard. "It's weird she hasn't shown up. Anybody call her?"

"I did. She didn't sound upset to hear the house was burning," Joy said.

"I know why." Anna sat back on her heels, blew her bangs off her sweaty forehead, and broke Kimberly's unspeakably horrible news to Lauren and Joy. "If the house burned down, Mrs. Scroogemore wouldn't have to pay for the demolition. She'd be thrilled."

Joy and Lauren stared at Anna, speechless. It might have been the first time since birth that Joy had not had an opinion.

"It's the truth," Anna said.

Finally, Joy asked, "She'd tear down this house?"

"More tenants mean more money. That's all she cares about," Anna said.

"How do you know about this?" Lauren asked.

"I just heard it from Jeff's assistant. He's the damned architect." The way Anna said "architect," the word smoldered with disdain. "His assistant said he was filing for permits at city hall today, and his new building would replace 'some old Victorian house.'"

"Maybe it's not ours," Lauren said.

"What other house could it be? We're the only one with a big enough yard," Anna said.

"That odious toad! I want to smack him," Joy snarled.

"Mrs. Scroogemore is as much to blame." Lauren's boa feathers looked even darker than before. "I can't believe Jeff would do that, Anna."

"Men betray you all the time. Ask my ex-husband, the Twit," Joy said.

"Jeff's not that type. He's a good man," Lauren said.

"As of now he's a vile slug," Joy said.

"Anna, what are you going to do?" Lauren asked.

"I don't know." Anna wrung water from a towel into a blue plastic bucket. "I'm too shocked to think straight."

"I'm thinking fine. You should get rid of him," Joy said.

"That would be a shame. They're great together," Lauren told Joy.

"Maybe not anymore." Anna took a deep, sad breath and closed her eyes for an extra-long blink. "I've never misread anybody so badly in my life. I trusted him. I can't believe he wouldn't have told me. He's always honest."

"*Was* always honest," Joy corrected.

Anna rubbed her towel over the floor. "I don't think I can ever trust a man again."

As she wrung out her towel, she glanced out the front door, which was open to let in fresh air. Jeff was running down the sidewalk toward her, his briefcase clutched against his heart.

CHAPTER 6

Panting for breath, Jeff ran up to the house, and Anna stepped onto the porch. Ash grayed her clothes. Her face was grimy, and her hair, an unruly mess. But she was there! In one piece! Unhurt!

"You're all right!" he shouted. As he hurried down the sidewalk, relief washed over him. He thought Anna had come out to meet him, as glad to see him as he was to see her.

"I'm all right, but Earnest isn't. He's at Dr. Nilsen's clinic," Anna said.

Jeff stopped. His stomach lurched. "What happened?"

"He inhaled smoke."

"Dr. Nilsen doesn't think he'll die, does he?"

"He doesn't know."

The news sent Jeff reeling.

He set his foot on the bottom step, intending to climb up to the porch, put his arms around Anna, and hug her like he'd never let her go. They could comfort each other. They could be strong for Earnest together.

"Don't. Come. Up. Here."

Jeff put his foot back on the sidewalk and stared at her.

Anna's voice was a dark, bruising purple. Red splotched her pale cheeks. The animation that was always in her face seemed to have dried up and blown away, so that her expression was frozen. Her jaw looked like it might splinter if she took a step toward him.

"Anna, what's the matter?" *She's got to be worried sick about Earnest. So am I.*

"Are you filing for a permit to tear down this house?"

Jeff tried to swallow, but his throat stiffened. "Where'd you hear that?"

"From Kimberly. Is it true?"

"Yes, but let me explain. . . ."

"I don't want to hear your excuses. They're too much for me right now."

"Just a minute . . ." Jeff said.

"You know I love this house. How could you?" The little tufts he loved to smooth in Anna's hair seemed to bristle.

"I meant only the best for you. For us," Jeff defended.

"How could you possibly think it would be best for us?" Anna asked.

"Because . . ."

"It's horrible."

"Just listen . . ."

"I don't want to talk with you today."

Anna would hardly look at him. She acted as if resting her gaze on him for longer than ten seconds would scorch her eyeballs.

On the way back to Seattle, Jeff stared out the ferry window. Puget Sound looked smooth as glass. The cloudless sky was the celestial blue that painters use for angels' robes. The sunny afternoon invited him to ignore all troubles.

But after seeing Anna, in Jeff's mind a storm of worry brewed, and gales lashed his thoughts. Earnest might be fighting for his life, and that was horrible enough. But Anna? Snippets of her last few statements hit him like needles of sleet.

"I can't trust you."

"I don't understand how you could have so little regard for my feelings."

"I don't think I can live with you right now. One of us has to move out of the condo."

She'd spoken the words, but the Anna he loved didn't seem to be the speaker. She'd turned off the faucet of warmth that always flowed from her. He wanted his Anna back, not the frozen woman who'd met him on the porch. He wanted her to let him respond, but she wouldn't listen.

Stunned, Jeff leaned his head against the window, so his breath fogged the glass. Was he at fault? Had he been insensitive? Truly, he didn't think so. He'd meant well. His intentions had been sincere.

Tonight he'd intended to unroll his architectural plans and show her where she, Lauren, and Joy could set up new shops in a modern building with decent bathrooms, central heating, earthquake proofing, and stairs you didn't have to take your life into your hands to climb. Jeff had wanted Anna to be pleased. He'd never dreamed that his goodwill could have gone so wrong.

Especially when Anna was always loving—sometimes to a fault. Once she gave every penny in her purse to a homeless woman in Seattle, a kind gesture, but what if she'd had an emergency—Jeff shuddered to think—or if she'd lost her ferry pass and couldn't get home?

Countless times she'd put his needs before hers like that. The summer before they'd gotten Earnest, they'd taken a six-mile hike in Southern California. Toward the end, they'd gotten lost and were nearly out of water. The trail seemed to twist and turn forever, and the sun beat down and burned right through their cotton shirts.

Jeff chided himself for not being prepared. His sweaty shirt stuck to his body, and he was getting a headache. From his daypack he pulled his and Anna's plastic bottle and its two remaining inches of water. "Here." He handed it to her.

"I'm not thirsty," she said.

"You've got to be. It must be a hundred degrees."

"No, really. I'm fine."

"Come on. I don't want you having a sunstroke on me."

"I don't need water. Honest. You drink it."

At first he refused. He wasn't about to hog up what little water they had. But as they continued to wander and she kept saying "no" every time he offered her the bottle, he began to feel like he might pass out—and he broke down and took a couple of slugs. She acted like she was some kind of drought-resistant camel till the trail finally looped around and they saw their car in the parking lot. Anna rushed to a hydrant outside the women's restroom and turned on the water full blast. As she gulped it from her cupped hands, it dribbled down her chin.

"I thought you weren't thirsty," Jeff said.

"I wasn't."

"You're pretty even when you lie."

Anna had been the only woman he'd ever known who'd sacrifice for someone else like that. It was still another reason for him to love her. And protect her even if he didn't understand her and if she was frustrating the hell out of him right now.

What am I supposed to do? Jeff looked out the ferry window at gulls who seemed to race each other across the water. They looked carefree and happy, as he and Anna and Earnest had been just hours before. Somehow Jeff had to get their pack of three together again. But how could he when Earnest was injured and Anna wouldn't listen to anything Jeff said? He brooded over that question all the way to Seattle.

As the crew was tying the ferry to the dock, Jeff decided that the only way he could stand his life being so out of control was to have a plan. First, as soon as he got back to his office, he'd call Dr. Nilsen and find out about Earnest. Until Jeff knew his condition, he could make no arrangements to help.

Second, Jeff would win Anna back. He couldn't do it with a grand gesture—he could hardly send her flowers, and she wouldn't accept a dinner invitation. No, subtlety and patience were the only way to go. No matter what she said or did, he would be as kind to her as she'd been to him on the California hike. It would be his turn to take care of *her*. And he would do whatever would please her. He'd go along to get along.

If she felt she couldn't live with him for a while, he'd move to an apartment, as big a waste of time and energy as that would be. He'd wait till Anna came to her senses and listened to reason. He'd wait for the Anna he loved to return.

Jeff was walking down the gangplank, when his cell rang. For an instant, he thought, *Great! Anna's calling*—until he remembered their "conversation," and he told himself, *Dream on. She'd never contact me now.*

Naomi Blackmore didn't bother to identify herself, but he would always recognize her voice because it boomed "entitlement." Without considering what she might be interrupting, she jumped right in with questions about Jeff's meeting at city hall.

"Everything was fine." He summed up the meeting with more confidence than he felt. "We're off to a good start."

"Excellent," she said. "While you were on Gamble, you must have heard about the fire."

"I stopped at the house. I'm on my way back to the office."

"Lots of damage?"

"I didn't go inside."

"I'm in Santa Barbara. I won't be back to see for myself for a week or two."

"Your insurance company can take care of it while you're away," Jeff said.

"I've already called them. It looks like the fire is a gift." Mrs. Blackmore chuckled. "I'm going for a cash settlement. If we get a permit, I'll use the money for construction. If we don't, I'll repair the house. Either way, I win."

Jeff flinched at the satisfaction in her voice. "What about your tenants? They can't stay if the house is badly burned."

"I hope they'll live with the mess for now. I want to keep rent coming in."

Mrs. Blackmore has no thought of trying to look out for anybody. She'd surely never refuse water so someone else could drink. Jeff didn't like her. Never had. Though he'd known her for months, he didn't call her "Naomi." Using her first name would mean familiarity he'd never want to have.

As Jeff told her good-bye, he conjured up an unsavory picture of her at her beach house, sprawled on a chaise lounge under a peppermint-striped umbrella. No inconvenience would dare appear on her horizon. The discomfort in her life would not fill a pygmy hamster's thimble.

One stamp of Mrs. Blackmore's feet got her what she wanted. Even her appearance showed she'd been cosseted all her life. Her helmet of perfectly highlighted hair. Her perfectly manicured nails, painted fire-engine red. Her gold necklaces, which shouted, *I'm richer than you are.* The nips and tucks that lifted her face so her sixty-year-old skin was as smooth as a stingray's belly.

CHAPTER 7

Anna flicked on Vincent's turn signal and aimed him toward the entrance to Dr. Nilsen's parking lot. She was desperate to see with her own eyes that Earnest was "hanging in," as Dr. Nilsen had said on the phone. She wanted to rest her cheek against his neck and soak up his steady reassurance—and she wanted to reassure *him* that everyone loved and missed him. She'd tell him, "We want you home."

Suddenly, Anna tightened her grip on the steering wheel and slammed on the brakes. Jeff was driving out of the parking lot and staring at her. She didn't want to see him. Not when hurt was sitting in her heart like a sad black toad. Jeff's mere presence upset her and made her want to run from him.

As his Honda passed Vincent, Anna riveted her eyes on the clinic's front door as if its olive green held answers to life's most crucial questions: *Why am I on earth? What's the meaning of my existence? What's going to happen when I die?*

In her peripheral vision, however, Anna saw every blue inch of Jeff's car move into the street. She was as aware of him as a compass needle is of north. But she wouldn't let him hurt her any more than he already had. She turned into the parking lot and left him in a cloud of dust.

★ ★ ★

Anna had expected Earnest to look downtrodden after inhaling smoke and burning his dear paw. But the sight of him in an ICU cage, too sick to get up and greet her, went beyond her expectation and made her feel desolate.

Though Dr. Nilsen had said he was giving Earnest IV fluids, she was not prepared for the dreadful IV bag and tube or the blue bandage over his catheter and shaved leg. For fear of alarming him, she tried not to shrink back at the white plastic cone fastened around his neck to keep him from chewing off the gauze around his paw. She might as well have been looking at his face through the large end of a megaphone—and Earnest's face was stricken.

He didn't seem stricken only for himself, though surely pain was mixed into his expression. His face also seemed stricken for her. His glazed eyes spoke frankly of his worry and distress: *If I'm stuck in this blasted cage, I can't protect you. I'm not living up to my responsibilities. I'm sorry.* As if to underscore his regret, Earnest flopped over, and his cone banged against the cage wall.

"Oh, Earnest. It's okay." Anna sank to her knees and reached inside to pet him. When he tried to lick her hand, his cone hit her wrist.

This cone is a satanic invention, said his dark look.

"Don't worry, Sweetie. You won't have to wear it forever." Anna stroked Earnest's shoulder. "And you don't have to worry about me. I'm fine. Honest." Her first lie to her beloved dog.

Anna usually kissed Earnest's forehead, but the cone made that impossible, so she kissed her fingertips and pressed them on his front paw. As she patted it, an arresting thought occurred to her. Maybe Earnest was also stricken because she had not come to visit him with Jeff. Earnest would have expected them together. He'd want to see his family. Maybe he was as worried about that as about her.

I don't understand, said his crinkled forehead.

How could Anna explain?

She dared not trouble Earnest with her distress, which was probably seeping out of her in ill-smelling scarlet waves. She couldn't tell him that she and Jeff had not come here together because he'd shocked her to the core. Nor could she point out that she was worried sick about the house. The fire was not its only trouble. So was the threat of demolition.

Anna bit her lip. She would never burden Earnest. In order to heal, he needed peace, not strife. Yet surely he sensed that something highly disagreeable was happening. He was too smart not to read the signals.

"Everything's going to be fine. You'll see," Anna said.

The troubled cast in Earnest's eyes said he was not so sure.

In the waiting room, Dr. Nilsen's fish were zipping around, showing off their vigor. But the doctor looked tired. Stubble shadowed his cheeks, and the edges of his eyes seemed blurry—surely he'd seen too much injury and illness for one day. His shoulders looked stiff from lifting and cajoling dogs. He curled his fingers around his stethoscope's chestpiece and he leaned against the wall.

"Your boy's doing pretty well," he said. "He's a good patient."

"He looked sad," Anna said.

"That's because he doesn't want to be here. He'll perk up if he goes home."

"If?" The word fluttered in Anna's throat like a frightened wren.

"He's still not out of the woods. We'll watch him through the night and keep measuring his oxygen saturation. He'll be getting oxygen support through his nose."

"When can he breathe on his own?"

"Tomorrow, we hope."

"Did you x-ray his lungs?"

"Not yet. He seemed too stressed. We decided to wait till morning." Dr. Nilsen rubbed his tired eyes. "For now we've given him pain meds and a steroid shot in case his lungs are inflamed."

"Will he be okay?" The ever-haunting question.

"We hope so," Dr. Nilsen said. "I explained everything to Jeff. He can fill you in when you get home."

If you only knew. On the way through the parking lot to Vincent, hurt and worry clawed for supremacy in Anna's stomach. Then irritation at Jeff reared its head and joined the fray.

CHAPTER 8

Jeff was ripping up romaine lettuce in the kitchen when Anna unlocked the condo's door and crossed the tile entry. "Hi, Anna," he called. "I'm making us a salad."

No response.

Jeff kept ripping as she went into the bedroom and closed the door. When he'd half filled the wooden salad bowl, their first purchase as a couple, he cut a tomato into the small pieces Anna liked and tossed them in. He peeled and sliced a cucumber. "Anna?" he tried again. "Do you want Thousand Island dressing? Or Italian?"

More silence—until finally she muttered, "I'll make my own salad."

That's a start. Hope springs eternal. At least Anna had acknowledged Jeff's existence. He set two straw placemats on their round butcher block table and added napkins, forks, and knives in case he could lure her to dinner. "I'll broil chicken," he called.

This time without a moment's hesitation, she said, "Don't bother. None for me."

"Come on, Anna." Jeff started toward the bedroom to try to coax some reason into her. "You've had a hard day. I'm trying to make you a decent meal. We need to talk."

"The only thing I want to talk with you about is who's moving to another place."

"You won't talk about Earnest?"

"With Dr. Nilsen, not you."

Jeff opened the bedroom door.

"I really need my space right now. If you come in here, I'm leaving," Anna said.

"If you leave, how can we talk about who's moving?"

"Okay, talk." Clearly intending to stay as far as possible from Jeff, Anna backed up against his blue upholstered club chair in the room's farthest corner.

"You don't have to worry. I'm not carrying the Ebola virus," Jeff said.

Anna replied with a frown. Usually, she smiled even if she didn't mean to. It was her nature—she couldn't help herself. Her lips turned up of their own accord.

But not tonight.

"Are you moving out, or should I?" she asked.

"I hate for either of us to leave here. If you'll just listen to me for a minute, you'll change your mind."

"I don't think I'll ever change my mind."

"Look. I have the best intentions for my project. I want you to be glad about it."

"Are you moving to another place, or should I?" she repeated.

Jeff held up his palms toward her, a signal of surrender. *Go along to get along.* Anna needed time to calm down. He wouldn't press her now. "If you're sure you want me to move, I'll do it."

"When?"

You don't have to be in such a hurry. "I'll look for a place tomorrow."

Without a "good," "fine," or "thanks," Anna walked into the bathroom and closed the door behind her. The lock's click said, *Good-bye.*

★　★　★

At the kitchen table, Jeff crunched his romaine. The noise echoed through the silent room and made him feel lonely. Being alienated from Anna was awful enough, but the condo felt even lonelier without Earnest, especially after Jeff had just seen him at Dr. Nilsen's clinic.

Normally, at dinnertime, Earnest lay under the table and rested his chin on Anna or Jeff's foot as if to proclaim, *These are my very own humans, and nobody else can have them.* Or Earnest curled up beside the stove and did his impersonation of a giant cannelloni bean, his legs tucked under and his chin pressed toward his haunch. Or he rolled on his back on the crimson bed in the kitchen corner, his legs flopped out, exposing himself in his flasher position. Though he pretended to sleep, he pricked his ears and eavesdropped on Jeff and Anna's conversation.

Tonight, if Anna had deigned to eat with Jeff, however, there'd have been no conversation for Earnest to overhear except Jeff's attempting to connect, followed by Anna's shrinking further behind her Great Wall. Their conflict would have stressed Earnest, and he would have planted himself between them like a referee and waited for them to make up. Maybe it was better for him not to witness the rift, though he might have nudged Anna toward a little guilt for being unreasonable and bringing friction into their house.

Which was no longer theirs. At least for now, it would only be hers. Jeff shook his head, bewildered.

He refused to get discouraged, however. He had faith. Squaring his shoulders, he finished his dinner. Though worried about Earnest, Jeff whistled cheerfully so Anna could hear, and he washed his dishes and put them away. To keep Anna from starving in the bedroom, he clumped loudly into their study and opened and closed file drawers so she would know the kitchen was free. He sat at the desk, his back to the door so she could walk, undetected, through the living room. Giving her privacy for her dinner and her withdrawal into herself was the gentlemanly thing to do.

Jeff Googled "craigslist Gamble Island, WA, apartment rentals," and three listings appeared on the screen. Not exactly an abundant choice, but Gamble was a small place. He'd make do.

When he glanced at the first listing's depressing lead photo, he reminded himself that this move would be temporary. He need not be picky about where he lived. He repeated this to himself. Twice. He studied the listing.

The photo showed an empty white room that looked like the inside of a cat carrier. The only hint of a window was a feeble streak of light on the white shag rug that had met countless parades of dirty shoes. The picture's caption was "A Place to Call Home." *Maybe if you're a needy cat,* Jeff thought.

The photo for the next listing showed a kitchen—a stainless steel sink, a faux wood floor, clean white appliances, natural wood cabinets. Not bad. But the caption troubled him: "GOBBLE UP THIS GREAT APARTMENT before somebody else does! Remodeled just with you in mind! But HURRY!! Don't miss out!" *Why the rush?* Surely tenants were not elbowing each other out of the way to get to this ordinary place. As Jeff sensed the landlord's desperation, wariness ridged his forehead.

"Super Cute," the third option, required courage to consider. The photo showed a bathroom with hot-pink walls and lime-green cabinets. Gold veins ran though the cracked white tiles around the sink. Fuchsia whales with long black eyelashes swam across the moldy shower curtain. As an architect, Jeff needed harmonious colors, preferably in subtle shades. He needed taste. But the caption *did* promise "Location! Location! Location!"

Jeff leaned back in his chair, stretched his arms toward the ceiling, and laced his fingers behind his head. He heard Anna rustling around in the kitchen and smelled her canned chicken soup. He'd have liked to talk with her, but he knew better than to try. Now his task was to move out. He'd be honorable about it.

When Jeff woke the next morning, the sun was shining on his face because he'd forgotten to close the living-room shades. As he lifted his arm to shield his eyes, a sharp pain hammered his back. The sofa had not been long enough for his six-foot-two frame, and he'd hunched over all night. The blanket, which he'd resurrected from the storage locker, hadn't been warm enough, either. His cramped position and the chilly air had stiffened him, and every time he'd wakened in the night, he'd brooded about Earnest and Anna.

In their spacious queen-size bed, Anna had slept like a princess with no pea, but Jeff reminded himself not to be resentful. He listened to her showering and imagined warm water running down her lovely body. In their former routine, she'd taken the bathroom first while he made the bed. Then he'd shaved and showered while she fed Earnest and put together their usual hurried granola and tea. After a loving good-bye kiss, Jeff rushed to the ferry, always eager to get back to her.

Today no breakfast would be forthcoming. Sadly, there would be no kiss. He lay there feigning sleep till Anna came out of the bathroom and headed for the kitchen. As she passed the sofa, he rose up and said, "Good morning."

Her face was stern. No "good morning" back.

"Anna, do we have to be like this?"

She went to the kitchen, clunked the toaster on the counter, and stuffed in a slice of bread. Jeff wanted to follow her and take her into his arms, but he squashed that desire. The timing would be wrong. It was too soon to express those feelings.

He threw back his blanket and climbed off the sofa in his boxer shorts and tee shirt. His pajamas were in the bedroom, which Anna had clearly defined as her private domain and which last night he'd not wanted to invade. "Are you finished in the bathroom?" he asked politely. *A little chivalry might help.* He paused, hoping for an answer. "I take your silence as a 'yes,'" he said.

Jeff went into the bedroom. Their bed looked rumpled, thrashed in—Anna's night must not have been any more restful than his. To remind her what a good guy he was, he quickly smoothed out the sheets and blanket and covered them with the linen spread they'd bought together. He took clean underwear from the dresser and Dockers and a fresh shirt from the closet, and he went into the bathroom, which, he was grateful, did not have hot-pink walls and lime-green cabinets. After showering and shaving, he was about to make an assault on Anna's new territory, the kitchen, when the phone rang.

"How is Earnest?" Anna asked.

Jeff hurried to the bedroom extension.

"Earnest's x-rays look pretty good. There's not much carbon on his lungs. We stopped the oxygen this morning," Dr. Nilsen said.

Wonderful. "Dr. Nilsen, this is Jeff," he said to alert him that he was on the line. "Does that mean Earnest can come home?"

"I'd like for him to stay here another day so we can watch him. We'll keep monitoring his oxygen saturation. If he maintains it on his own for twenty-four hours, we'll know he's rounded the corner."

"Do you think he will?" Anna asked.

"He's giving every indication he's okay."

Relief!

"I'll visit him at lunch," Anna said.

"He'll be glad to see you," Dr. Nilsen said.

"I'll be there after work," Jeff said.

Dr. Nilsen paused for slightly longer than a blink and then said, "Fine." But the small delay was enough to indicate that their arriving separately again had registered with him. As it would Earnest.

CHAPTER 9

"Come on, sweet Edgar. Don't die on me. This bath should make you feel better." Anna gently washed the plant's rubbery leaves with a sponge and soapy water, then dried them with a towel. Free of smoke, his leaves looked greener and, though drooped, were thick and tough. Anna patted them, as she might have patted Earnest's paw. "You've got to fight. I need you," she said.

In the sink she sprayed water on Constance's shriveled fronds and hoped there might still be life in her. From a plastic bag, Anna shook soil into a clay pot, which would be Constance's new home. "I won't give up on you. As you revive, I'll be here cheering for you." Anna set her in the soil and added more around her roots.

Anyone but Anna would have tossed these plants into the ever-growing pile of rubbish on the lawn. But she could never give up on her dear old friends. To her, plants were like people. They had personalities and needs, and they commanded respect. She liked their quiet dignity as they witnessed life around them. They had a silent steadiness.

One morning Jeff had watched her watering and whispering to her begonias in their condo windowsill. He'd said, "They're growing into giants. Soon you'll have to beat them back."

"I love them."

"They sure know it." Jeff had smiled the smile that got Anna every time. She'd crossed the kitchen and kissed him.

How her life had changed in just one day. Now that she'd lost all trust in Jeff, kissing him would be impossible. She branded him "thoughtless"—no, more than thoughtless. Insensitive. He had a rhino's hide. And when she remembered Kimberly's revelation yesterday, Anna had to admit that Jeff had flat out ambushed her. She'd never have predicted it in a thousand years. *How* could *he have done such a thing?*

Feeling crushed, Anna pressed down Constance's soil so she'd sit tall in her pot. Anna watered her, carried her to the corner, and set her on her pedestal. "You be brave. You need to get strong again," Anna told the fern. Constance may have been wounded, but she was proud.

Earnest's now-gray lily pad reeked of smoke. If Anna washed it, the corduroy cover would be fine, but the pillow inside would fall apart. She was about to haul the bed out to the rubbish pile, but then she reconsidered.

Throwing away Earnest's lily pad would be like throwing *him* away. Such a disloyal act might indicate she'd given up on his recovery and didn't expect him back. *Jeff is the disloyal one, not me,* she thought. She set the bed down. Gently. With care. For now, no matter how bad the smell, she'd keep the lily pad exactly where it was.

Luis Ramon wore blue coveralls, Reeboks, and a Seattle Mariners baseball cap turned backward. When he spoke, his gold tooth flashed. He handed Anna a business card for Serve-U Restoration in Seattle. "I come from insurance company. You burn, we earn." His whole face crinkled when he laughed.

"What can I do for you?" Anna asked.

"I do estimate to clean."

"Fantastic! We're desperate for help." Anna was so grateful that she felt like hugging him.

"Estimate only. Boss says no work," he said.

"I thought you cleaned."

"We do. Not here."

"So you'll just make an estimate? That's *it?* We won't see you again?"

"Sí, señora."

As Luis measured walls and wrote down numbers in a spiral notebook, Anna grumbled to her disappointed self. This morning Gamble's building inspector had declared the house a mess, but habitable if electricity were restored. Now, clearly, Mrs. Blackmore had decided not to bother cleaning up, so she surely wouldn't bother with repairs. A tightwad like her wouldn't put a pinched penny into a house that might be demolished in a few months. Anna should have known. She should have turned her back on hope.

Anna called an official meeting—like those that she, Joy, and Lauren used to have around their kitchen table to count their savings for the house. But since the kitchen was gone, their meeting place was Plant Parenthood. Their agenda was the future.

"Exhibit A for my fight against the ash avalanche." Joy gave her broom's dingy gray bristles a halfhearted kick. She'd walked in, leaning wearily on the handle. With a groan, she sank into a metal folding chair. Side-by-side, Anna and Lauren dangled their legs from a Chinese-red table.

"I'm thinking the universe is telling me to forget my shop and find a regular job," Joy said.

"You don't want to do that. You wouldn't have time to finish *Wild Savage Love*," Lauren said.

"We've stuck with you while John and Penelope fell in love in Cornwall. Now that Murdon's captured them, you can't leave us hanging. We have to know what happens," Anna said.

"It's all bad," Joy said. "They're chained up in the brig of the Evil Murdon's slave ship. He's got the hots for Penelope, so you know where that might lead. As he heads for the Barbary Coast, a storm blows in and everybody's getting tossed around and sick, but John and Penelope can't reach each other."

"You can't leave those poor people in misery like that forever. They have to escape. There has to be a happy ending. You can't give up the story," Lauren said.

"I'm not sure." Devoid of her usual spunk, Joy hung her head. Ashes sprinkled out of her hair and landed on her shoulders. "I'm discouraged."

"We all are, but we can't let a fire defeat us," Lauren said.

"I don't see how I can reopen my shop. I don't want to be the starving Queen of Smokeland." Joy covered her face with her hands, perhaps the only place to hide from her bad luck. "Total bummer," she mumbled against her palms.

Lauren thumped her hiking boots' heels together. For work clothes, she wore a camouflage jumpsuit with an emerald-green ascot. "We need to figure out what we're going to do."

"We can't till we find out what Mrs. Scroogemore has in mind. If she won't let us stay here for now, that changes everything," Anna said.

"I've called her twice," Joy said. "The rancid scumbag. If she gave a flying flip about anybody but herself, she'd get back to us."

"I don't understand why she's avoiding us. Where do you think she is?" Lauren asked.

"Who knows? Maybe robbing orphans' piggy banks in Florida," Anna said.

"I wish an alligator would drag her into a swamp and do her in." Joy brightened at the prospect.

Anna flicked an ash off her blue chambray shirt. "I think we should forget about her for a minute and decide what we want."

"I want George Clooney to prostrate himself at my feet while Brad Pitt nibbles my earlobes." Joy chortled.

"I'm serious," Anna said. "I'd like to stay here with both of you and keep going as long as we can. And I still want to buy this house."

"I'm in," Lauren said.

Two pensive lines appeared between Joy's eyebrows. "I don't know."

"You can't bail out on us. We'll help with your shop," Anna said.

"Mrs. Scroogemore could boot us out tomorrow," Joy pointed out.

"What if she boots us out in a few months, after she gets a permit? Would we fight?" Lauren asked.

That paved the way for more what-ifs and more hard questions.

What if Mrs. Blackmore did *not* get a permit? If Anna, Joy, and Lauren had spent their savings getting their shops up and running, how would they scrape together money for an offer on the house? How could they afford repairs?

What if Mrs. Blackmore let them stay for now but did nothing for the house? How could they get electricity? How could they fix the burned wall of Joy's shop? How could they clean all the walls so customers wouldn't gag at the smoke?

When Anna pondered these repairs, Jeff rudely pushed his way into her mind, a camel's nose under her tent. Every summer in college he'd worked for a contractor. Jeff could fix anything.

He knew about wiring, painting, and plumbing. Putting up Joy's new wall would take him just an afternoon. Anna squeezed her eyes closed to banish him from her thoughts. No matter his skills, she would never ask him for help. Not after what he'd done.

"We can't tell what's ahead. We have too many unknowns," Joy said.

"We know we want to save the house and buy it if we can. That should be the goal," Anna said.

"Hear, hear," Lauren said.

"It seems impossible," Joy said.

"Even so, we can't just lie down and die," Anna said.

Joy rolled the broom's handle between her palms. "I hope you're not lying down and dying about Jeff, Anna."

"What do you mean?"

"Letting him get away with being such a despicable piss-ant," Joy answered.

"He's definitely hurt me," Anna admitted.

"*Hurt* you? He's clobbered you. A betrayal like that de-serves a whap to his kisser," Joy said.

"You're probably right," Anna said.

"I'm more than right. Don't you think so, Lauren?"

Lauren swung her feet and seemed thoughtful for a mo-ment. "Anna, you do have a right to be mad."

"She has a right to be outraged. He betrayed her big-time. I'd kill him," Joy said.

Anna glanced at the floor. Though she'd mopped it twice, tracked-in ashes were everywhere. She felt like one of those ashes herself. Trampled. Pulverized, really, if she were honest with herself. Joy was right—Jeff *had* betrayed her, and she was more than hurt. When she looked at his betrayal square in the eyes, she realized how resentful she was.

★   ★   ★

For the rest of the afternoon, Anna smoldered, but she did not welcome her resentment. It felt like a burglar who'd crawled through her window and was rifling her home. However, there the feeling was in all its spiked and prickly glory, and she had no way to ignore it. A healer might say that her spirit was enflamed and she had a fever of the soul.

Seeking calm, Anna climbed up to the turret, which as a child had been her secret thinking spot. As a renter for the last few years, she'd sought refuge here with Earnest. She found comfort in the quiet, and she liked looking down on Gamble's roofs from the perspective of the floor-to-ceiling windows.

Now smoke had left a gloomy gray film on them, and the rest of the turret was equally dreary. But she told herself that the white wicker rocking chair could be repainted, and the brass floor lamp's lotus-shaped base could be polished to a shine again. Earnest's faux oriental rug could be cleaned. A little mopping, scrubbing, and window washing could revive the room in a weekend.

Opposite the windows, Anna sank, cross-legged, to the floor and leaned against the wall. She counted her breaths for a while and then unscrewed the rusty lid of the Mason jar that held the time capsule, which Ted Carcionni had saved. A thick layer of dust clouded the glass and kept her from seeing the objects inside. But the capsule inspired awe because it linked her tangibly to the house's past. As she shook out the jar's contents, she felt that whoever had built the house was reaching out to her through the mists of time.

In a letter, James Williams, an attorney, explained that he'd come from Minnesota and built the house in 1880 for his wife and their seven children. A photo showed the children standing in front of a one-room clapboard schoolhouse; on the back he'd listed their names. He'd enclosed a dollhouse's ladder-back chair, a bullet, a clamshell, and a lock of hair. He'd also put in a page from the *Gamble Crier*. Al's Grocery advertised eggs for thirty cents a dozen; milk, eight cents a quart; and ham, thirteen cents a pound. James Garfield had been elected U.S. president, and a new steamship was traveling from Gamble to Seattle.

The time capsule drew Anna close to James Williams and his family. She could almost hear their laughter and their weeping, and feel their spats and disappointments, which lingered in the house. Perhaps members of their family had been born and had died here. Maybe they'd danced to photograph records in the living room and made apple pies in the kitchen. Certainly, the family's love for each other still hung in the air, just as Anna and Grammy's did.

Whenever Anna came to the turret, she felt Grammy's love as she had when sitting on her lap and leaning back against her chest. "I love you more than the sun and sky and all the flowers on the earth," Grammy would say as she folded Anna in her arms. "If my love were an ice cream cone, it would be big enough to hold the whole world."

Dear house, I can't let people raze you to the ground. But I'm not sure what to do, Anna thought.

A little confusion never hurt anybody, the house replied in Anna's heart—the exact words Grammy would have said.

What if we try to save you, house, but it all comes to a dead end? Anna asked.

You have to risk for what you want. You don't live on an island named Gamble for nothing.

Anna nodded. That was true.

As so often happened in the turret, a memory came to Anna as if carried on the wind. One cold fall day she and Grammy had been driving back from a Huskies game. Grammy was cranky because they'd lost, and she kept muttering, "Blast! Drat! Crumb!"

A mist rolled in, and the windshield wipers squeaked across the glass. As the Chevy traveled along Alaskan Way, wisps of fog swirled before the headlights, slid like ghosts across the hood, and billowed behind the car.

No matter how hard Anna squinted or how many times she wiped the windshield with her fist, she could see only a few fearsome yards ahead. Grammy must have sensed her apprehension, because she patted her knee. "Don't worry. If we're careful, we'll be all right."

"I hope," Anna said.

To distract her, Grammy launched a philosophical discussion, as she did from time to time. "A drive through fog is like life, you know."

"How come?"

"We're bumbling along in the car, and we literally can't see behind or ahead. It's the same when we go through life. As we muddle day to day, we can't see the past or future; they exist only in our memory or imagination. All we have to live is the present moment—in life and in this car. Understand?"

"I think," Anna said.

"I can ponder today's wretched Huskies score till the cows come home. Same with wondering about next week's game. What matters is right here, now, with you. The fog forces us to focus on it."

Grammy turned up the defroster so the fan whirred behind the dashboard. Anna felt the wipers' rhythm, steady as a pulse.

"One thing's for sure. Surprises are waiting for us out there in the fog of life," Grammy added. "We must hope for the best and expect even more."

That had been Grammy's mantra. Anna had heard her say it dozens of times. The words echoed in her mind when she got up and cleaned a circle of the turret's window with her fist, just as she'd cleaned Grammy's windshield to see out on that long-ago afternoon. For now, when Anna's future was uncertain, the present seemed a safer place to be. Predicting what lay ahead for herself *or* the house was as pointless as worrying about it. She'd try to muddle along in the present, a step at a time, and hope for the best. As for expecting even more, she wasn't sure.

CHAPTER 10

———⁂———

Jeff raised a disapproving eyebrow as he looked around the apartment's living room. *What an awful place. But beggars can't be choosers.*

He tried not to recoil from the walls—hot pink, shocking pink, tickle-me pink. Whatever you wanted to call it, the color prevailed like an infectious rash that had spread from the hot-pink bathroom. At least Mr. Ripley, the landlord and a retired Marine, had painted the baseboards and window trim a civilized white. In order to stay on Gamble near Anna, Jeff could make do here if he had to.

He could clean the last tenant's toothpaste off the bathroom mirror easily enough, and a little bleach could send packing the kitchen sink's mold. Though tattered, the red-and-brown plaid sofa was serviceable. Jeff didn't really want to look at the mattress—he could always set his sleeping bag on top of Mr. Ripley's ruffled pink taffeta bedspread. And there was a balcony for Earnest to loll around on. He wouldn't mind looking down on a gas station.

What mattered most was that the apartment was furnished. Without moving much from the condo, Jeff could stay here for however long—and he hoped it would be short. More important, he also hoped that Earnest could live here. Mr. Ripley, who had gray sideburns and a paunch, was the only Gamble landlord on craigslist willing to consider a pet, and Jeff had come running after work with Earnest's photo.

"Here he is. He's a fantastic dog!" From his wallet, Jeff handed Mr. Ripley the picture, which he took with the tips of his stubby thumb and index finger. He acted like Earnest had mange that might crawl out of the photo. "I can't bring him here right now because he's at the vet's. But you can see how handsome he is," Jeff said.

"I don't care what he looks like. I care how he behaves. How do I know this dog won't rip up my apartment?" To Mr. Ripley, Earnest was surely fanged and bent on destruction.

"Earnest is a Lab. The friendliest, most well-behaved breed. He's at the clinic because he inhaled smoke. He's a hero. He rescued people in a fire."

"The one on Rainier yesterday?"

"Yes." Plant Parenthood was just two blocks from this apartment.

"Does the dog shed?" Mr. Ripley asked.

"I brush him every day."

"Bark?"

"Rarely. The only time he loudly voices an opinion is when he's being protective."

"How much does he weigh?"

"About eighty pounds, but he's surprisingly graceful. He doesn't break things. He's never attacked another dog."

Mr. Ripley eyed Jeff with misgiving. "Usually, I have to meet the pet in person."

"You'd love Earnest. Everybody does. Really." *No pleading. Keep the desperation under wraps.* "If you want someone to vouch for him, I can get a reference from his vet. It's Dr. Nilsen. Do you know him?"

"Never had a pet. Don't much like animals."

"Right," Jeff nodded.

Mr. Ripley studied Earnest's face with the focus of a general trying to decipher the secret code of an invading army. "I don't know. I guess he seems okay."

Great.

He handed the photo back to Jeff, picked up his backpack by the door, and pulled out a legal-size paper. "I'll want a four-hundred-dollar deposit, and here's the year's lease you need to sign."

Aargh. On the phone Jeff had not asked about a lease. He'd hoped Mr. Ripley, like many landlords on their friendly island, rented with only a deposit and a handshake.

"Could the lease be month-to-month?" Jeff asked. *Otherwise, he'd have to break it to move back to the condo.*

"The shortest I ever allowed was six months, and that was for my brother-in-law," Mr. Ripley said.

"What if I paid a higher rent each month?"

"Like how much?"

"Say fifty dollars?"

Mr. Ripley seemed to consider this offer for a moment. "You could move out in a month or two and leave me stuck with this place in the middle of winter. Nobody rents in the rain."

"Um . . ." As Jeff collected his thoughts, his gaze went to fly specks on the window. Eye contact was hard when he edged too close for comfort toward deception.

If he had his way, he'd move out of here in a week and forfeit the rest of this month's rent. Yet he valued honesty and decency, and he wouldn't want to leave this man in the lurch. On the other hand, Jeff didn't know how long Anna would take to come to her senses. He might have to live here for a couple of months or more. If his future truly were not definite, he wasn't misleading anyone.

"I want to live here. I'll keep it clean. I'll pay the rent on time. Earnest and I won't cause you trouble."

When Mr. Ripley exhaled, his belly jiggled slightly. "Oh, all right."

"Thanks." Jeff clapped Mr. Ripley's beefy shoulder as he took the lease. He quickly looked it over, signed it, and wrote out a deposit check. Mr. Ripley gave him a key.

"Anna?" Jeff called.

He could tell just from stepping inside the condo that she wasn't home. Evening shadows darkened the living room, and something felt askew. Instead of the usual warmth, there was an unsettling emptiness. Now that Jeff wasn't exactly living here, the room itself didn't seem the same, either.

Sure, against one wall was the same white denim sofa he'd slept on, and, across from it, the same love seat with a whisper of pink like a blush. The his-and-hers wingback chairs. Anna's plants. Jeff's landscape paintings. Earnest's wicker bed and its royal-blue pillow. The shelves where Jeff and Anna's books mingled together.

But Jeff felt like he was trespassing on someone else's property, and he didn't quite belong here anymore. Uneasy, he went to the bathroom and packed his toiletries bag, including Pepcid for stressful days like the last two, and ZzzQuil if the stress kept him awake. From the bedroom closet he got pajamas and a change of clothes. Tomorrow after work he'd come back for more.

He stopped in the kitchen and made a chicken sandwich, which he ate standing at the counter. In the quiet, he could hear himself chew. He felt slightly furtive. If Anna came home and found him, he should probably bolt out the door.

In the garage, he stopped at his and Anna's storage locker and rummaged through the camping gear. In a plastic bin he found their sleeping bags, and it did not escape his notice that they seemed to be snuggling, as he and Anna had on camping trips when they'd zipped the bags together.

Pulling his bag out of the bin and leaving Anna's behind depressed him. *Easy, man,* he comforted himself. *You'll be camping with her again before long.*

He told himself again that his move was temporary. He would soon be back in his and Anna's bed. As usual, Earnest would start the evening snoring innocently on the rug. But as the night got cooler and Jeff and Anna's sleep got deeper, Earnest would sneak up on their bed and wriggle between them so they made a sandwich, Earnest the ham and Jeff and Anna the bread. Those were the coziest times, the three of them cuddled up together in their nest. Jeff warmed at the memory. What he wouldn't give to sleep like that tonight.

CHAPTER 11

⁂

No one would have known that Earnest had inhaled smoke. He pranced down the hall the best he could with his burned paw and plastic cone, and he burst into Plant Parenthood to reclaim his kingdom. But then he paused, moved his head around, and peered out the cone at Anna's shop.

He looked up at her with a puzzled expression. *What the devil has happened here?*

"The fire, Sweetie. Remember?"

Earnest aimed his charcoal-lump nose toward the floor and tried to sniff his way to what had been Anna's houseplant jungle. Now only Edgar and Constance greeted him, with sagging leaves and withered fronds. Earnest circled the half-filled garbage bags, the empty flower buckets, and the chests and tables, now denuded of their merchandise. He bumped his cone against the base of Anna's sink, where sooty metal Buddhas were soaking in soapy water.

Anna held up Earnest's gray lily pad so he could see. "Smoke got your bed. I'm going to throw it out, but don't worry. Last night I ordered you a new one online."

For now, Anna set her sleeping bag on the floor and patted it to encourage Earnest to nestle in for a nap. She did not mention that she'd gotten her bag from the storage locker that morning, and Jeff's had been missing. Or that she'd not seen him at the condo last night. Later today Earnest would get home and realize that his family was divided. She dreaded the distress that would cause him.

Her own distress was enough for them both. Two days after learning of Jeff's deception, shock and resentment still churned through her—but now also sadness, and sometimes she felt numb. Her feelings must have emanated from her with an odor as arresting as ammonia because Earnest cocked his head and watched her, his face somber.

His pensive eyes informed her that he had noted her unhappiness, and his conclusion was, *I smell a rat.*

"You get some rest, Sweetie. That's your job right now. You've had a huge ordeal."

What's going on? What are you not telling me? asked his forehead furrows.

"Here, Earnest. Lie down."

Winston Somebody—Anna didn't catch his last name— looked like a hedgehog. He had small round eyes, a pointed nose, and a salt-and-pepper flattop that grew in the manner of freshly mowed grass. He walked into Plant Parenthood and introduced himself, but shrank back to the doorway when Earnest came to greet him.

Winston glared at him as he would have at a weevil. "Does he bite?"

"In that cone, he couldn't if he wanted to. He's just trying to say hello," Anna said.

"Get him away." Winston waved his arms. He could have been fanning poison gas.

How absurd. "Here, Earnest. Come back to the sleeping bag."

Earnest looked insulted. From deep inside his cone, he shot

Winston a black, distrustful look. Earnest sat with his front paws extended so his body made a tripod—the better to spring forward and bark if Winston tried anything funny.

"At least he obeys," Winston sniffed. He edged back into the room, as far away as possible from Earnest. "I'm an adjuster for Seaco Insurance. I need to estimate the damage here."

"Be my guest." Anna picked a Buddha out of the sink. As she squeezed a soapy sponge over his head, gray dribbled down his robe and left behind shiny brass trails. Anna dunked him back into the water and wiped the sponge over his face and arms.

Slinking around the windows, Winston glanced repeatedly at Earnest to make sure he wasn't gearing up for an assault. He walked the shop's perimeter, then stepped behind Anna's counter, a protective barrier in case Earnest decided to lunge at his throat. He smoothed a hand over the wall and grimaced at the residue. "Looks like the main problem in here is from smoke."

"That's true of the whole house except the kitchen," Anna said.

"It's going to need a lot of fixing."

"When will you do it?" Anna asked, though she assumed Mrs. Blackmore didn't intend to fix anything.

"I don't do repairs. I estimate them."

"So you have no idea when the electricity will be turned back on?" Anna asked.

"That's an easy question. Not till the house is rewired."

Disappointed, Anna groaned and gripped the Buddha. If a fig had fallen from his Bodhi tree and bonked him on the head, his scowl would not have been as dark as hers. "We're desperate for power," she said.

"Lady, you don't want power here till the wiring's repaired. It's not safe. It caused the fire in the first place."

Winston's news danced down the counter and brushed

Anna's face with the pleasure of a long-desired kiss. "The *wiring* caused the fire?"

"According to the investigator's report."

"So it was faulty!" *Our Mr. Coffee is innocent! Mrs. Scroogemore can't sue us! Maybe we can sue her . . . but, then, she'd never sell us the house.*

Winston fixed his beady hedgehog eyes on Anna. "Look, I'm not supposed to talk with you about this stuff."

"I'm glad you did."

"Forget I said anything. And forget turning on the electricity. Trust me. The wiring needs to be brought up to code."

At the end of the day, when Anna left for home with Earnest, they paused at Lauren's poetry post for her latest September poem. Each month she usually put up only a single poem, written by one of her many community contributors. But this poem was her own, posted without delay, she said, because she wanted to make an important point. Anna pulled a copy from the Plexiglas box and read:

The Fire

The fire began with a single spark,
Which caused electric wires to arc.
Hiding in the kitchen wall,
This monster sought to consume it all.
He devoured the cookbooks, the kitchen table.
His crackling flames threatened the gable.
His evil smoke breathed the first alarm.
With smoke he meant to do his harm.

Smoke swirled throughout our treasured place,
Smell and soot left in our space.
The monster's appetite was cruel.

Yet his destruction becomes my fuel.
Give up? Not in my DNA.
We live to fight another day.
Begin again, I tell my soul.
That's who I am. That's how I roll.

CHAPTER 12

"Earnest!" In the condo's entry, Jeff sank to his knees and hugged him.

Wriggling with happiness, Earnest nuzzled Jeff despite the evil plastic cone, which would have vexed Saint Monica, the patron saint of patience. At last home from the clinic, Earnest squeaked and wagged his tail as if he thought it could lift him into flight. He unambiguously declared, *I'm thrilled to see you! I love you! We're finally all together again!*

Jeff said, "We were worried about you, Earnest."

We. Without thinking, Jeff had used the word. For three days he and Anna had not been a "we"—they'd split into an "I" and an "I."

Jeff looked around the living room. "Is Anna here?" he asked Earnest. Jeff got to his feet. "Anna?"

No answer.

He found her stirring Earnest's evening yogurt into his extra-nutritious kibble, whose expense took a firm financial commitment. When Jeff reached the kitchen doorway, she did not look up.

"So, how you doing?" he asked cheerfully despite the scrunch at the edges of her eyes. He'd seen it before, when she fought back tears. He wanted to hold and comfort her.

But as she kept stirring, the scrunch hardened, and the tears' unexpressed sadness seemed to give way to irritation that was written all over her face. She pressed her lips together in a tight, straight line.

Jeff reminded himself not to let her ill feelings spoil his intent of going along with her wants and needs. For now, she was in the driver's seat, and he was glad to run behind Vincent and cough in the exhaust. *Sometimes you have to sacrifice in the present to achieve a future goal,* he thought. No matter how mad she got, he would not veer from his plan to wait out her huff and welcome her back.

"I'm fine," she finally said. "Have you come for the rest of your stuff?"

"That was my plan, but I wish you'd dissuade me."

"Not likely." Anna unfastened Earnest's cone and set it on the counter. She placed his supper on the floor.

As he began to inhale his food—he didn't chew, he vacuumed—Jeff pointed out, "Smoke didn't ruin his appetite."

Anna let the words roll by her. She stared out the window at fir trees, gray-black in the gathering dusk.

Jeff took the hint. "Okay, so I'll start packing."

He went to the bedroom and piled clothes on his and Anna's bed. From the garage's storage locker, he hauled back two suitcases and five Bekins moving boxes, which he assembled with tape. Slowly, he packed—underwear, towels, sheets, his pillow, some architecture books, and two Stephen King novels he hadn't gotten around to reading yet. He rummaged through the bathroom for extra razor blades and shampoo. From the kitchen, where Anna was studying her tea as if her entire future hinged on how long her chamomile bag might float, he got a frying pan, sauce pan, cereal bowl, mug, spatula, knife and fork and spoon, and two glasses. He took a beer and a package of cheese from the refrigerator and put them in a paper bag.

As Jeff packed, Earnest, wearing his cone again, hobbled behind him from room to room. He tilted his head, the better to observe what disappeared into each box. Though he'd seen Jeff pack a suitcase for out-of-town business trips, he'd never seen him load items into large cardboard cubes. Their novelty clearly pricked his concern. *What are you doing?* asked his suspicious glances. Earnest's worried eyes wrestled Jeff's resolve to the ground.

Guilt over what he was about to do to his dog pained him—guilt he didn't deserve. The last thing he wanted or intended was to upset Earnest, and now his routine would be disrupted, and he wouldn't understand Anna and Jeff's separation even for a short time. Jeff didn't know how to convey to him that Anna wanted it this way, that *he* wished he didn't have to leave.

He supposed he could make up for Earnest's disruption with ferry rides, or trips to the office, where his colleagues would fawn over him. Jeff could set him by the goal line at Saturday morning practices of the tyke soccer team Jeff coached. Earnest loved little kids. He would be happy. Jeff hoped.

He carried the boxes and his drafting stool and table to his rental truck. He took his two paintings off the wall. (They'd never look right with Mr. Ripley's hot pink, but at least they'd add a civilized touch.) Jeff went back for the clock radio but decided that he could wake up by his cell phone and Anna needed the morning alarm. From the dresser's top, he took a photo of Earnest leaning against Anna's leg while she was browning hamburger.

Finally, as Anna remained in the study, ignoring Jeff, he went to the kitchen pantry. He lifted the cover of Earnest's kibble vat and poured scoopfuls into a plastic bag. He took five cans of Earnest's gourmet chicken and a bag of Cheetos, for which Earnest would gladly give a year of his life. Jeff removed Earnest's leash from the hook by the back door.

"Let's go, Bud," he called.

As Earnest padded over to him, Anna rose from her chair. She looked angrier than a threatened mother grizzly, her claws unsheathed. "What are you doing?" she growled.

"Earnest is coming with me."

"He is *not*."

"Of course he is."

"Earnest is staying here. With *me*."

"That's ridiculous. He's my dog. I adopted him at Second Chance. I filled out the form and paid the fee."

"He's mine," Anna seethed. "How could you be so callous? If you take him away, you'll upset him more than the fire did."

"You think my *leaving* won't upset him?"

"Earnest needs his home."

Earnest clearly heard his name being tossed back and forth because he moved his cone from Anna to Jeff, the better to read their faces and smell their smells, which shouted *Danger! Trouble! Bad news!* He narrowed his eyes to screen out the emotions that flew around the kitchen. As he crouched down and flattened back his ears, his face went dark, like blowing out a candle.

Jeff stopped himself from saying more. In this situation no one would win, especially not Earnest. Right now what mattered most was keeping him secure. Jeff told himself, *Traipse lightly on the eggshells. Don't get Anna's dander up any more than it is. Go along to get along.* But he'd never imagined that going along would mean leaving behind his dog.

"Fine. You keep him," Jeff said gently. For Earnest's sake, Jeff kept his voice calm, hardly what he felt. He hung the leash on its hook, replaced the cans on the pantry shelf, and poured the kibble into the plastic bin.

"Bye, Buddy." Jeff squatted down and hugged him as he had when he'd arrived, but, for both of them, the joy seemed to have drained out of the gesture. Jeff patted Earnest's side and got a hollow, empty sound. Earnest seemed stiff, tense. He might have been holding back feelings he didn't understand.

Collateral damage. To my best friend. Damn. If Jeff let himself, he could be as mad at Anna as she was at him.

But he wouldn't let himself. Back to his plan. He smiled at Anna, who seemed to have launched a new career in glowering. "See you, Honey." He headed toward the door with Earnest at his heels.

"Wait a minute," she said.

He stopped, turned around. *Please, say you don't want me to leave. Please, let's go back as we were.* "What's the matter?"

She held out her hand, flat, palm up. "I can't live here if I could come home and find you in the living room. I need the key."

What the hell? This was Jeff's condo as much as hers. He'd signed the lease with her. He'd paid most of the deposit and sometimes her half of the rent. Besides, giving her the key was too final. Being Mr. Nice Guy was getting old. Fast.

But then he thought, *Humor her. Let her keep the damned key for a few weeks. What difference does it make?*

As he worked the key off the chain she'd given him for Christmas, its four-leaf clover dangled upside down and seemed to spill out Jeff's luck. He dropped the key onto Anna's palm, patted Earnest, and said a pleasant good-bye. Without looking back, Jeff walked out the door.

CHAPTER 13

Earnest limped to the bedroom and sniffed Jeff's side of the bed. He examined Jeff's empty half of the closet and plodded into the living room. He stopped at the love seat, where Jeff and Anna often cuddled under a quilt and watched TV, and he circled the wingback chair, where Jeff read his nightly *Seattle Tribune*. After searching for Jeff's drafting table in the study, Earnest checked Jeff's place at the kitchen table.

Then Earnest started his restless patrol again. He would not stop pacing. His whimpers let Anna know his feelings: *Where is Jeff? I am upset and confused.*

As Anna watched him, her heart melted. It wasn't fair for Jeff to tarnish Earnest's shining spirit. Jeff could ruin *her* life, but Earnest's? And just so Jeff could chase ambition? His professional success was not worth a louse's toenail of the anguish he was causing their dear, sweet dog.

Earnest came to Anna. From deep inside his cone, he looked up at her with undeniable torment that asked again, *Where is he? What did you do with him?*

"Sweetie, I haven't done anything with Jeff. He's moved out." There was nothing else to say. She couldn't gloss over the truth when Earnest could decipher nuances of behavior and read minds.

Anna wanted to point out that Jeff had been a jerk, but she stopped herself. After a breakup, parents weren't supposed to disparage each other to their children, and surely that rule also applied to sensitive dogs.

All she could think to do was to distract Earnest. From a ceramic cookie jar, she picked out one of the vile cow's hooves that Jeff bought for him in spite of Anna's guaranteed recoil. To her, there was something gruesome about his gnawing on a hoof, but, to him, it was the golden key that unlocked Nirvana's door. Barely touching the hoof, she set it on the kitchen floor. She expected Earnest to be ebullient. He'd chomp it with abandon and forget that Jeff was gone.

To aid the chomping, she removed Earnest's cone. He glanced at the hoof, then up at her so the whites under his eyes looked like dejected supine crescent moons. *I'm on to you. You can't bribe me,* said his pressed-back ears.

Earnest picked up the hoof in his teeth, escorted it to the study, and dropped it where Jeff's drafting table had been. As Earnest walked away, he offered his unambiguous view of Anna's method of distraction: *Phooey on your hoof. I don't want it. I want Jeff.*

Earnest limped to Jeff's wingback chair and curled up in his cannelloni bean position next to where Jeff normally placed his feet. Earnest could not have made plainer where he stood on the matter of Jeff's absence: *It is terrible. Unacceptable. Cruel.* Earnest closed his eyes and retreated to a dark and tangled mental forest.

When the phone rang, a small, sad, sorry piece of Anna wished the caller might be Jeff. Because of Earnest, she was torn. Part of her felt like a huffy begrudger, who wanted Jeff banished from her life. But another part felt like a wounded lamb, who wished Jeff would come home and reassure Earnest so he'd be himself again and they could go back to being a family.

However, Anna mentally grabbed herself by the scruff of her neck and told herself that the wounded lamb had to go. She would serve it on a platter with asparagus for Easter dinner before she would think again of getting together with Jeff. Wanting him home was out of the question.

Anna picked up the kitchen phone.

"Boy, have I got good news for you." Joy laughed the low and lusty laugh of her villain Murdon when he'd snatched Penelope away from the Cornwall pub. Lately, Joy had gone back to writing, much to the relief of Anna and Lauren. When Joy was working on her novel, she sometimes acted like her characters.

"I could use some good news." Anna sat at the table and twirled a fork between her thumb and index finger.

"Divine justice comes to Mrs. Scroogemore! Tee-hee! Lightning strikes the old bat!" Joy said. "I hinted that she was negligent about the wiring and we might sue her if she didn't let us stay in the house for a third of the rent. She agreed as long as we'd move out quickly if she gives notice."

"What about rewiring?"

"She said she can't afford repairs. Can you believe that?!" Another Murdon chortle. "She said there's a separate electrical panel in the garage that some tenant put in for his shop. If we buy those long orange extension cords at the hardware store, we can get electricity from the garage into the house."

"Would that work? Is it safe?"

"Lauren called her electrician cousin. He said the setup would be weird, but okay for now," Joy said. "The buzzard woman said she'd have her lawyer write up some paper for us to sign. She refuses to be responsible for our safety."

"Typical." Anna rested her elbow on the table. "At least now we have some time before we'd have to move out."

"Exactly. Mission accomplished, except I want her to suffer. I want cannibals to get a crack at her. I want them to broil her in her St. John's suit."

"Oh, well," Anna said.

"You don't sound very happy. I thought you'd be ecstatic."

"Jeff just moved out. He tried to take Earnest. At least he backed off."

"Uh-oh. Red flag. I read in *New Divorce Magazine* that couples fight for custody of pets," Joy said. "Maybe he's playing nice before he goes to a lawyer."

"You think he'd actually *do* that?" Anna sat up straight.

"You never know. You should line up Mad Dog Horowitz. He's the lawyer who freed me from the Twit," Joy said. "Here, I'll give you the number."

As Anna wrote it down, conflict bit into her again, but this time in a new way. Now instead of the huffy begrudger versus the wounded lamb, she was of two minds about Earnest. He needed to live in his familiar home and come to work with her as usual. He needed Anna.

But if she were truly honest, he also needed Jeff.

Anna was the gentle one, Earnest's devoted caretaker, who fussed over him, wiped his muddy paws, knew all his friends, fed him, walked him, and bathed and brushed him. In thunderstorms she soothed him, and on hot days she carried water in Vincent to quench Earnest's thirst. She broiled him chicken breasts when he was sick and baked him peanut butter pupcakes every year on his "gotcha day," when she and Jeff had adopted him.

Jeff, on the other hand, was Earnest's playmate, his mentor of manly pursuits, such as body surfing, fetching a Frisbee, romping through wetlands, and balancing in a canoe. Jeff played rough games with Earnest, the favorite being tug with Monty, who started life as a plump toy rabbit but became a pink fleece scrap.

Outside in a deck chair, Jeff held out Monty, tantalizing, teasing. Earnest bit into his hind feet while Jeff grabbed his ears, and back and forth, man versus dog, they went. Earnest growled tenacious playful growls. With all his mighty eighty pounds, he yanked Jeff from his chair. Jeff jerked back and hauled Earnest by his teeth across the grass. Finally, Jeff let loose so Earnest won. He pranced around the yard with Monty in a victory lap.

Countless times, Anna had pushed Monty's stuffing back into his fleece suit and sewn him up. Though the rabbit was only a piece of fabric now, Earnest still adored him. *He also adores Jeff,* Anna thought. *The tie between them is as strong as steel.* It wouldn't be fair for her to break it, but it wouldn't be fair for Jeff to have Earnest, either. What was she supposed to do? King Solomon couldn't slice through Earnest and give half of him to her and half to Jeff.

She told Joy good-bye and fished out what was left of Monty from Earnest's toy basket. She would entice him into a few tugs, even if they wouldn't measure up to his mano-a-dientes bouts with Jeff. When she went to the living room, however, Earnest's closed eyes put her on notice: *Do not disturb.* Anna turned around and set Monty back in the basket with Earnest's balls, Frisbees, Kongs, and Nylabones—his macho toys from Jeff.

CHAPTER 14

Jeff was stacking papers into orderly piles on his office desk when his boss, Brian Cooper, knocked at the open doorway. "Here's your application for the ideas competition." He handed Jeff a folder from Seattle's chapter of the American Institute of Architects. "Send in your drawings. Cedar Place has a great chance to win."

"Thanks." Jeff set the folder on his desk next to a leather-framed photo of Anna and Earnest on a bench outside Gamble's library.

"The project going okay?" Brian asked.

"I filed for the permits. Now we wait."

"Who's your planner?"

"Randy Grabowski."

"I've heard about him. Sadistic bastard, supposedly," Brian said.

"That's about it."

Jeff covered his mouth and stifled a yawn. Last night Anna had grabbed on to his brain like a bulldog and wouldn't let go till dawn. "Got a minute?"

Brian checked his watch. "Meeting at eleven." He leaned his shoulder against Jeff's shelf of binders for products and codes. "What's up?"

Jeff stood and closed the door, which was nearly always open. Brian looked puzzled by the need for privacy. His bulbous nose and rolling hills of cheeks belonged on an applehead doll, but they were deceiving. Under his salt-and-pepper eyebrows, his eyes were stern.

Jeff cleared his throat. "I've enjoyed working on Cedar Place. You know that. But I'd like to hand it over to someone else."

Brian's thin lips parted in surprise. "That makes no sense. It's your chance to prove yourself as a lead architect."

"Something's come up." Jeff's gaze went to the tight chevrons in the carpeting. "Anna and two of her friends rent the Victorian house we're tearing down on the property."

"So?"

Jeff hurried through an abridged version of the women's dreams and plans. He explained why he'd put off telling Anna about the project and how she'd found out. "She's upset. She's broken up with me. I moved out last night."

Brian pinched the bridge of his nose as he seemed to collect his thoughts. "You've got a great design. It's a turning point for you, and it's going to take you places," he said.

"Couldn't somebody else here manage it?"

"You don't change horses midstream, Jeff. Your client— what's her name? Blackmore? She could move to another firm."

"I don't think she'd do that. She likes what I've done. She could finish up here with someone else," Jeff said.

"You know as well as I do that you have to mollycoddle clients. If you skip out on Mrs. Blackmore, she's going to feel betrayed."

Jeff's shoulders fell. "That's how Anna feels. 'Betrayed' is the word she used."

"She'll get over it. Mrs. Blackmore won't. Cedar Place is a

lucrative project for us. It's important for the firm's success. You need to see it through."

Brian checked his watch again. "Look, I don't have time today for foolish decisions. I can promise you'll regret it if you quit your project. That's how things work in this firm," he said. "We value you. You've got a great future here. You don't want to lose it. Bailing out would be a big professional mistake."

"Okay," Jeff said, though it was unclear what he was agreeing with. He felt as if he'd shrunk from a confident six-foot-two adult to a small, chastised child.

As Brian walked out, he told Jeff, "Think carefully about what I've said."

Thinking carefully, but bruised by Brian's threats, Jeff slumped into his chair. He knew that a bad professional reputation would sink its claws into him and never let go. If he handed over Cedar Place to someone else, Brian would fire him without a reference, and Jeff would be blackballed in his search for a new job. He had no choice but to see Cedar Place through to the finish.

He stared at two cacti that Anna had insisted he keep in his office—because workplace greenery was supposed to increase productivity by fifteen percent, she'd said. One cactus slumped in its pot like a dejected biscuit, and the other, a frequent source of mirth for Jeff's male colleagues, jutted up like a triumphant penis. *The cacti pretty well sum up the dynamics between me and Brian,* Jeff thought. At least he'd always know he tried to get off the project.

On the wall above Jeff's desk hung his University of Washington diploma, which had always added honor to his life. Today, however, the parchment only reminded him of how hard he'd worked to support himself through school. He'd served in dining halls, mopped floors in the chemistry lab, collected tickets at the Varsity Theater, sold shoes at Murphy's, vacuumed Rent-a-Wreck cars. In summers he'd worked for a contractor, who built shopping centers in Puyallup and Issaquah. Jeff nearly cut off his fingers with a table saw, and he hurt a disk in his back when helping raise a roof beam that an ox might have buckled under.

Every day Jeff had told himself that he would wear like armor the character he was building. He would get through the University of Washington *and* the School of Hard Knocks. He would make something of his life, as men he'd met along the way had encouraged him to do: his high-school basketball coach; his university adviser; Uncle Fred, who'd missed his family's alcoholic gene; Brian Cooper—before he'd threatened Jeff about his job today. They were his collective father figure, the one he'd needed, but missed growing up. Jeff's father had fallen in love with the bottom of a whiskey bottle and had been a rotten provider.

When Jeff was seven, he'd been invited to a birthday party. The parents of his best friend rented an entire roller-skating rink, called Skateland, and his second-grade class would be there. Jeff had only skated in the street on his cousin's rusty skates. To him, the rink would be a palace. He imagined flying across a gleaming wooden floor, disco music blaring, lights shining like stars from the ceiling, just as he'd seen on TV.

On the Saturday morning of the party, Jeff barely touched his cornflakes. His stomach was already making loops and zipping around the rink. He stationed himself at his apartment window so he could spot his ride as it pulled into the parking lot. He would run down the stairs.

Just before nine o'clock, finally—*finally!*—the car arrived. Jeff leapt to his feet.

His mother, thin from standing at a grocery store's cash register all day, stepped in front of him. "Stay here, Jeffrey. I'll be right back."

Two stories down, Jeff watched her, a miniature mother, walking to the car. She leaned toward the driver's open window, her hands cupped over her knees. As she talked, the cold turned her words to fog that drifted away. Jeff's impatience scraped his stomach. His mouth tasted sour.

The driver rolled up her window. As the wipers tossed raindrops off her windshield, she drove away. Jeff's mother waved. When she returned to the apartment, Jeff's lower lip was quivering.

"I told her you were sick," she said. "We couldn't afford a birthday present."

Jeff went to his room, a converted walk-in closet. He stayed there all day.

His father arrived for dinner, his face flushed, his gait unsteady. On nights like this, Jeff knew to eat in silence and disappear. But his mother needled, "Jeff missed a skating party because we couldn't buy a present. Such a shame."

His father shoved a bite of tuna casserole into his big mouth and waved her away as if she were a pesky fly. "Just as well he didn't go. He'd have fallen down and broken his ass or something. We couldn't pay the doctor bills."

Anna was the only person Jeff had ever told this story. Without a word, she'd taken his hand and kissed his palm. He'd never felt so close to anyone as he had to her at that minute. He'd felt exposed and vulnerable, but she'd made it all right.

Chapter 15

All the cleaning was getting old, first purging ashes from Plant Parenthood and now purging Jeff from the condo. With the vacuum cleaner, which Anna and Jeff had bought together—*so who owned it now?*—she assaulted dust bunnies that had burrowed under his drafting table before he'd taken it away. In the closet she went after bits of his ferry passes, dirt from his running shoes, and paper clips from his office. An ill wind had blown all his detritus to the closet floor. *Such an imposition!*

His now-empty side of the closet seemed to glare at Anna like an accusatory eye, as did the two faded rectangles on the living-room wall, where his paintings had hung. But what did they have to glare at her about? Jeff was the one to blame.

In the bathroom, Anna curled her lip, disgusted, at globs of toothpaste on his drawer's plastic liner. For a tidy man, the globs were out of character. *He might have left them there on purpose to harass me.* He'd also left half-finished bottles of Listerine and cough medicine, tubes of sunscreen and athlete's foot cream, and half-empty vials of prescription pills for his allergies to povertyweed and prickly lettuce.

Unwilling to keep these reminders of Jeff—*the lingering smell of his shaving cream is bad enough!*—Anna shook open a plastic trash bag. She would fill it with his belongings, then either throw it away or drop it off at Jeff's apartment, *if* she learned where it was, and *if* she could guarantee he'd not be there. Into the bag she tossed the bottles, tubes, and vials. She added socks from under the bed and belts coiled like snakes at the back of a closet shelf. She threw in his baseball hat, lodged between the wicker headboard and the mattress.

But what about photos lined up across his dresser? There was a picture of her and Earnest, searching for sea glass on Heron Harbor's beach. She supposed she could blot out the thought that Jeff had aimed the camera and clicked the button—and she would keep the photo here. She couldn't say the same about the one of her and Jeff in the Village Green's gazebo, plastered together so a thread couldn't slide between them. Anna dumped that photo in the trash bag.

She picked up an eight-by-ten walnut-framed picture of her, Jeff, and Earnest in Waterfront Park on his first gotcha day. She and Jeff were sitting yoga-style in the center of a Blazing Sun quilt. Between them, Earnest, in a pointed wizard hat, was lying in his roosting-chicken position after having gulped down a broiled hamburger patty and two pupcakes with peanut butter frosting. Earnest, Jeff, and Anna were smiling.

On that afternoon, Earnest's favorite pastime, picking blackberries with his teeth, had worn him out. He'd set down his chin in the center of the quilt's star and watched a fuzzy black caterpillar inch toward his nose. When the creature got so close that Earnest crossed his eyes, Jeff caught it in a paper cup and gently poured it on the grass at the edge of Earnest's blackberry thicket. "Take care of yourself. Have a nice day," Jeff said to the creature.

Anna laughed. How many men would rescue a caterpillar? She'd loved his courtesy and kindness.

But now he'd shown his true nature. *The fork-tongued*

weasel! Still, Anna couldn't bring herself to throw away the picture of that special afternoon. She looked at the photo one last time and hid it facedown at the bottom of her sweater drawer.

She had more to sort through, including linens, dishes, and cookware. And what about dividing their herbs and spices, whose jars Jeff had lined up in the cupboard alphabetically after searching for oregano one night? Would he get the allspice; she, the bay leaves; he, the celery seed? It was too much to consider in one morning. Her purge was going to take longer than expected. For now she had other pressing tasks.

Such as wiping their financial slate clean and putting all the condo accounts only in her name. From a drawer of the file cabinet, she pulled out last month's bills, called Puget Sound Energy, and was put on hold. As the wait dragged on, to amuse herself, Anna added up the amounts due for the phone, water, cable, electricity, and garbage pickup. Though she'd paid her half each month, the total stared her in the face and shocked her. She gaped at the number as people do when driving by a freeway wreck.

When she and Jeff had divided expenses, they'd seemed manageable. Sometimes after a slim-pickings month at her shop, he'd bailed her out and paid the bills himself. But now just as she was trying to get Plant Parenthood going again, she'd be responsible for the full amount of the bills *and* rent. Without Jeff, she was up a financial creek.

"Puget Sound Energy." The customer-service woman sounded bored.

"I need to change a joint account so it's only in my name," Anna said.

"You have the account number?"

As Anna gave it to her, she heard the smack of gum.

"You're Anna Sullivan?"

"That's right. You need to take Jeff Egan off the bills. He's not living here anymore."

"Break up?"

"Um . . . yes." *If you really want to know.*

"I've been getting lots of calls like yours. Maybe Mercury's in retrograde." A click of computer keys. "So Jeff Egan's off the account now. Anything else I can do for you?"

Help me win the lottery. Lead me to buried treasure. Find me a consumptive aunt who will die and leave me a fortune.

Anna pictured herself at the top of a circus tent, swinging from a trapeze by one finger—and no safety net was there to catch her.

Every time Anna had turned into Puget Sound Bank's parking lot, Earnest had marched his front legs in place on Vincent's seat. He'd hardly been able to wait to dash inside for a Milk-Bone from Marion, his faithful teller. Today, however, he sat there with a brick's enthusiasm and seemed hardly to notice he was about to enter his mansion of treats. Anyone could read his perspective on the situation: *ho-hum. I'd just as soon go home.*

Anna had to coax him out of Vincent. Earnest didn't even seem happy to be free of his plastic cone. Inside, he did not dash across the polished floor and skid to a stop at Marion's counter, as he usually did. He walked there with a slump. Anna could have tied a rope around his middle, pulled up, and corrected his posture.

Less than a year from retirement, Marion slumped too. Counting her days, hours, and minutes to freedom, she seemed too burned out to iron her blouse or tuck loose wisps of hair into her disheveled French twist.

"How's my adorable boy?" Marion placed her elbows on the counter, leaned over, and held out a Milk-Bone. Normally, Earnest rose on his hind legs, rested his paws on the counter's edge, and presented his teeth for a chomp. But today he stood there, four paws on the floor. "What's up with him?" Marion asked.

"Jeff moved out."

"Are you kidding me? I'd have bet an extra year on this job that you two would get married."

"Not going to happen." It felt strange to say it out loud.

"That's terrible. No wonder Earnest's not himself."

"I'm hoping he'll snap out of it."

"Here, give that boy his biscuit." Marion handed the Milk-Bone to Anna.

To get Earnest to take it, she pushed it between his two horse-shoes of teeth and mentally urged, *Don't be rude*. He dropped it to the floor, no more enthused about it than he'd been about the former hoof, which Anna had finally returned, without a tooth mark on it, to his treat jar.

Just then, a man in a navy sweat suit stepped in line behind Anna, and Marion shifted into business mode. "So what do you need today, Anna?" she asked.

"I want to move twenty-five hundred dollars from savings to checking."

If the man had not been waiting, Marion might have exclaimed, "Whew! Savings takes a hit." But she only nodded, official.

Anna handed her a withdrawal slip, and she gave Anna a receipt, which she took with a leaden heart. Her savings for the house had been sacred, but now she needed money for plants and flowers—and the condo's rent and bills.

After collecting the money off Marion's counter, Anna picked up Earnest's biscuit, which lay on the floor like a small, wounded soldier. "Maybe he'll be hungry later," she said.

CHAPTER 16

On the first Saturday afternoon in his new apartment, Jeff's objective was to settle in quickly and ignore his hot-pink walls. He'd think of this apartment as a bad hotel he had to stay in for a short time. Though Jeff's confidence in his and Anna's relationship had faltered since she'd taken his key, he held on to the prospect that soon she'd stop freezing him out. For now, however, he understood how the man inside the shaken glass ball felt about the blizzard.

Jeff leaned his paintings against the living-room wall because he had no hammer for his nails. *Something to pick up at the condo.* He set up his drafting table across the room and started to unpack his books. He looked around. No shelves. Okay, he'd leave the books in the box—they'd be easier to move back to the condo. *Shelves or no shelves aren't the end of the world.*

In the bedroom Jeff unpacked his clothes. Since shopping was torture for him, his wardrobe was sketchy—two suits, about a dozen shirts, and a few sweaters, sports coats, and pairs of slacks and jeans. He had a parka, overcoat, down vest, rain slicker, and handful of ties, mostly from Anna. For the last few days, he'd worn the same pair of slacks and one of those ties with whatever wrinkled shirt he pulled out of a cardboard box. But his rumpled look couldn't go on forever. He needed his and Anna's iron. *Another thing to pick up.*

In a neat row Jeff lined up his four pairs of shoes on the closet floor. He opened the top drawer of Mr. Ripley's dresser to put in shorts and tee shirts. Jeff stopped. He stared.

Long hairs lay, like irksome threads, on the bottom of the drawer. He pursed his lips with distaste. *So the former tenant had been a brunette. Irish? Japanese? Salvadoran?* Whoever she was, Jeff wished she'd vacuumed the damned drawers before moving out.

Having no vacuum cleaner here, he dampened a paper towel and wiped up the hair. To clean this place, he should have the vacuum cleaner, which, like the iron, he and Anna had bought together. What were they going to do? Borrow these essentials back and forth? Buying new ones for a short time would be a waste of money. In this situation, how was anybody supposed to win?

Besides the hammer, iron, and vacuum cleaner—and Anna— the other crucial missing thing was Earnest. Jeff had not seen him for three days, which felt like three months. Tomorrow Jeff would go to the condo, borrow him for the afternoon, and take him for a romp in the woods. Afterward, they'd stop here, and Jeff would show him the balcony and give him a Granny Smith apple—Earnest went wild over the crunch.

Except Jeff had no paring knife to cut the apple here. Where would the list of missing essentials end? *Another thing to pick up at the condo.*

Jeff thought, *What a pain in the ass this situation is getting to be.* But then he told himself, *Patience, patience. The Romans took a while to build their city.*

Jeff knocked on the condo door. When his neighbor bounded along the sidewalk in his running shoes and baseball cap and found him there, pathetically trying to get inside his own place, Jeff felt like a fool.

"Lost your key?" the neighbor asked.

"Yes." *But not in the way you think.*

"The manager can let you in."

As the neighbor jogged on, Jeff thought, *Damn. This is my home as much as Anna's.* From the beginning, they'd rented it together, and this very month he'd paid his usual half of the rent. Legally, he had a right to live here till the end of September. He wished he'd not so amiably handed her the key.

Jeff knocked and called again. "Anna?" Besides picking up Earnest, he'd intended to tell her that he'd asked Brian to take him off the project. He'd wanted her to see she meant so much to him that he'd been willing to tarnish his professional future for her. *But damn her! He couldn't talk with her if she wouldn't answer the door.*

This morning Anna hadn't answered the phone, either. He'd called. Three times. In the garage he'd just parked next to Vincent, so he knew she was inside. He'd have to be brain dead not to understand she was avoiding him.

Impatient, Jeff pounded the door with his fist. Still, she didn't come. "Anna? I know you're in there. Open the damned door."

When Jeff pressed his ear against the wood for signs of life, he heard Earnest whimpering on the other side—so near and yet so far. Each whimper felt like a stab from the paring knife Jeff had intended to collect here today.

Anyone could recognize the anguish Earnest was expressing: *I know Jeff is there. Why isn't he coming in? I'm confused, and I don't like it. I'm not sure what to do.*

Jeff closed his eyes and pressed his fingertips against his temples. His cheeks felt hot. His mouth was dry. He had a right to be annoyed when Anna was acting like he didn't exist, and,

far worse, when she was upsetting his dog. But for today, as
hard as it was, he resolved to continue as Mr. Go-Along-to-
Get-Along. He would keep his annoyance in check.

It was building up, though, and sidling precariously close to
resentment. Anna couldn't just cut him off with a quick and
heartless scissor snip. Whether she liked it or not, their damned
iron and vacuum cleaner kept them entangled, to say nothing
of nearly three years' memories and feelings. And Earnest. He
mattered most. Anna couldn't let her pettiness reduce him to
whimpers.

Biting his lip in frustration, Jeff rested his forehead on the
door. For Earnest's sake, he stopped knocking. "It's okay,
Buddy," he said.

On his cell, Jeff called what used to be his and Anna's land-
line. He could hear rings in the living room, but no footsteps
moving toward them. After six rings, the voice mail clicked on.
Another shock. That morning his voice had been on the
recorded message, but now Anna said, "I can't come to the phone
right now, but if you'll leave a message, I'll call you back."

She's not wasted any time, Jeff thought bitterly. He'd stood by
and let her elbow him out of the way and take over their
condo and his dog—and now she was usurping their life. He
called her cell. *No answer, of course.* After another recorded message, he said, "It's me. As you know, I'm standing at the door. I
want to see Earnest." Jeff paused, not sure how hard to push. If
he alienated her more than she already was, they'd never work
out this mess.

"We need to talk," Jeff continued. "I realize you're trying to
claim Earnest, but he's mine. You can't hold him hostage just
because you're mad at me. I paid for his adoption. I've footed
most of his food and vet bills. I'm responsible for him."

Jeff wanted to say he was *legally* responsible, but the word
might sound too much like he was gearing up for a court
fight, and that would sound the death knell for their relation-

ship. He held out hope that he and Anna would somehow get back together.

Nevertheless, he was vexed. A few days ago his patience had been as thick as the Sweet Time Bakery's mile-high chocolate cake. Now it had thinned to a razor's edge.

CHAPTER 17

Anna was weaving lavender wands when the first customer of her newly opened shop walked in. Perhaps the sandwich board that she and Lauren had set out next to the poetry post that morning had drawn him. They'd attached blue and white balloons and printed in triumphant red letters HURRAH! WE'RE READY FOR BUSINESS AGAIN!

"Welcome. May I help you?" Anna asked as Earnest rose from his new emerald-green lily pad and sized up the man.

He could only be called a hunk, though a rose by any other name would smell as sweet: heartthrob, babe magnet, eye candy, stud. His muscled chest bulged under his cotton turtleneck, the same turquoise as his eyes. His chiseled features might have graced a *GQ* cover. *Too bad Joy's not here to see him.*

"I want to surprise my girlfriend. Do you have flowers I can leave on her car seat?" he asked.

"Sure. Any idea what she'd like?"

He paused as he considered the question. His lips were seductive. Sexy stubble darkened his cheeks. "I've never given flowers to a woman before. What do other men get?"

"Depends on what they want the flowers to say."

His turquoise eyes lit up. His smile was pure bad boy. Anna

would have bet the statement that this hunk wanted the flowers to make was *You're hot, babe. Let me ravage you again tonight.*

"Are you looking for something romantic?" *Of course, he was.* She'd asked just to help him out.

"Romantic. Yes! Sure! That'd be great."

"Red roses maybe? I have some that are actually called Romeo. They're fragrant and sensuous. Women love them."

"Good." The bad boy smile again.

Anna took her bucket of Romeos from the refrigerator, which was now running by an extension cord from the garage. She set them on the counter. She'd make him the Humdinger, her standard amorous bouquet. It was luscious, the opposite of her chaste Virtue Special.

"Here, smell," she said.

He sniffed—heartthrob nose to voluptuous rose. "Perfect."

"A dozen?"

"Sure."

"I'll have them ready in a few minutes."

Anna counted out the roses, placed them on cellophane, with a tissue paper lining, and folded the corners over the stems. The man wandered around the room and examined her new plants and freshly washed Buddhas and angels. He squatted down and petted Earnest, who'd gone back to his new lily pad as if he were a Mongolian prince claiming his yurt. With entitlement, Earnest sprawled languidly on the corduroy, like he thought the customer had come to pay him homage and any minute yaks would arrive bearing Granny Smith apples and cheese.

As Anna stapled the cellophane in place, she thought of the hunk's girlfriend showing up at her car and finding his roses. Surely she'd be pleased. Women liked surprises. Anna did.

Last year after breakfast one morning, she'd dropped her favorite teacup on the kitchen's tile floor. The cup, almost large enough to house a goldfish, shattered into more pieces than Humpty Dumpty had. As she picked them up, she complained to Jeff, "I don't know how I'll ever find another cup like this. I never see this size anywhere."

That evening when she came home from work, he was waiting for her on the love seat, unusual because she nearly always got home first. "Ready for a treasure hunt?" he asked.

She started hunting right there in the living room by poking through throw pillows.

"Cold," he said.

She looked behind books in the shelf.

"Totally cold."

She searched through Earnest's wicker toy chest.

"Icy."

Jeff and Earnest followed her into the bedroom, where she reached into drawers, got on her hands and knees and checked under the bed, and searched coat pockets in the closet.

"Colder, colder, colder," Jeff said until she walked into the den. "Warmer. Now you're getting somewhere."

Hidden at the back of a file-cabinet drawer, Anna finally found a cup exactly like the one she'd broken. On his lunch hour, Jeff had tracked it down in Seattle—a supremely considerate surprise.

Unlike his supremely *inconsiderate* surprise three weeks ago when he'd given her the shock of a lifetime, wrapped in betrayal and tied with a bow of deception, Anna thought as she tied her own red bow around the roses. Now Jeff's surprises were still coming in the form of demanding phone messages that she'd never expected from him. Every night he called and said that Earnest was his and he wanted him back, and she knew Jeff well enough to read his voice's growing impatience. Now that her shop was open for business again, he might show up at any time and take Earnest away—and she couldn't stop him. Lately, that prospect had provoked sweaty, bitter dread.

"Here you go." Anna handed the bouquet to the hunk, whose credit card revealed the unhunkworthy name of Dudley Spitz. "I hope your friend likes the roses."

"Oh, she will."

As soon as he'd swaggered away, Anna found Mad Dog Horowitz's number in her wallet. She picked up the phone.

CHAPTER 18

———

"Jeffrey? What's going on? I called your condo, and Anna said you'd moved out. Is that true?"

Jeff closed his eyes. How to answer his mother, Madge? He'd intended to phone her, but he kept putting it off. He and Anna had been separated less than a month, and he wasn't ready to talk about her with anyone. Though she was being impossible, he wasn't ready to call it quits with her, either.

Perhaps his resistance to calling it quits—or to contacting Madge—stemmed from his parents' divorce. It had bruised Jeff. He didn't have a single memory of them happy together, and he'd sworn never to follow their footsteps into a bad relationship. Nevertheless, he wasn't ready to accept or admit that his and Anna's had failed. It was too soon for that.

"Yes, it's true. I'm living in an apartment." Jeff slumped back into Mr. Ripley's plaid sofa.

"What happened?" Madge asked.

"A misunderstanding."

"What kind of misunderstanding?"

"A dumb one."

"Most are. Why was yours dumb?" Madge asked.

"Because it didn't need to happen."

His mother had a streak of battering ram that used to infuriate his father. She could pinch up her thin face, fire off questions like grapeshot, and make people squirm. She should have been a lawyer instead of a grocery-store checker—and now co-manager, with her boyfriend, of a Sun City, Arizona, video arcade. Her specialties would have been stomping over boundaries and assaulting people's privacy.

"I don't mean to be nosy. I respect your right not to talk about it," she said, in retreat.

"Thanks," Jeff said. "Talk's a waste of words right now because I don't know how things are going to shake out."

"Are you okay where you're living? Is it clean? Safe?"

"It's got hot-pink walls."

"I like that color. *People* magazine said that Oscar de la Renta designed hot-pink clothes. Even swimming suits."

"I'll bet he didn't paint his walls hot pink."

"You never know."

Jeff heard a thunk, and then his mother came back on. "Sorry. Dropped the phone. Hard to talk and wash dishes at the same time," she said. "Jeffrey, are you all right?"

"I'm fine."

"Sure?"

"You don't have to worry about me."

"Anna was a nice girl."

Was. He didn't like the past tense.

Anna was a nice girl. Indeed. She was. *She is.*

Jeff had met her one Saturday morning after stepping out of the shower. He heard a knock on his door and grabbed his robe. Another knock. And another as he hurried, dripping, across the living room. He thought the person was impatient, rude.

When Jeff opened the door, a blonde with gorgeous blue-gray eyes was peering at him over the top of a fan-shaped spray of gladioli that seemed bigger than she was. His first thought was of a nightclub singer, prancing across a stage with a huge feather fan, but the legs of this woman were a little thin for that job.

"Sorry to beat on your door. I was afraid I'd drop this." The gladiolus fan tilted to the right.

"Need some help?" Jeff straightened it so the water wouldn't spill. "Let me hold it." To give her arms a rest, he took it from her.

"Thanks." Her smile was lovely. "Good luck tonight. I hope lots of people bid on my arrangement and your auction's a big success."

"I don't know anything about an auction."

"Not for the wildlife shelter?"

"No, and I didn't order these flowers," Jeff said.

"Aren't you Eddie Baker? This is 203-C Erickson Avenue, right?"

"Right, but I'm not Eddie Baker."

At the unexpected news, she widened her gorgeous eyes and reeled him in, hook, line, and sinker. When she got flustered—and looked adorable—she scraped off his scales, filleted him, and rolled him in cornmeal. *Amazing for her to land on my doorstep. A gift out of the blue.*

"There must be some mistake. I'm sorry," she said.

"No problem. Why don't you come in? We can look up Eddie Baker in my phone book." Maybe that sounded like "come in and see my etchings," but what was he supposed to do?

As she followed Jeff into the kitchen, he thought how vulnerable she was. For all she knew, he could be Charles Manson, and a machete could be stashed behind the stove.

He set the gladioli on the kitchen table. "You know, you shouldn't be so trusting of men. There's a lot of evil in the world."

"I could tell in a second that you're a good person." Another smile. Those pretty teeth.

What a way to start a Saturday.

Suddenly, Jeff remembered he wasn't dressed. Water from his hair was trickling down his neck, and he had nothing on under his robe. He grabbed its front to insure he didn't flash this lovely woman. He, who prided himself on being calm, turned nervous.

He rummaged through a kitchen drawer. "I can't remember where I left the phone book. It has to be around here somewhere."

Eventually, he found it in the den, and Anna found out where Eddie Baker lived. And soon Jeff and Anna found out that they liked each other. A lot. Slowly, over time, their "like" tiptoed close to "love."

On Valentine's Day, near their seven-month anniversary, Jeff took Anna to the Seattle Aquarium. As little kids hung over the tide pool's edge and splashed their hands in the water, Anna petted the limpets, hermit crabs, and sea stars. At the harbor seal display, one biologist tossed herring down the gullet of Alice, and another brushed the teeth of Humphrey. A boy in a Nemo sweatshirt begged, "Mommy, can we have a harbor seal?" Everybody in the bleachers laughed.

Jeff pulled Anna through the crowd to the giant Pacific octopus tanks. In one swam Delilah, her arms flowing behind her, graceful as a ballerina. In the other, Inky clung to his glass wall by his suckers, his eight arms spread out like a red sun's rays. When Jeff and Anna moved close, he aimed his eyes straight at them as if he were making sure they hadn't concealed a harpoon under their coats.

"Big things are happening here today," said a docent, who looked like a school marm in a long flowered skirt. "The diver in Inky's tank is about to remove the passageway's partition between him and Delilah. They've been yearning for each other for a long time, and now they can finally mate."

"Imagine a hug with sixteen arms," Anna whispered.

The diver slid away the partition, and the horny Inky picked up Delilah's pheromones and came to life. He charged through the tunnel, sprang on her, and covered her with eager arms so no one could tell where he ended and she began. All anyone could see was writhing and swishing.

Love was definitely blooming. Sperm would join eggs, and babies, in the form of plankton, would be in Inky and Delilah's future. At last, their longing satisfied, they could cohabit for a while.

Jeff led Anna past the otters, spinning and zooming through the water. In a quiet corner near the whale display, he put his arms around her as ardently as Inky's around Delilah, and Anna wrapped hers around Jeff's neck.

"I've been thinking we should move in together," he said.

"I've been thinking you should be the one to bring it up."

"I'm bringing it up. Want to get a condo?"

"I'm so glad you asked."

As Jeff kissed Anna's smile of agreement, Roman candles showered silver stars inside his heart. "I love you, Anna."

"I love you too."

Their two years of living together had been the happiest of Jeff's life. No pleasure could compare with waking up each morning and finding Anna beside him. Jeff could not understand how a love so deep could have gone so wrong. Their breakup was ridiculous. Somehow he had to get that through to her. He had to try one more time.

He would call Anna again and leave her another message, and this time he would not mention that he wanted Earnest. Jeff would tell her that he was going to sit in front of their condo door till she opened it and let him in to talk—and, if necessary, he would go on a hunger strike. She had to let him explain his side, he'd say. Then if she still wanted to break up with him, he'd reluctantly agree. He was a man of his word, he would remind her. He would be honorable. When they first met, she'd said he was a good person.

Before hanging up, he'd tell her that he loved her.

CHAPTER 19

———— ❧ ————

Anna had expected Sheldon "Mad Dog" Horowitz to remind her of a pit bull, or at least a Rottweiler. He'd be muscular and menacing. He'd foam at the mouth and lunge at throats.

But what she met across the broad expanse of his oak desk was a Chihuahua of a man—short, slight, skittish. He had a small snub nose and translucent ears; from the window behind him, the sun shone through his ears and exposed small veins.

This is Mad Dog? Is Joy crazy? The dissonance between his name and appearance jolted Anna. Nevertheless, she poured out her fears about Jeff's demanding phone messages. "I'll do anything for custody of Earnest," she said. She'd brought him so that Mad Dog could understand why this fight was so important.

Earnest had stationed himself at the door in his tripod posture, his front legs propping up his torso, the easier to bolt and run. The tension he picked up from Anna had put a grim look in his eyes. His preliminary verdict of this meeting was unmistakable: *Get me out of here. I have no wish to consort with a Chihuahua.*

Mad Dog stopped taking notes and tossed his gold fountain pen on his yellow legal pad. "We need to talk about what could happen with a case like this," he said. "First, tell me, where did you and Jeff get Earnest?"

"We adopted him from Seattle's Second Chance Shelter."

"Do you remember in whose name?"

"Jeff filled out the form, so I guess it was his."

"He also paid the fee?"

"Yes."

Mad Dog seemed to prick his translucent ears at this information. "That could be a problem."

"Problem" jangled Anna's nerves. "Jeff earns more than I do so he usually paid for extra things like that."

"Hmmm." Mad Dog leaned back in his leather chair, which swallowed up his small frame. "If Jeff signed and paid for the adoption, he's got ownership papers. They make your case more complicated. If you get a judge who views Earnest as personal property, like a sofa, he could rule that legally he's Jeff's dog."

At this shattering news, Anna's heart drooped like a parched prayer plant. "It didn't occur to me that we should adopt Earnest together. I never dreamed Jeff and I would break up."

"Most couples say that. It's why lawyers recommend a prenup for pets. Sadly, dogs and cats outlive the average relationship, which is only about two years and nine months."

About the length of Jeff's and mine. Anna shrank back in her chair. "Doesn't it count for anything that Earnest comes to work with me every day? I'm the one who feeds him. I bathe and brush and walk him. He's nearly always with me. He's like my child."

"Who pays his vet bills?"

"I do once in a while, but mostly Jeff."

"What about food?"

"We feed Earnest the most expensive kibble and canned food. So Jeff always buys it."

Mad Dog made a quick note on his pad. "Okay. You're responsible for Earnest's care, and you spend more time with him. But Jeff's responsible for him financially. A judge could conclude you're equally important to him."

Back to the prayer plant droop. "I guess you could put it that way."

"Let me tell you how things work." Mad Dog pressed his fingertips together, forming a peak. "If you go to court, a lot depends on what judge you get. They're all over the map with pet-custody cases. Judges who see dogs as property could rule that you have to sell Earnest and divide the proceeds.

"Some judges acknowledge a dog's emotional value. Some consider what's best for the dog. A few hate these lawsuits and rule as quickly as they can, in which case Jeff's adoption papers would give him an advantage. But more sympathetic judges might rule in your favor as Earnest's main caretaker. Or they could make you and Jeff share custody."

Anna's feathers ruffled. "I'll *never* let Jeff have Earnest, and I won't share him."

As she made this angry decree, she glanced at Earnest, and his feelings were as visible as the veins in Mad Dog's ears. He was pressing his body against the door as far as he could get from the unsavory Chihuahua. The ridges in Earnest's forehead said he'd been listening to the consultation, and it had upset him: *Do not sell me! I want fresh air. Take me to the dog park!*

"How do we know what judge we'd get?" Anna spoke quietly so as not to stress Earnest more.

"We don't know. And the hearing isn't always pretty," Mad Dog said. "One judge I know makes the dog come into court, has the parties call it, and rules in favor of the one it goes to. A poodle got so scared it went to the judge. Could be difficult for a dog."

And a nightmare for Earnest, who tries so hard to do the right thing. "I could never put Earnest through that. Maybe I should forget custody."

"Absolutely not! We'll handle whatever comes up. That's what *I'm* here for." Mad Dog seemed to puff up into a Doberman. He jutted out his jaw, and a vicious glint shone in his eyes. When he smiled, he exposed teeth too large for his face—strong, pugilistic teeth—snatchers, rippers, and grinders.

"I'd like to take on Jeff. You can't let a former boyfriend push you around. We can win!" he said.

"So there's hope?"

"*Certainly,* there's hope!" Mad Dog barked. "You said Earnest was like your child?"

"Yes."

"I'd argue that he's your child substitute, and he should be considered according to child custody laws. As his major caretaker, you're his mother!"

"But maybe that's not enough to counter Jeff's adoption papers."

"Don't worry. We'll get around them," Mad Dog said.

Anna wound her fingers around Earnest's leash, lying in her lap. "If we went to court, how much would it cost?"

"Depends on how long and hard we have to fight. Litigation's not cheap," Mad Dog said.

"Do you have a ballpark number?"

"I can give you an example. Ten years ago a Phoenix couple spent over a hundred grand. They called in animal behaviorists to testify. The husband commissioned a study on canine bonding, and the wife hired a camera crew for a video of her walking and playing with the dog. It was the Cadillac of pet-custody trials, but you get the picture."

Yes, Anna got the picture. The astronomical expense was as far out of her reach as the top of a hundred-year-old fir tree—if a termite were giving her a leg up.

Her expression must have revealed her dismay, because Mad Dog tucked his killer teeth behind his lips and disguised himself again as a Chihuahua. "You'd better think about this. Going into litigation is a big decision. Clients have told me that fighting over their dog emotionally drained them more than fighting over their kids."

"I don't want anything to upset Earnest," Anna said.

Apparently, Mad Dog's lust for combat *had* disturbed Earnest. He'd turned his back to them and pressed his nose against the door. His body said in the starkest terms, *You can't trust a Chihuahua. This is unseemly. I want to go home.*

"Is there anything you can do to keep Jeff from calling me all the time?" Anna asked.

"He *is* the one who signed the adoption papers." Mad Dog hung the threat over her like Damocles's sword.

"You can't make him back off? File a restraining order?"

"I'll write him a nastygram. It'll take some of the starch out of him." Mad Dog chuckled, the glint back in his eyes. "Some bushwhacking will soften him up before we close in for the kill."

CHAPTER 20

Over the phone, Randy Grabowski sounded like the imperious despot of an inconsequential country. "You have to do a more detailed traffic impact study," he said.

"Why?" Jeff asked.

"Because cars will turn off Rainier to park behind your building. They could hit pedestrians."

Hardly likely. "I see," Jeff said.

"If the study finds a problem, you'll have to come up with another parking plan. We also want a traffic count."

Are you joking? Our traffic engineer will fall asleep waiting for passing cars. "Given the location, do you think the count is necessary?"

"If I didn't think so, I wouldn't ask."

Grabowski's demands irritated Jeff, itches he couldn't scratch. He thought, *Go ahead, Grabowski. Jerk us around. It's part of my job.*

Jeff glanced at Anna's photo on his desk. He'd let her jerk him around about Earnest, but that was about to end. This morning he'd left her the voice mail he'd thought about all week. He'd told her that at eight tonight he was going to sit at her door till she let him in, and, once and for all, they'd end their misunderstanding. "I love you," he'd said.

Jeff told Grabowski, "I'll get back to you with the traffic study. Six weeks?"

"I'd say more like three. A month, tops."

You say, "Jump," and I ask, "How high?" "We'll do our best."

Jeff was hanging up the phone when his assistant, Kimberly, set a certified letter next to his phone. From Horowitz, Mason, and Drudge, Attorneys-at-Law. It wasn't Mrs. Blackmore's firm, but maybe she'd changed lawyers.

Expecting a complication from Mrs. Blackmore, who was an expert in making Jeff's job harder than it needed to be, he opened the letter. Expensive stationery typical of lawyers. The smell of ink. Letterhead in bold black print that bristled ego.

As Jeff read, his gaze became intense enough to slice the paper. He couldn't be reading right. He started again. Each of Sheldon Horowitz's words could have been a bullet Jeff was biting—and he was cracking teeth: "Harassment." "Stalking." "Over the line." "No contact." "With Anna *or* Earnest."

No contact with Earnest! Some lawyer dared tell Jeff he couldn't see his own dog? Who the hell did Sheldon Horowitz think he was? What lies had Anna told him?

Jeff turned Anna's photo around to face the wall. Suddenly, it sickened him to look at her. All week he'd thought of her with tenderness, and he'd just left his loving message, which he'd regret to his dying day. Never would he have believed she'd sic a lawyer on him. And the preposterous claims! Harassment? Stalking? Where had she come up with those? She'd gone beyond the realm of decency into the land of ambush.

Reeling from shock, Jeff buried his face in his hands. He'd been a fool to trust Anna. To love her, he'd been out of his mind. He was embarrassed to have been so stupid. And to think he'd wanted to marry her!

He may have been wrong to leave that damned message, but, come hell or high water, he was going to get Earnest back.

Slowly, Jeff's shock expanded like combustible gas. It seeped into his mind, filled its darkest corners, and blazed into fury.

As his face turned fiery red, Jeff muttered, "This is war."

From the sideline, Jeff clapped his hands and shouted, "Go, go, go!" His tyke soccer team of five-year-olds, the Mini Kickers, ran around the field, their skinny chests heaving under small green jerseys. From brightly colored camping chairs along the sidelines, mothers and fathers yelled, "Control the ball, Duncan!" "Behind you. Look, Joey!" "Kick it! Kick it!" Alan Biggs, an attorney and Jeff's co-coach, who was even taller than he was, encouraged from the other side of the field.

Usually, Earnest, as team mascot, watched from the touchline. However, for the fourth Saturday in a row, he hadn't come to Heron Harbor Park. "Not feeling well" to explain his absence no longer cut it. His missed games were more reason for Jeff to be angry.

Both teams ran to the center of the field and clumped together. Jeff and Alan's boys were trying to get the ball and score with only forty seconds left in the game. They were behind, but another goal would win it. Jeff yelled, "Come on! You can do it! Let's go!"

Alan's son, Bobby, broke away from the others. He had the ball! He kicked it with the power of his entire forty-five pounds—but in the wrong direction, toward his own team's goal.

"Stop! Stop!" Alan shouted.

"Go back!" Jeff yelled, and pointed to the field's other end.

The Mini Kickers' parents wailed, "Turn around! Wrong way!" Pandemonium reigned.

Bobby kept kicking the ball toward the wrong goal. Clearly, he did not realize his mistake. He must have seen glory ahead, and he was determined to reach it. He closed in on the cross-bar, took careful aim, and with one last triumphant effort, he sent the ball into the Mini Kickers' net and scored for the opposing team.

Bobby jumped up and down and waved his arms in victory, but slowly it seemed to register on him that he was the only person cheering. He looked at his father, then Jeff, then his teammates' sullen faces, and Bobby's grin slumped in confusion. As a sun of understanding rose in his vulnerable brain, his lips rounded to a small O of horror. He seemed to shrink, then crumble into small, embarrassed pieces.

Jeff ached with sympathy for him. When the referee blew his whistle to end the game, Jeff hurried down the field to assure Bobby that we all make mistakes, nobody gets it right every time in life, lapses of judgment happen every day. As Jeff himself had just learned by going along to get along with Anna and telling her he loved her in his damned voice mail message. He'd headed for the wrong goal and run the wrong way. His mistake had been far worse than Bobby's.

After Alan's wife took Bobby home and everyone had left, Jeff and Alan leaned back in their camp chairs with Cokes for a postmortem about the game and a last shot at sun before the autumn rains.

"I'll give Bobby a pep talk when I get home." When Alan set the heel of his size-fourteen running shoe on his chair's seat, his long, thin leg looked like a collapsible yardstick.

"I was proud the other kids didn't make Bobby feel bad. Maybe all our talk about good sportsmanship is paying off," Jeff said.

"I wish Earnest had been here. He'd have made Bobby feel better."

"Yeah . . . well." Jeff flicked sweat off his Coke can. "I think I need your help to get Earnest back."

"Where is he?"

"Anna's holding him hostage." Jeff let out a long and angry breath. He explained the whole miserable business, starting with his move from the condo and ending with Sheldon Horowitz's letter.

Alan's nervous laugh surprised Jeff. "What's so funny?"

"Horowitz. Anna's not messing around. He's a hard-nosed bastard. People call him 'Mad Dog,'" Alan said.

"Great." Jeff's fury heated up a few degrees. "He accused me of stalking. Can you *believe* that?"

"He's setting up a paper trail. He's warned you. He'll be waiting to see if you do something stupid."

Jeff shook his head. "But Earnest is mine. I want him."

"If it means a legal fight?"

"What choice do I have? Anna's brought in Mad Dog." Jeff spat out the name through contemptuous lips.

Alan fixed Jeff with his intelligent eyes. "You'd better think carefully. Litigation costs you."

"I have deeper pockets than Anna does."

"There's also a big price to pay in time and energy," Alan said. "You'd be asking for more sleepless nights than you can imagine. If you think you're angry now, wait till Mad Dog goes after you."

"It'll be worth it when I get Earnest back."

"But you might not. That's the thing. Mad Dog's a diabolical genius at finding creative ways to screw people."

Dismayed, Jeff looked at the harbor. On the beach, a heron was scratching fleas, and a golden retriever scared ducks into flight. The water was rough. Small white caps bobbed in the waves.

"So Anna has a maniac to represent her. What am I supposed to do?" Jeff asked.

"I'd go to mediation. You and Anna could meet with a neutral third party who'd help you figure out what to do with Earnest. It'd be a lot cheaper than a trial." Alan rolled his Coke can between his palms.

"Anna and I could never compromise about Earnest," Jeff said.

"You'd be surprised. When push comes to shove, people usually work out their differences."

"What if we don't?"

"You declare an impasse. And you have the pleasure of watching Mad Dog grind you up and spit you out in court."

Perish the blasted thought. Jeff took his last swallow of Coke and crushed the can in his fist. Maybe mediation was the wrong goal. He could end up as vulnerable as Bobby Biggs, running in the wrong direction. But what choice did Jeff have?

"I don't know." He wiped his hand over his face, covered his mouth.

"You don't have much to lose."

"Can you set it up? Go with me?" Jeff asked.

"If you want. The trick is to get Anna there," Alan said.

"She won't talk with me. You'd have to track her down." Jeff watched the golden chase another duck.

"I'll give it a try," Alan said. "No guarantees."

CHAPTER 21

Anna was putting together a Weep-No-More bouquet of sunflowers for Edna Cartwright, whose husband, a freighter captain, had died of a heart attack on the way to Singapore. Edna's neighbors had gone together to order the flowers, and Anna wanted them to cheer her. She stroked the yellow petals and whispered, "Go out into the world and do your job."

As she fluffed a matching bow around the Weep-No-More's vase, the phone rang.

"Can I order some flowers?" The man's voice was as rich as butterscotch. If he were a late-night radio host, women would fantasize about him.

"I take phone orders if you have a credit card," Anna said.

"Do you deliver?"

"At the end of the day."

"Great. I want you to take some flowers to my wife."

"Any special occasion?"

"It's for a secret anniversary."

"Oh . . ." *Secret!* Anna's imagination leapt to its feet. The flowers could mark the day he and his wife robbed their first bank, or divorced their former spouses and ran away together. If the latter, Anna could deliver the Humdinger or another of her specialties, the Floral Smooch. Anna also made an arrangement called the Golden Glow, of orange gerberas, gold cushion mums, and red daisies. That would work.

"What flowers would your wife like?" she asked.

"I'm not sure."

Anna searched her mental catalog. He'd make it easier if he told her what the secret was—but, then, maybe she didn't want to know. "Do you want roses? Lilies? I could do a mix."

"I'll leave it up to you."

Yikes.

Anna took the man's credit-card number and home address. He told her that his card should say, "Remember, Sweetheart?" He added, "Don't forget the question mark."

Later, Anna was still trying to decide what bouquet best fit a question mark, when Joy showed up in pink skinny jeans and a black lace top. "Where's Earnest?" she asked.

"At the library. Today's his day to encourage kids to read aloud," Anna said.

"Right. I forgot." Joy settled on the stool next to the counter and rested her hands on her knees. "Slow day. All I've sold are a few motley birthday cards. I'm trying not to get freaky about my poverty."

"You'll sell some gifts tomorrow." Anna brushed ribbon trimmings into a pile on her counter. "I need some help. A man just ordered his wife flowers for a secret anniversary. I can't decide what to put together."

"What's the secret?"

"He didn't say. I was thinking the day they eloped."

"Way too tame. It's got to be more delicious. Sex has to be in there somewhere." Joy held out her hand, palm down, and examined her coral-pink polished nails. "At the very least it's the first time they made love. Maybe in some weird place like a hot air balloon or on a McDonald's bathroom floor."

The wheels of Anna's mind began to turn. "In a Macy's fitting room. Under the bed. On a golf course. In an aerial tram."

"You got it. Now what about flowers?" Joy asked.

"Some dark, exotic ones. Black calla lilies. Queen of the Night tulips."

"Queen of the Night would fit right in for sure," Joy said.

Anna rested her fists akimbo and shook her head. "The problem is my inventory's low. I don't have any dark, exotic flowers."

"Make the Humdinger. If you gave that wife a dandelion and crabgrass bouquet, she'd be thrilled because her husband remembered the secret. The Twit never remembered anything. Including that I was his wife."

Anna threw the cuttings from Mrs. Cartwright's sunflowers into a plastic garbage can and wiped her hands on her blue apron. When she glanced out the bay windows, she saw a man hammering a sign into the front yard. His beard looked like the fur of a cadaverous alley cat.

"Joy, look." Anna went to the window between Constance and Edgar, who'd lately perked up.

Joy crossed the room and peered out. "Boy, would Lauren ever like to get her scissors on that ghastly beard. A whole family of hamsters must be nesting in it."

"The sign can't be for politics. There's no election," Anna said.

By the time she and Joy stepped outside, the man had put his hammer into his backpack and started down the street. The sign he'd left behind was plastic-coated poster board stapled to two stakes. Across the top was printed, NOTICE OF APPLICATIONS FOR DEMOLITION AND BUILDING PERMITS. Naomi Blackmore was listed as the applicant/owner, and Randy Grabowski as the head planner. The proposal was described: "Remove current residence and construct a commercial building."

"I can't believe it," Anna fumed.

"This makes it official. Those putrid worms," Joy said.

"I feel sick."

"It's no surprise. We already knew Jeff filed for Mrs. Scrooge-more's permits."

"This sign's a finger in our eye." Anna could practically hear bulldozers flattening Grammy's house. She could smell dust and see wood scraps, glass shards, and brick rubble over-flowing Dumpsters. "It's not fair."

"Hey! I just bought us some kettle corn." Lauren hurried down the sidewalk, wearing animal-print harem pants and her Salvation Army Eileen Fisher sweater. As she got closer, she stared at Anna's and Joy's faces. "Who died?"

"Look." Anna pointed at the sign as if it housed flesh-eating bacteria. "It's Jeff." As Lauren quickly read the sign, Anna added, "I'm not sure what we should do."

Lauren put a soothing arm around Anna's shoulders. "We'll think of something. We'll fight."

"But how?" Anna asked.

"Bring on the tar and feathers," Joy suggested.

"We'll find a way, Anna. Don't worry. We must have months before they'd come after the house," Lauren said.

"That sign can't hurt us. It's just words," Joy said.

"Yes, but we have to stop Jeff," Anna said.

"Here. Have some comfort food." Lauren held out her bag of corn.

Anna popped a kernel into her mouth. "I want to rip down that sign and burn it."

"That wouldn't accomplish anything," Lauren said.

"It would show how mad I am," Anna said.

"We have to keep calm and strategize," Lauren said.

"And never give up." Joy grabbed a lusty handful of corn and spilled kernels on the sidewalk.

Anna narrowed her eyes and said, "This is a fight to the finish."

CHAPTER 22

The office of the mediator, Lincoln Purcell, occupied the first floor of a white historic house, which looked like Mrs. Blackmore's minus the turret and plus five fluted columns, thick as telephone poles. His assistant escorted Jeff and Alan to a mahogany-paneled library. Though French doors looked out to a rose garden, the room was dark. At a trestle table in the center of the room, Jeff studied the floor-to-ceiling shelves of leather-bound books, their spines as stiff as his was.

Alan looked through notes on a yellow legal pad while Jeff listened to ticks of a grandfather clock. Anxious for the damned mediation to begin, he thrummed his fingers on the table—until he heard Anna's voice, then toenails clicking on oak.

"Earnest is here!" Jeff jumped to his feet to rush into the hall.

Alan grabbed Jeff's sport coat sleeve and pulled him back into his chair.

"I want to see my dog. It's been six weeks," Jeff protested.

"Shhhh," Alan warned.

Too late.

Earnest barked, quick staccato barks, every one of which ended in an exclamation point. *I heard Jeff! He's here! He's here!*

Earnest's nails skidded on the hardwood as he charged the library door. *It's me! Let me in! I want to see Jeff!*

Again Jeff got up, and Alan yanked him down. "Don't go out there. You and Anna will fight. You can see Earnest later. Now's not the time."

Jeff heard a gladiatorial shuffle of paws and feet and knew that Anna was tugging Earnest's collar and trying to lead him down the hall. Resisting, he cried and fought his way back to the door. He whimpered and sniffed at the crack underneath as if he couldn't get enough of Jeff's smell.

As Jeff ground his teeth, he shook hands with agony. It crowned every other awful feeling he'd had since moving from the condo. His best friend on earth was out there, and he'd doubtless concluded that Jeff didn't care enough to open the door. Hurting Earnest's feelings like that was torture.

"Come on, Earnest. Heel!" Anna sounded exasperated.

The more exasperation for her, the better, Jeff thought.

Suddenly, Earnest let out a small but urgent shriek. Someone might have hit him or stepped on his paw.

Alan grabbed Jeff's sleeve before he could leap up again. "Mad Dog must be out there," Alan said barely loud enough for Jeff to hear over Earnest's protests.

"If he so much as touches my dog . . ." Jeff said.

"You've got to go with the flow today. Zen. One minute at a time. Let this play out," Alan said.

Inside Jeff, wild horses reared back on their hind legs to stampede the hall, but his respect for Alan made him pull in their reins and stay seated. Still, his long separation from Earnest infuriated him. It had been Anna's power play, aided and abetted by Mad Dog.

As Anna dragged Earnest away, Jeff buried his face in his hands and seethed. Every cell in his body quivered with anger. How in hell had Anna manipulated him into this situation?

Never again.

★ ★ ★

Lincoln Purcell lumbered into the library like an amiable grizzly. He had broad shoulders, a chest as thick as a refrigerator, and thighs like hams. Somewhere in his past had surely been a football. His round Harry Potter glasses rested on a nose that veered slightly to the left, perhaps broken by knocking heads with fellow bruisers on the field.

He greeted Jeff and Alan with handshakes strong enough to drain the life from flesh, then fit his heft into a Windsor chair at the table's head. "So we're going to try and work out Earnest's future today," he began. And for the next few minutes the three men discussed Earnest as if they'd just met in a sports bar.

Purcell listened with enthusiastic ears, and Jeff relaxed. "You'd wear out your arm throwing sticks for Earnest. He's a black hole for retrieving," Jeff said.

"You love him, don't you?" Purcell said.

"He's my family," Jeff said.

Purcell leaned forward. He flattened his palms against the tabletop and spread out his fingers like asterisks.

"I've talked with Alan"—Purcell nodded at him—"and with Sheldon Horowitz, Anna's lawyer. So I have a good idea what brings you and Anna here today. I don't intend to dictate that one of you wins and the other loses. My role is to see you through the mediation process and try to help you help yourselves."

"That's pretty much what Alan's told me," Jeff said.

"I'm sure Alan also explained that I'm not the one making decisions about your agreement today. Neither are your lawyers. The outcome is entirely up to you and Anna. It's your responsibility to get beyond your conflict."

"That's not possible when we hate each other," Jeff said.

"But you both love Earnest."

"That's why we're here."

"Then let me explain why it's best for you to work this out with me." Purcell reached into his pocket for a handkerchief and began cleaning his glasses' lenses. "If you don't come to an agreement, your only recourse is court, and a judge will be interested only in legal issues. He won't work out an accommodation like you two could do today, and I wouldn't be surprised if he'd rule that you and Anna had to share custody."

Jeff slammed his hand on the table. "I refuse to share Earnest with her! And how the hell would she pay his expenses anyway?"

"Temper that. If the judge ordered you to share, you'd refuse at your peril," Alan warned.

Someone on the street could have heard Jeff's exhale of pent-up angry steam. *No way in hell will Anna get Earnest.*

Purcell put on his glasses again and returned the handkerchief to his pocket. "Usually mediators keep parties in separate rooms, but I'd rather get you both in my office so you can work out what's best for Earnest together," he said.

The last thing Jeff wanted was to sit in the same room with Anna. "Does she agree?"

"Yes," Purcell said.

Jeff would have preferred vacationing in a garbage dump to talking with her, but at least he could see Earnest. "To hell with it. All right."

When Jeff opened the door to Purcell's office, Earnest barked and whined and tore across the room. He took a flying leap, hurled himself at Jeff, and nearly knocked him down. Whimpering, Earnest bucked and thrashed and danced around Jeff's legs. He circled Purcell's antique desk, wingback chairs, and oak file cabinets, and returned, wriggling with excitement. Jeff could hardly sweep him into his arms and hug him.

Oh, where have you been? I thought I'd never see you again, said Earnest's whines. Jeff felt them as palpably as silk brushing his cheeks. *I love you! I've missed you! I'm thrilled you're here!*

Jeff set him down and kneeled beside him. He buried his face in Earnest's neck and smelled his doggy smell. "My buddy," he murmured. Jeff mentally promised him, *I'll never let Anna keep you from me again.*

Purcell pulled out a chair for Jeff at the conference table and motioned to him that the meeting would start. Only when he took a seat next to Alan did he glance across the table at Anna and Mad Dog, a skinny runt whose audacity still made Jeff burn. He dismissed Mad Dog as too loathsome to consider, but he locked eyes with Anna, three feet away, the distance for quarantine, but not nearly far enough for Jeff. He intended for his glare to make her look away. But she glared back, defiant.

"Why don't you take turns telling each other in a polite, respectful way how you'd like to resolve your conflicting interests in Earnest," Purcell said.

"That's easy," Jeff blurted out as Earnest wriggled under the table and lay down between Jeff and Anna's rows of toes. It did not escape his notice that Earnest was touching him *and* Anna. To link them together again as a family? Or to block them from kicking each other?

"My resolution to the conflict is to walk out of here with Earnest and take him home with me where he belongs," Jeff said through clenched teeth. "I adopted him. I have the papers. He's mine."

Streaks of war-paint red appeared on Anna's pale cheeks. The tufts in her hair looked like small bayonets. Her eyes shot twelve-penny nails at Jeff. His shot them back.

"Anna? I expect you'd like to take Earnest home too?" Purcell asked.

"I want Earnest with me like he's always been. I watch

after him. He sleeps in my bed. I take him to work. I don't want Jeff to disrupt his life."

"You've disrupted his life by keeping me away from him. You think he's happy about that?" As Jeff pointed an accusatory finger at Anna, his look of revulsion said she ranked lower than a rattlesnake scale.

Mad Dog puffed out his chest and snapped, "Mr. Purcell said to be respectful, Mr. Egan. I don't like your tone."

"I'll use any tone I please."

Alan tugged Jeff's sleeve again. "Easy," he whispered. He could have been coaxing a man-eating glimmer from the eyes of a tiger.

"Okay, let's just stop here for a second." Purcell formed a time-out "T" with his brawny hands. "I see anger in this conversation, but I'm not ready to conclude we're wasting our time. I'm asking you again to act like two adults who have the responsibility to reach a satisfactory resolution. Since you both want Earnest, I'd like to hear from each of you how you might share him."

"Earnest is mine. I don't have to share him with anybody," Jeff said.

"Edicts like that aren't going to advance our discussion," Purcell said. "Let me put it this way: If I had the power to decree that you two share Earnest, what terms would you find acceptable? How could you work together?"

The silence, through which ran a streak of petulance, was the temperature of sleet. Jeff listened to the clock ticking in the library, and imagined punching Mad Dog in his feeble little chops. Anna wrapped her fingers together in an agitated pretzel.

"Hostility serves no purpose here," Purcell reminded them. "Let me backtrack. Can we figure out *anything* you agree on?"

As Jeff considered the question, he slipped his foot out of his loafer and wriggled his toes in Earnest's fur. *Fighting with Anna would only hurt Earnest,* Jeff thought. Though he would never get over his fury, he owed it to his dog at least to contribute to this process.

"When one of us is with Earnest, the other should stay away. I'm sure Anna feels the same," Jeff offered.

"Do you, Anna?" Purcell asked.

"Absolutely." Anna flashed Jeff a look that would wither iron.

"Anna, can you agree that Earnest loves Jeff?" Purcell asked.

"Yes, I'll give him that."

"How do you know Earnest loves anybody? He's just a dog. Dogs have no feelings," Mad Dog said.

Go twitch your rodent whiskers elsewhere. "Have you ever had a dog?" Jeff demanded.

Before Mad Dog could answer, Anna interjected, "Really. I can tell. Earnest loves Jeff."

At least she's finally being honest.

"So if Earnest loves Jeff, wouldn't it be best if they could spend time together?" Purcell asked Anna.

"Yes, I guess," she said, begrudging.

"Any thoughts about where Earnest would be happiest living?" Purcell asked.

"In my apartment," Jeff said.

"He'd sit there all alone. You're never home during the week," Anna said.

"What about that, Jeff?" Purcell asked.

"I guess she's right."

Jeff and Anna could not agree on much else. All morning Purcell tried to herd them to an orderly arrangement, but the discussion traveled off to varied destinations. Finally, when Jeff was starved for lunch, Purcell left the room. Twenty minutes later, he returned with a proposal, handed copies to Anna and Jeff, and said, "If this is acceptable, you can sign it and get on with your lives."

Jeff and Alan read the document together at the table, and Anna and Mad Dog moved to chairs across the room. As they mumbled together, Earnest, lying on Jeff's feet, began to pant as he often did when he was worried. From the number of times his name had been bandied about today, he must have concluded that something serious about him was going on. He may also have sensed that his future's road had forked, and he was anxious about which direction would be taken. Jeff reached down and patted him, but he kept panting. *Damned Anna.*

The proposal said that Anna would keep Earnest during the week, and Jeff would have him from Friday evening till Monday morning. Anna would pick him up at Jeff's apartment, and Jeff would pick him up at the condo. Jeff would get Earnest on holidays and vacations. Anna and Jeff would each pay for Earnest's food on their days with him, and they would split his vet care costs. If unanticipated problems arose, they would contact their attorneys.

When Jeff finished reading, mixed with his rancor were resignation and fatigue. Though he'd never forgive Anna for what she'd done to him and Earnest, he consented, as did she, to Purcell's proposal. Jeff signed away half his right to his own dog, then rose, drained, from the table.

The room filled with the shuffling of papers and twanging of briefcase latches. Earnest wriggled out from under the table and pressed his body against Jeff's legs as if he were begging not to be left behind. When Anna tried to attach the leash to his collar, he shrank back, timid and unsure. He hid behind Jeff.

Jeff hugged him. "I'll pick you up on Friday night," he promised.

As Anna pulled Earnest toward the door, he looked back at Jeff, his eyes confused. *Why aren't you coming home with us?*

Earnest's innocence ripped Jeff's heart into confetti. Guilt steamrollered him flat. He was responsible for Earnest, and he should have protected him from this misery. But Jeff had failed, and now Earnest was going to get shunted back and forth between two homes. It wasn't fair. He'd suffer. It was all Anna's fault.

If only you could explain mediation to a dog.

CHAPTER 23

On Friday night Earnest paced the condo, and for the first time Anna could remember, he sniffed his kibble, laced with canned duck and sweet potato, and he walked away. When he looked back at Anna, his eyes said as straightforwardly as he'd ever said anything, *Yuck.*

Because he'd always been a blue-ribbon porker, his indifference to dinner concerned her. So did his restlessness as he paced around the condo. She handed him a cow's hoof so he could gnaw away his nervous energy. But he refused it too. As a last line of defense, Anna got out his brush, the fastest way to make him happy.

A rampant hedonist, Earnest considered grooming a dog's equivalent to a bachelor's night in a five-star resort, including a six-course dinner with sirloin and ice cream, a postprandial walk on a golf course, and nubile nymphs gyrating on his minibar. All it took was one glance at his brush, and Earnest would lie on the floor, his legs in the air in his flasher position, and present his sides, chest, and belly. He would close his eyes and ready himself for bliss.

Tonight, however, Earnest bristled his eyebrows and gave the brush a mistrustful look. *Are you trying to lure me into ecstasy*

so I'll forget about Jeff? Earnest stationed himself at the front
door in the posture of a stone lion guarding a library. Clearly,
he knew that Jeff was coming.

At the mediation, Anna had heard Jeff tell Earnest that he'd
pick him up on Friday. It *was* Friday. Therefore, Earnest must
have an uncanny inner calendar, or he was one of those dogs
who knew when his person was coming home. *Except Jeff was
now only half of Earnest's person. And this was no longer Jeff's home.*

Now Anna would have to hand over Earnest to the dishonorable twit—as Joy would say—who had manipulated her
into sharing her own dear dog. For that, she would consider
him eternal scum. She was ready to spurn him.

Though she was mentally prepared for Jeff, at his inevitable
knock on the door, Anna jumped inside her skin. But Earnest,
as anyone would expect, went wild. He whimpered and
danced and nudged his nose against the doorknob, trying to
turn it and usher in his cherished alpha, his BFF, the most
wonderful man on earth. Earnest's rejoicing yips said, *Let him
in! Let him in!*

The yips threw dry straw on Anna's flames of jealousy.
Would Earnest be as happy if *she* knocked on the door? She
was his attentive caretaker. He was supposed to love *her* most.
He was *her* dog. But as he pressed himself against the door, she
felt like he was more Jeff's dog than hers, and her value to
Earnest might be about even with a tick's.

Grammy had once told Anna that she should never compare herself to another person, that everyone was unique and
equally worthy. But maybe in the eyes of a dog, some people
were more worthy than others. Maybe Jeff was Earnest's ba-
nana split, and Anna was the rancid whipped cream that got
stuck in the aerosol can.

Anna stiffened her shoulders, the better to meet her rival
for Earnest's affection. She marched across the living room, un-

latched the deadbolt with an assertive click, and opened the door just wide enough for Earnest to squeeze through. As he rushed to Jeff, she gave Earnest's haunch a final anguished pet.

"I assume I can pick him up at your apartment on Monday morning." Her words were more clipped than a poodle.

"Yes." Jeff did not address her by name, but his "yes" conveyed an entire thesaurus's worth of adjectives he might have chosen to accompany "Anna": repellant, abhorrent, detestable, appalling, revolting, repulsive.

She felt that his "yes" stomped on her self-worth. But, worse, she felt desolate that Earnest was gone. Except for his nights with Dr. Nilsen after the fire, tonight would be her first time in over two years to be alone in the condo.

Earnest's constant presence had become a part of her. She'd taken it for granted, like her next breath or tomorrow morning's sunrise. Tomorrow when the sun *did* rise, Earnest would not be snoring next to her, pressing down the mattress, and radiating warmth. She would not feel his moist nose nuzzle her awake so she would give him breakfast.

Anna backed toward the love seat and fell against the pillows. The condo's silence consumed her. She stared at the empty rectangles where Jeff's paintings had been. She was empty too. Lost, if you wanted to put a fine point on it. The only time she'd ever felt so alone was after Grammy died and her parents sent her to a Seattle boarding school.

CHAPTER 24

⟨❦⟩

Under a picnic table, Jeff found a stick the size of an extra-fat flute. *Perfect.*

He held it out to Earnest. "Look, Bud."

Would he beg Jeff to throw it? Or take it with a mighty chomp and swagger around, playing I-have-it-and-you-don't? For the first time ever, Jeff wasn't sure Earnest would show interest in the stick, for which his passion had known no bounds.

Since Earnest had wakened with his head on Jeff's pillow, he'd been moping. Normally the Canine Hoover, he had sniffed his breakfast and taken only a few desultory bites. At the Mini Kickers' soccer game, he'd flattened back his ears, a sure sign he was pensive, and followed Jeff around, a shadow in need. Earnest had hardly noticed that Bobby Biggs's ego still needed plumping after last month's score for the opposing team.

Now the kids and parents had gone home, and Heron Harbor Park was Jeff and Earnest's private bonding ground. Earnest had patrolled the blackberry bushes and seemed to accept that they did not produce in late fall. If he were willing, it was playtime.

"Here! Want the stick, Earnest?"

His eyes lit up. *Yes! A stick! A stick!* He tugged it out of

Jeff's hand and pranced around the picnic table, showing off his trophy.

Relieved at the enthusiasm, Jeff reached out to grab the stick. "Give it to me."

Earnest let him take it, but he stared at it so hard his body quivered. *Throw it! Throw it! My genes are programmed for chasing and returning! I am bred to fetch!*

Jeff raised his arm and hurled the stick into Heron Harbor, and the glorious retriever in Earnest sprang to life. He charged down the beach and lunged into the water, then paddled to the stick like a Knight Templar on a quest for the Holy Grail. Earnest gripped the stick in his mouth and paddled back to shore, victorious. He ran, dripping, up the beach, dropped the stick at Jeff's feet, and shook his body, baptizing Jeff with water.

"Good boy! The wonder dog!" Jeff patted Earnest's head.

Earnest fastened his gaze to the stick, then glanced up, his eyes pleading, *Please, please, oh please, Jeff! Retrieving is my mission. You wouldn't want me to go against my nature!*

Jeff picked up the stick, drew back his arm, and pretended to throw without releasing. Refusing to fall for the ruse, Earnest planted his paws in the sand and did not budge. But he trembled with anticipation—until finally Jeff threw the stick for real. Earnest shot across the beach and leapt into the water.

Again and again Jeff threw, and Earnest, tirelessly eager, charged into the harbor and fetched. He wagged his tail hard enough to light up Seattle for a week. His joyful face said, *Hurrah! My favorite game! I have Jeff all to myself!*

Only Anna had been able to lure Earnest from his obsessive compulsion for retrieving when she'd sat and watched him and Jeff on this very beach. Once in a while, she got up and snatched one end of Earnest's stick. Gripping the other in his mouth, he hung on like the fish hooked in *The Old Man and the Sea* as Anna dragged him around, his paws skidding through the sand. His flapping ears exclaimed, *Oh, wow! How great is this!* He never let loose of the stick till she did.

A pleasant memory, but to hell with her, Jeff thought as Earnest plopped the stick in front of him again. He wondered at Anna's ability to sneak into his mind, boot him out of the present, and drag him back to the past as surely as she'd dragged Earnest around the beach. Jeff would not allow it. He shoved her out of his thoughts and threw Earnest's stick with extra force. Earnest swam out to get it.

After what felt like one-hundred-and-thirty-seven-thousand throws, Jeff's arm began to tire—far sooner than Earnest's determined legs. "What do you say, Buddy? How about a Granny Smith apple?"

That temptation alone might not have enticed Earnest from the game. But when Jeff turned around and walked to the picnic table, Earnest responsibly followed. He dropped the stick as Jeff handed him an apple slice. Though not so gleeful about it as in the past, Earnest looked pleased about the crunch.

"I wish we could be together every day. All I want is to make you happy." Jeff handed him another piece. "On Monday you're going to have to go back to Anna. You know that, don't you?"

Earnest munched his apple. He raised the top of his ears and cocked his head the way he did when he was listening.

"I hate that I can't have you with me all the time. But that's the way it is. I couldn't stop this horrible arrangement."

Earnest cocked his head to the other side. His eyes looked sad. *I love you, man.*

"I love *you.* I want you to know that," Jeff said.

Earnest's expression matched his name—serious, honorable, sincere. He looked so vulnerable that Jeff could not continue. He swallowed against the lump gathering in his throat. His heart felt like every beat took effort.

CHAPTER 25

⁓

With a serving spoon, Anna scraped out her pumpkin's pulp and seeds. She emptied them on newspapers spread over her counter, around which she, Joy, and Lauren perched on stools. Tonight they were combining their monthly financial meeting and annual carving party. As house treasurer, Anna officially began:

"Our October finances are grim. We all know our individual savings accounts to buy this house have taken a dive. But now we also have to worry about our stash for expenses. It's down to zero. Halloween decorations wiped us out."

"Our whole kitty's gone? That's *it?*" Lauren's carefully plucked eyebrows rose toward the ceiling.

"That's it," Anna said.

"What about Christmas decorations? I don't have a whole lot of money to put in. My sales are pathetic," Joy grumbled.

"Your regulars will flock to you for Christmas presents," Anna said.

"If they don't, I'm doomed. I'll close," Joy said.

"And then what? How will you eat?" Lauren asked.

Joy shrugged as if food were a minor matter. "I'll finish *Wild Savage Love.*"

Lauren, who had a degree in English literature, drew zigzag

lines across her pumpkin's face for future teeth. "Joy and I have been working on her plot," she told Anna. "I keep telling her that John and Penelope have to escape before Murdon sells them into slavery."

"Where are they now?" Anna asked.

"In Tunis. Murdon's ship just landed, but they're still in the brig. The slave market's a block away. They can hear the moans and screams of desperate captives. Penelope is freaking out," Joy said.

"That's sad," Anna said.

"Exactly. You're supposed to grieve for them," Joy said. "Slavery's going to drag out the suspense. John and Penelope have to suffer for a while."

"Maybe they've suffered enough. How would *you* feel if you'd been kidnapped and locked up for months on a foul, nasty slave ship?" Anna emptied another scoop of pumpkin on the newspaper.

"I like happy endings," Lauren said.

"Give John and Penelope time. After they're sold, they'll find each other again. Birds will tweet," Joy said.

Lauren stuck a paring knife into the edge of what would be a tooth. "Joy, what are you carving?"

"Leonardo DiCaprio."

"How could that possibly be Leonardo DiCaprio?" Lauren asked.

Joy turned her pumpkin around to show his eyes, nose, and sexy grin. "In case you need enlightenment, this is a goatee." She'd drawn it and his eyebrows with a black felt-tip pen.

"Oh, I get it." Lauren carved another tooth. "My pumpkin's Hannibal Lecter." From a black tote bag, Lauren pulled out a tennis shoe and the lower third of a jeans leg stuffed with cotton. "These are going to stick out of his mouth. He's already eaten the rest of the body."

"Pretty scary," Joy said.

"Mine's not." Anna, who'd been concentrating on her pumpkin, showed them the leaves and flowers she'd drawn on it. No face.

"You don't have your heart in it," Lauren said.

"Too much to worry about right now," Anna said.

"What besides this house and money?" Lauren asked.

"Isn't that enough?" Joy asked.

"I'm worried about Earnest. Look how thin he is. His ribs are sticking out," Anna said.

When Earnest heard his name, he opened one eye. He cocked an ear. Clearly, he'd been eavesdropping because he rose from his lily pad and walked to the counter.

Anna reached down and petted his shoulder. "I can get him to take a few bites of broiled chicken, but forget kibble."

"He's upset. His life has changed," Lauren said.

As if on cue, Earnest stared at the floor like all his friends had come down with ague and keeled over dead, and he was alone. His tail sagged at half-mast. He turned despondency into an art form.

"Maybe he'll perk up tomorrow. He loves Halloween. He thinks every trick-or-treater has come to visit him," Anna said.

"Is he going to be a bumblebee again this year?" Joy asked.

"A zebra. I wanted him to be a unicorn, but all I could afford was black paint for his stripes," Anna said.

When she reached down to pet Earnest again, he walked away as if he didn't care what he was going to be disguised as. *Zebra schmeebra,* said his posture's droop. He flattened back his ears and hunched his shoulders. If his heart had been a piece of paper, "bummer" would have been written on it.

At 4:00 p.m. on Halloween, Gamble's merchants turned the downtown into a trick-or-treater's mecca. In front of stores, they handed out candy to passing crowds. At intersections, Rotary Club volunteers in iridescent vests directed traffic. The organist at Grace Congregational Church played spooky music that floated through the air from speakers hidden in the steeple.

Everyone wore costumes, including dogs, who were often disguised as bats, tigers, and sharks. Anna's economic straits had driven her to turn her last year's princess dress and crown into a fairy godmother outfit. For a magic wand, she'd bought a dowel, and on the end she'd glued a silver star. In her pocket was fairy-dust glitter she intended to throw on children.

At three forty-five Anna poured bags of 3 Musketeers, Mars bars, and Reese's Peanut Butter Cups into black wicker baskets. As she carried them to the porch, a small pain flashed above her eyebrow. Her grueling day had caught up with her. Since breakfast, she'd had no time to sit down.

More people than expected had wanted Halloween flowers, and she'd almost run out of ceramic pumpkin vases and the tiny metal spiders she stuck on gold and orange mums. Also in demand had been her "Boo Bouquet," which included ghosts she'd stayed up making till 3:00 a.m. with four-inch squares of sheets. She'd stuffed their heads with cotton, tied white string around their necks, and stuck them from wire among roses and carnations.

Earlier today Anna had given an extra ghost to Tommy, age ten. It was a reward for writing the October poem for Lauren's community poetry post—about Igor, the Venus flytrap, who after the fire had replaced the unfortunate Fang.

MY FRIEND IGOR
by Tommy

Igor is a plant who loves to eat.
He catches flies to be his meat.
His hungry jaws stay open wide

Till a bug begins to come inside.
Then, SNAP! Igor has caught his lunch.
The bug is now a tasty crunch.

On the porch, Anna handed Lauren and Joy their candy baskets. Lauren had turned her little black cocktail dress into a witch's costume, applied black lipstick and nail polish, and put on a pointed hat that made her a scary seven feet tall. Joy wore a sexy gypsy outfit—a low-cut peasant blouse with a tiered skirt, and a gold scarf, knotted above her left ear.

Earnest seemed to have decided to be a misanthropic zebra. He clumped to the corner next to the front door and lay down under long cobweb wisps and man-sized ghosts, which hung from the beadboard ceiling. He ignored children streaming down the sidewalk: three girls disguised as bottles of mayo, mustard, and ketchup. A boy dressed as a mouse with his mother, a cat. A jellyfish carrying a clear plastic umbrella from which hung Saran Wrap strips for tentacles. A flock of angels left over from Christmas pageants.

Tommy arrived as an orange felt traffic cone, and Sam, his golden retriever, wore a George Washington wig that his mother had found in Gamble Playhouse's costume bin.

"Earnest, come here," Anna called. "It's your best friend, Tommy. Say hello."

Usually, Earnest bounded over and licked Tommy's face, but tonight he struggled to his feet as if lying on the porch had exhausted him. He plodded over to Tommy, whose face he couldn't lick anyway because it was mostly hidden behind orange felt.

"Is he sick?" Tommy asked.

"I don't think so. But lately he's not been himself," Anna said.

"Why?"

"I'm not sure."

"I'll visit him tomorrow."

"You do that. He'd like it." As Tommy turned to leave, Anna waved her magic wand and tossed fairy dust on him. "Any particular wish?"

"That Earnest would feel better," Tommy said.

Wrenching words. From the mouths of babes. "That's my wish too."

As Tommy made his way back down the crowded sidewalk to Rainier, Anna glanced across the street. In front of Sawyer's Restaurant, Jeff was hurrying along in a parka and blue muffler, his eyes as straight ahead as a Marine's in parade formation. Doubtless, Jeff had just arrived from work and was headed to his apartment. Also doubtless, he intended to avoid Anna—because he looked like his neck might break if he turned his head.

Tonight's Jeff contrasted sharply to the Jeff she'd loved last Halloween. With relish, he had thrown himself into haunting the house and scaring the children. He'd cut out cardboard gravestones, painted "RIP" on them, and lined them up in the front yard. On the porch he placed coffins he'd made out of wooden crates from Hall's Imports down the street. Jeff recorded scary noises and screwed colored lightbulbs into upstairs lamps. From a Seattle party store, he rented a fog machine.

When the big night came, thanks to Jeff, red and orange lightning flashed in upstairs rooms, and wails and screeches pierced the dark. Fog billowed out the windows and front door. Occasionally, Jeff leaned from a window above the porch, shone a flashlight under his chin, and laughed, "Heh-Heh-Heh!" Then he dangled a plastic skeleton by the neck a nd cackled like a deranged chicken. He shrieked and rattled his Honda's snow chains. Some of the kids had been too afraid to come to the porch, so Lauren had handed out candy on the street by her community poetry post.

The memory of that happy night warmed Anna. But the warmth lasted only a moment before the mediation's fight over Earnest invaded her mind. For the last ten days she'd brooded about Jeff's aggression, his unfair usurping of her dog.

Anna quickly stepped in front of Earnest to block his view. If he saw Jeff, he'd dash across the street to him, and she would not give him the satisfaction of knowing Earnest missed him.

Anna patted Earnest's stripes. "Good boy. Good zebra."

Pain flashed again above her eyebrow.

CHAPTER 26

⟨⟨⟨⟩⟩⟩

With the latest *Gamble Crier*, Jeff fanned the broiling steak's aroma toward Earnest, who was sprawled on his side across from the oven door.

"Sniff, Earnest, sniff. How good can it get?" *Fan, fan.*

The smell wafted straight toward his nose, which Jeff wanted to quiver with excitement. But Earnest's nose stayed resting on the floor like a wet coal lump rescued from a snowman's eye.

"This steak is for *you*, Earnest. The whole thing. You don't have to share a bite." Jeff fanned again. "I've seen you lunge after a measly sliver, and now you'll have twelve ounces! You like steak better than cheese!"

Jeff might as well have been hawking Styrofoam. Earnest did not raise his head. His listless gaze explained his position: *I am not hungry. I have important moping to do.* To emphasize that point, he moaned, a discouraged rumble from deep inside his chest.

Jeff also felt discouraged. "Okay. Maybe you'll feel better about it when it's in your bowl."

He broiled the steak to medium rare, which was supposed to extract from Earnest whines and anticipatory leaps around the kitchen. But in disappointing silence, Jeff cut the meat into tempting bite-sized pieces, set them on a plate, and put them into Mr. Ripley's refrigerator, where duct tape held up shelves inside the door. While waiting for the steak to cool, Jeff opened the *Gamble Crier* he'd been fanning and reread an op-ed piece he'd skimmed in Thrifty Market an hour before. The editor's sentiment wasn't any better the second time. "What a misguided jerk," Jeff mumbled to himself.

Now that Grabowski had put his sign in front of Mrs. Blackmore's house, Cedar Place's permit applications were public knowledge. And biased, provincial Gamble citizens, such as the editor, were already sniping at the project. The town did not need a big commercial building, said his op-ed piece, and more would surely follow. "Developers are only out for profit. Next thing we know they'll want to build a Walmart here. We can't sit back and let them ruin our small town," he said.

The narrow-minded editor would lead the charge against Cedar Place. He'd print readers' letters against the project and toss those in favor into his trash. Opposition loomed, and it unsettled Jeff. It was another thing he couldn't control, like the Gamble permit process and Lincoln Purcell's mediation.

To hell with it. He folded the *Crier* into a lopsided square. Intending to deposit it on his closet's newspaper pile, he walked into his hot-pink living room and, as usual, shuddered at the damned color. As he passed his oak drafting table, so out of place in the pink brothel he called home, his eyes went to the right front leg.

A foot from the floor was a ring of chewed wood, wet with saliva. Splinters, like bits of toothpicks, were scattered on the rug. The leg looked like a beaver had been gnawing it for dam purposes but had not yet finished the job.

There was only one beaver-like animal in the apartment, and he was in the kitchen. He'd assaulted the leg when Jeff had left him for fifteen minutes to buy his steak. Earnest had struck at lightning speed, then innocently settled on his kitchen bed as if he'd never heard of a drafting table. He must be protesting something. Or mad at Jeff. Or scared to be left alone in the apartment. *What is* wrong *with him?!*

Separation anxiety, that's what.

Earnest's sensitivity had gotten the best of him. Once a stable, secure companion, he'd become erratic and temperamental. He'd given in to neurosis and acted out his fears. Maybe he was afraid of being abandoned again, or maybe sudden change had upset him. As Jeff and Anna's former family rock, he was unused to being handed back and forth. Jeff could not be mad at him. Anna was the one to blame.

Damn. When will this mess end?

Jeff tossed the *Gamble Crier* on Mr. Ripley's red-and-brown plaid sofa and went back to the kitchen. Earnest did not look at Jeff or raise his head. He did not seem inclined to apologize for his destructive act, either. He might not even have remembered it now that he was busy attending to gloom.

Unsure what to do for him, Jeff turned to the steak. "Okay, Earnest. You ready for some rapture?"

He took the steak out of the refrigerator and felt the pieces, warm enough to be delicious, but not too hot for Earnest's mouth. Jeff poured them into Earnest's white ceramic bowl and set it in front of him, like he was King Farouk, who ate a hundred oysters in one sitting.

"Service with a smile. You don't have to stand up to eat!" Jeff said. "I've heard of starving dogs in Afghanistan who'd kill for one bite of steak, and you've got at least fifteen here."

With all his heart, Jeff wanted Earnest to be a gleeful glutton again. Jeff wanted Earnest to dive at the bowl, gulp down the steak, and look up at him with Oliver Twist's entreating eyes, begging, *Please, sir, I want some more.* Jeff wanted Earnest to get back to his old self.

Earnest rolled over to his sphinx position. At first he looked at the steak as if it were a personal affront, but then the smell coaxed him into nibbling pieces. But he did not inhale them, as Jeff had hoped. Nor did he finish the feast. *You can't make me happy with food,* said his chin as he set it on his front paws to mark the end of dinner.

"Do you eat at Anna's? Are you only sad with me? Would you rather be with her?" Jeff asked. Or was Earnest an equal opportunity dog who spread the worry around to both of them? Jeff would talk with her about it—if they were speaking to each other. Tonight was the first time since Mad Dog's letter that he wished they were.

Later that night, Jeff brushed his teeth and avoided looking at the eyelashes of the whales cavorting on the shower curtain. They irritated him. He washed his face, stepped into his flannel pajamas, and went into the bedroom. He turned on Mr. Ripley's lamp, a ceramic owl with a burlap shade sticking out of his head.

Lying in the half circle of light cast on Jeff's pillow was a cow's hoof that Earnest had not yet finished chewing. Only he could have set it there, though he'd never brought anything but himself to bed before. At first Jeff thought Earnest had meant the hoof as a bread-and-butter gift to say, *Thank you for the steak.*

Then Jeff decided that Earnest had wanted to leave a message. He might have been pointing out, *I'm sorry for gnawing on your drafting table. I meant no harm. I couldn't help myself.* Or he may have wanted to tell Jeff in the only way he could how important Jeff was to him. The cow's hoof might simply be saying, *I love you, man.*

Though Jeff did not know Earnest's intentions, he did know that he loved his dog. More than anything. *People may disappoint you, but Earnest never would,* he thought. Jeff found him in the living room, not far from the site of the drafting table massacre. "Thanks for the cow's hoof, Buddy. Come on. Let's go to bed."

CHAPTER 27

Dr. Nilsen was smiling when he came into the exam room. He washed and dried his hands and threw his paper towel into the trash. When he looked down at Earnest, his smile faded and his forehead creased. "Earnest, you've lost weight."

"Seven pounds according to your scale," Anna said.

"That's worrisome."

Dr. Nilsen squatted down and handed Earnest a biscuit. Though he took it politely, he set it down uneaten and turned his head away. *I'd rather not.*

"He'll hardly eat anything," Anna said. "Yesterday he licked my ice cream cone, and this morning he ate a piece of cheese. But he won't look at his kibble."

"So you're holding out for the good stuff, are you, Earnest?" Dr. Nilsen asked. "We've always had to worry about keeping your weight down, not fattening you up."

Dr. Nilsen quickly checked Earnest's gums and teeth. He took his temperature and looked into his ears, then coaxed him to stand and prodded his belly. "He seems okay except for his weight."

Anna laced her fingers together. "I took him to the library for his reading session with the kids. He always loves it, but he lay there in a funk."

"He's like that all the time?"

"Lately, pretty much. Do you think he could be upset?"

"Sure. Earnest is emotional. His feelings are transparent. He could be telling you he's depressed." Dr. Nilsen leaned against the sink and shoved his hands into his lab coat's pockets. "Anything stressful going on at home?"

Anna had dreaded that inevitable question. *Of course, there is stress at home.* And there was no pill to cure Earnest of Jeff and Anna's split, which was Earnest's problem, she suspected. Today's trip here was to confirm it.

Anna explained that Jeff had moved out, and they were sharing custody of Earnest. "I think maybe he doesn't like going back and forth between us." She glanced at her loafers' stitching. "He might be grieving for his former life when he was happy."

"That makes sense. You've got a sensitive animal here," Dr. Nilsen said. "Any chance you and Jeff will get back together?"

"No way. Never." Anna fired off that edict. "We're definitely mad at each other."

"Earnest's picking up every bit of it. If you're sure you won't reconcile, you've got to find a way to help him feel better," Dr. Nilsen said. "Can you take him out together and pretend you got along? You need to show him nothing terrible has happened and his world is still secure."

Taking Earnest anywhere with Jeff felt like a prison sentence. But Anna could not let her beloved dog pine himself into a skeleton. "I guess if Jeff agrees, we could take Earnest for a walk."

"That's worth a try before we put him through a lot of tests," Dr. Nilsen said. "Look at things from his point of view. He may feel like he's failed because he hasn't kept his pack together. Seeing his family disintegrate is a real hardship for a dog. His world's fallen apart."

Guilt. "You think a walk is enough?"

"It'd take more than one. You and Jeff need to get together

every week till Earnest starts eating again. He needs a lot of attention right now."

Weekly walks would be forced marches, but she was willing for Earnest's sake. "I don't know how Jeff is going to respond."

"He'd do anything for Earnest. If he hesitates, have him give me a call," Dr. Nilsen said. "If Earnest stops taking treats, bring him here right away so we can x-ray him and do a blood panel. And bring him in if the walks don't work. You don't want him to get too thin."

Dr. Nilsen held out his hand to Earnest for a shake. As he offered his paw, for the first time in days Earnest brightened. Though he may not have understood Dr. Nilsen's prescription, he seemed to pick up concern and goodwill.

"As a vet, I sure wish breakups never happened. Believe me, they take a toll."

Guilt again. It gouged large chunks out of Anna's heart.

Before Anna turned the key in Vincent's ignition, she told herself, *Get it over with. You have to do it for Earnest. You can't put it off.*

She got out her cell and texted Jeff:

Dr. Nilsen says we should walk Earnest together. Saturday @ 3? Broken Arrow Park?

She hesitated. The screen's bright blue "send" crooked a finger at her and beckoned, *Press me.* When she still hesitated, the button shook a fist and urged, *You are a lily-livered wastrel if you won't take this step for Earnest. You know what's right.*

Anna inhaled and steeled herself. She pressed. The text flew through the ether to Jeff.

There. It was done.

CHAPTER 28

Jeff rested his elbows on the picnic tabletop and looked around Broken Arrow Park. Anna was nowhere to be seen. *She's probably late just to hassle me,* he thought. *She wants me to shiver in the cold. If it rains, she'll really be happy.*

When something plopped on the grass behind him, he turned around. Earnest was hovering over his stick, begging for another throw. He stared at the stick, then at Jeff, then back at the stick. Earnest's eager eyes said, *Oh, please, please! We've only played fetch for half an hour. That's not enough!*

"Okay." Jeff picked up the stick and threw it into the empty Little League diamond, and Earnest tore after it, a blond streak across the grass.

A Native American village had once been located on this very spot. It was surrounded by meadows, beyond which was a dense wood of evergreens and maples, their autumn leaves now shed. The park was called Broken Arrow because of early Suquamish skirmishes here, but you'd never guess that anyone had fought in such a peaceful place. Joggers ran on the gravel path around the park's perimeter. Children, bundled up against the cold, played on swings and slides. P-Patch gardeners dug up shriveled vegetable plants and put their plots to bed for winter.

Externally, all was calm. Internally, Jeff felt uneasy, on guard.

He did not look forward to seeing Anna. He'd answered her text with a single word: *Fine.*

That had been as much as he could bring himself to say when his warm feelings for her had blown away like so much dust. Earnest was the only reason he'd agreed to meet. If Dr. Nilsen thought Jeff and Anna should walk their dog together, he was willing. Whatever it took for Earnest.

After a dozen more stick throws and impatient glances at his watch, however, Jeff considered leaving. Finally, Vincent sputtered into the parking lot. Earnest pricked his ears and dropped the stick at Jeff's feet. When Anna opened Vincent's door, Earnest dashed to her before she jumped to the ground.

He wagged his tail and yipped. *Oh, you're here! You're here!* He pressed against Anna's knees.

She bent down and kissed his forehead. She was always leaving lipstick prints—and Jeff was always washing them off. Now he'd have to do it again when he and Earnest got back to his apartment. Anna was inconsiderate. *One more strike against her.*

Jeff took his time sauntering across the grass. When he reached Anna and Earnest, he did not say hello. He did not smile. He stood there, wooden, his feet planted in the parking lot's gravel.

But Earnest sprang to life. No one could have missed his joy that the two people he loved most were together. He ramped up his yips to ebullient cries. His ears flapping, he circled Anna and Jeff again and again as if he were lassoing them together and staking out his family's boundary. He leapt in the air and rolled in the grass, then pranced around them, swishing his tail.

Earnest's pure, innocent rejoicing tugged at Jeff. It was contagious. How could he not get into the spirit of joy when his best friend was so happy? Jeff fell to his knees, grabbed Earnest, and wrapped his arms around him. Anna kneeled down and hugged him too. Across his back, her arm brushed Jeff's.

His forehead grazed hers. Soon their petting hands touched; and when Earnest wriggled, they accidentally petted each other. Their breaths mingled into one exuberant cloud.

As Earnest whined and wiggled, Jeff's and Anna's eyes met. He smiled at her as warmly as the old days. When she smiled back, she glowed. But then Jeff pictured the twitch of Mad Dog Horowitz's rodent whiskers and remembered signing away half his right to Earnest. Jeff drew back into himself, a clam slamming his shell closed. The softness around Anna's eyes hardened.

Their play was over. The curtain fell on *The Importance of Loving Earnest* and rose on *The Iceman Cometh*. Without looking at each other, Jeff and Anna got to their feet. Jeff attached Earnest's leash to his collar.

"Come on, Earnest." Jeff would talk with his dog but damn well not with Anna.

Though Earnest obeyed, his mood shifted. Obviously, he had picked up Jeff and Anna's huff, and he did not approve. Disappointment radiated from him as he walked stiffly between them down the gravel path.

"I want to tell you something," Anna said.

"Fine."

"When I picked up Earnest last Monday, he was filthy. You'd taken him where he'd stomped through mud, and his fur was stiff with saltwater."

"So?"

"So I was late to work because I had to take him home and bathe him."

"What a shame," Jeff said.

"You're being snarky."

"So what?"

Earnest raised his head and gave Jeff and Anna a shriveling look. He curled his lip, and for the first time ever, he growled at them. He hooded his eyes as if the very sight of them annoyed him, and he let them know in the harshest terms, *Your scrapping is intolerable. You are the rat finks of the Western world.*

Earnest stepped off the path and walked on the grass as far away from Jeff and Anna as his leash would allow. His stand on the matter of their barbs was irrefutable when he lifted his leg and drowned the thorns of a Nootka rose bush.

"Dr. Nilsen said we should act like everything's fine so Earnest will feel secure." Anna's words sounded irritated, flea-bitten.

"How can we act like everything's fine when it's not?"

"We should talk."

"I have nothing to say to you," Jeff said.

"I don't have anything to say to you, either."

Jeff wanted to tell Anna to take her hornets' nest of anger elsewhere. But he decided if she wanted talk, he would give her talk. He would fill the air with words so Earnest might think they were conversing and he would feel better. No problem.

The first words that came to Jeff were from the Gettysburg Address, which his sixth-grade teacher, Mrs. Watkins, had made him memorize—and which would be imbedded in his brain forever. He began: "Four score and seven years ago our fathers brought forth on this continent a new nation, conceived in liberty, and dedicated to the proposition that all men are created equal."

"All right!" Anna seemed to understand his ploy. "London Bridge is falling down, falling down, falling down."

Like our relationship. "Now we are engaged in a great civil war, testing whether that nation, or any nation so conceived and dedicated, can long endure."

With contempt, Anna rolled her eyes. "Rain, rain, go away. Come again another day."

"We are met on a great battlefield of that war. . . ."

"No kidding," Anna interrupted. "Humpty Dumpty sat on

a wall and had a great fall. All the king's horses and all the king's men couldn't put Humpty together again."

"That government of the people, by the people, for the people, shall not perish from the earth."

"Little Miss Muffet sat on a tuffet. Along came a spider and sat down beside her."

Earnest, being a perceptive and intelligent dog, looked at them like they were lunatics. He yanked them off the path to a rhododendron bush, under which he found a sniff-worthy mole-hill. But Anna and Jeff stayed stuck on Grudge Mountain.

CHAPTER 29

———— ❧ ————

One evening after Joy and Lauren had gone home, Anna stayed late with Earnest to get ready for Thanksgiving. As usual when a holiday approached, Grammy was on her mind. Tonight Anna was remembering Grammy's favorite motto, "Waste Not, Want Not," because it had inspired the Thanksgiving bouquets Anna planned to make.

Grammy had taught her to piece old clothes into quilts and braid lavender stems into wands for birthday gifts. She and Anna had picked up neighbors' windfall apples and turned them into sauce. They'd gathered fir swags and pinecones in the woods for Christmas wreaths. "Free gifts are everywhere. All you have to do is find them," Grammy had said.

If there were ever a time when Anna needed free gifts, that time was now—when her savings were dwindling, Christmas expenses were looming, and her wholesale floral supplier had sent a cringe-inspiring bill. To save money on arrangements, Anna had been drying Queen Anne's lace she picked on road-sides, magnolia leaves that old Mr. Webster let her cut from his tree, and every flower that didn't sell in her shop. On walks in the forest with Earnest, she'd collected pinecones and pods to tuck into bouquets. For vases, Anna had hollowed out small pumpkins left over from Halloween, and bought pitchers and mugs from the New to You Shop.

Now all she needed were gourds for centerpieces and she'd be set. She roused Earnest from his lily pad and drove to Thrifty Market, where she left him in Vincent with a promise to buy him people crackers. Since his last walk with her and Jeff, he'd deigned to pick at his kibble, but he'd not yet returned to his vulture days. He'd let her know he wanted treats.

In the market, Anna rolled a grocery basket to the pet supply department. Late in the day close to Thanksgiving, Thrifty Market was packed, and shoppers zoomed along the aisles like kamikaze pilots. She dodged and wove to the back of the store, grabbed Earnest's people crackers, and moved on to the produce, where she picked out gourds in primitive shapes that seemed to have to do with sex and war: torpedo, phallus, belly dancer, fertility goddess, and pregnant hand grenade.

Since she was near Thrifty's flower stand, she aimed her basket down the aisle to check out her competition, though the skimpy selection had never rivaled hers. She expected shopworn African violets in plastic pots and weary irises clumped together with rubber bands. But when she turned the corner, she froze. She felt as if this year's Mr. Universe had whomped her on the back and knocked the breath from her.

An entire alcove of the store had been transformed into a new "Floral Department," spelled out in gold letters nailed to the wall. Containers of vibrant long-stemmed flowers were lined up below shelves of sumptuous plants and brightly colored vases. Anna's eyes moved from roses and carnations, to tulips and lilies, to mixed bunches, tastefully designed. Off to the side was a sleek chrome counter, behind which a newly hired florist filled orders. An eagerness to please seemed to float through the upscale air.

Clearly, Thrifty Market was giving Anna a run for her limited money. The owner was kicking her while she was down. If Earnest had not been waiting for his people crackers, Anna would have left her basket in the floral department and fled. But she could not disappoint her dog. She reminded herself to breathe as she made her way toward the three grocery checkers at the front of the store. Her hands cold from shock, she got in line. She looked around.

Of all the countless nights she'd come here—and after the floral department ambush—wouldn't you know that this would be the night when Jeff was moving through the line to her left? And wouldn't you know that when he reached the pretty blonde checker with the bouncy ponytail, he beamed at her? His smile never faded as she lifted orange juice and bananas from his basket and her long red nails punched in the costs on her register.

Gimlet-eyed, Anna watched the woman lean toward Jeff and hang on his every word. As he gazed at her, the outside edges of his eyes slanted like they did when he focused on an attractive woman. When she spoke, he laughed too loud. *He was flirting! How could he?!* Anna turned her head to keep from seeing more, but then she looked back, an iron file helpless against a magnet.

She may be mad at Jeff, but she had not gone blind, and he was still an attractive man. It took no more than the sight of him to resurrect the pleasure of his arms around her, the solidity of his chest, and the shelter of his broad shoulders. But she would *not* let herself dwell on his assets. No, sir! Not till hell froze over.

Anna told herself that there were other good-looking men in the world. More busses would come to her station, more cookies would appear in her jar, along with more tools in her shed. If there were more fish in the sea, Anna would not settle for a shark—and that was what Jeff was. A shark! Rather than dwell on his broad shoulders, she would think of sharp killer teeth.

However, as Anna carried her torpedo and hand-grenade gourds through the parking lot, Jeff's laugh and the upscale air from the floral department seemed to waft through Thrifty's door behind her. What had she done to deserve tonight's double whammy? Well, she would not let either whammy gnaw at her. Definitely not. Still, by the time she reached Vincent, her spirit had shriveled like brown edges on the leaves of an unwatered plant.

CHAPTER 30

───── ❦ ─────

Nothing like a holiday to dredge up loneliness. As Jeff rolled his shopping basket toward Thrifty Market's frozen foods, he felt like the last person in America with no Thanksgiving plans. All the happy people shopping for their Norman Rockwell dinners stoked his isolation. He might as well have washed up on a Pacific island, and the only sign of human life was Amelia Earhart's skeleton.

Jeff reminded himself that friends *had* invited him for Thanksgiving dinner tomorrow, and he'd turned them down. He'd not wanted to leave Earnest alone in the apartment after his assault on the drafting table's leg. Jeff would never let him get anxious like that again. Tomorrow they would celebrate Thanksgiving together.

Jeff had bought a turkey roast for them. At the Creamery he'd get blackberry cheesecake ice cream—as close as he could come to the blackberries Earnest liked to bite off bushes—and Jeff would serve him his own little bowl. For trimmings, they were going to share a frozen turkey dinner. Jeff stopped in front of the freezer's glass door and studied the brands—Stouffer's, Lean Cuisine, and Hungry-Man. Each package heralded a scrumptious meal on a china plate, but, what awaited him in-

side the cardboard wrap, besides a turkey slice, was a compart-
mented plastic tray of overcooked dressing, potatoes, and veg-
etables.

The pickings would seem puny after last year's feast with
Anna. They'd smoked a turkey on his outdoor barbecue, which
she still had, and he intended to get back, though he hadn't
drummed up enthusiasm for grilling on his balcony over the
gas station. Jeff had mashed the potatoes, and Anna had pro-
duced a lumpless gravy that would have brought Martha Stew-
art to her knees. In honor of her grandmother, Anna had also
made a green bean casserole as close as she could get to the one
she remembered as a child, and a pecan pie that she and Jeff
polished off in two days.

I'm going to miss that dinner, Jeff thought as he studied the
dismal frozen offerings. If he were honest, he also missed other
things. He'd lost plenty since he and Anna had broken up. First
and foremost was the obvious: He'd lost the woman he loved
and their family of three.

He'd lost the condo, and he'd sunk to a seedy apartment.
He'd lost three years of history with Anna; there was no one to
look back with on their shared pleasures and traditions. And
his routine had been blown out of the water—no more tending
Earnest together, or waking up to Anna's breakfast, or washing
and folding her sweet-smelling laundry on Saturday afternoons.
No more late-night movies, dancing around the living room,
conjugal trips to the bedroom. NO MORE SEX! Heaven
only knew how horny Jeff was.

He tossed the Hungry-Man dinner into his basket with
the turkey roast and thought that his list of losses could nudge
him off a cliff to a canyon of depression. But Jeff would *not*
give in to that. *What's done is done. You can't go home again,* he
told himself. It was time to leave Anna behind and move on.

Jeff stopped in the produce department for Earnest's Granny

Smith apples. Two women were picking through the Honey Crisps. One was too old for him, though she looked damned good for fifty-something. The other, as curvy as a Delicious apple, had sumptuous breasts that were fighting a mighty battle against her tight black-and-white-striped sweater. Jeff's eyes moved from the single pearl on a gold chain around her neck to her cleavage, which looked like a shadowy tunnel down which his hand could slide to paradise. A hint of her spicy perfume floated across the apples toward him.

Indeed, it was time to get on with his life.

At his apartment, Jeff sat at his computer, which he'd finally taken from the condo one Friday night when collecting Earnest—along with his file cabinet, TV, wingback chair, carving knives, and toaster oven. As the computer screen lit up, he felt as if he were about to shoot a gun into the air and start a race, though he, a horny man, would be the only contestant. At the finish line would be a sexy woman who would love and value him. The thought of someone waiting for him out there brought a flush of excitement.

On his Web browser, Jeff typed in NorthwestSingles.com and clicked on the site. So far, so good. He chose Fun2BWith for his username and lookingforsome1 as his password. He typed in his birth date and e-mail address, then got down to details, such as his range of income (seventy-five to a hundred thousand), occupation (creative/artistic profession), and education (BA). He paused at body build. Was he slender? Average? Athletic? How was he supposed to answer? He checked "average," then "never married" and "no kids."

Choosing his preferences for women piqued his anticipation. He clicked on "blonde," "blue eyed," "slender," and "liberal" before he realized that he was describing Anna. He paused and fixed his eyes on the brick wall across the alley behind his apartment. Was he looking for Anna's replacement? Could you substitute one woman for another? Definitely not, he decided, no more than he could substitute another Lab for Earnest. Better to strike out into unknown terrain.

Still, Jeff had always liked blondes, and he saw no harm in sticking to his established taste. He returned to checking preferences—"social drinker," "nonsmoker." (*Anna again, but so what?*) When Jeff got to the pitch he was supposed to make about himself, the challenge nearly made him turn off the computer and forget his quest. But no teacher brandishing a red pen would mark up his statement, he told himself. He forged on.

He was looking for someone fun, thoughtful, and caring, he said. And someone interested in spending quality time with him. He wanted a companion for hiking, camping, cross-country skiing, and going to art exhibits, concerts, and movies. And he loved his dog, so anyone he met could not be scared of Labrador retrievers. That was essential.

Finally, Jeff uploaded his firm's Web site photo of himself looking respectable at his office drafting table. Relieved to finish, he sent off his application and imagined it zooming with fervor to NorthwestSingles.com. Forty-five minutes later, his computer pinged to let him know an e-mail had arrived in his inbox. NorthwestSingles.com had approved him and sent his four allotted matches for the day. Hunting season had begun!

With a quiver of anticipation, Jeff studied the first woman. She looked wholesome. She might have spent summers rubbing sticks together for Girl Scout campfires. She wore wire-framed glasses, so if Jeff kissed her, they'd both have to whip theirs off in unison. Not a problem. She said she was ready to fall in love and was looking for fun with an active, confident, clever man.

So they both wanted fun, but Jeff wondered if he could consider himself clever. Then he decided it was not for him to say. When he saw that the woman had listed her occupation as creative/artistic, his heart stood at attention. He marked her as a favorite.

Next was a woman whose user name was VIVACIOUS!—all caps and an exclamation mark that no one could ignore. She was pretty in her low-cut black dress. So far so good. However, she said that she was "extremely intuitive and could read people like a book" so she needed an honest man. *What would happen if someone lied to her?* But Jeff was honest, and he didn't lie. He marked her as a favorite too.

Then came a woman who had cheeks slightly on the chipmunk side, but that was not enough to rule her out. She'd checked off her body type as "a few extra pounds," however, and in her bio she wrote that she loved cake and mentioned twice that she enjoyed trying new recipes and cooking new foods. Among her hobbies, she listed cooking, dining out, and watching cooking shows. Maybe all she did was eat. Jeff left her at her table and pressed on.

The final match showed the photo of a woman who said her name was Alice Spanker, she had a career in a "fun industry," and she liked to do backflips. *What am I supposed to do with all that?* Equally problematic, she was sticking out her tongue. Most likely for an invitation? She wrote, "I want a man willing to stomp on all spiders." *She doesn't want a boyfriend—she wants an exterminator.* No favorite for her.

Jeff leaned back in his chair and rubbed his eyes. Two favorites out of four possibilities today. Fifty percent. He couldn't complain. He'd send messages to the first two women, and tomorrow morning he'd see if they replied. Now when he woke, he had something to look forward to. It was not like rolling over in bed and snuggling up to Anna, but he'd see where NorthwestSingles.com led.

CHAPTER 31

Earnest dashed across the muddy terrain, thrilled to get to Anna. *You're here! You're here!* His eyes flashed joy. His tail wagged prestissimo. Though he'd seen her yesterday, anyone would have thought it had been a century ago. *You're here!*

"Hi, Sweetie!" Anna hugged him, wiggling, as Jeff strolled toward them. Unlike Earnest, he did not seem glad to be going on the walk today. But as he came closer, his lips turned up into a slight hint of a smile. "Hi," he said.

"Hi." Anna turned her own lips up into a slight hint of a smile back. It was a reflex, really. When someone smiled, she couldn't help but respond.

Lately, their walks had been businesslike and civil, though hardly warm. At least Jeff had not recited the Gettysburg Address, and Anna had not resorted to "Rain, Rain, Go Away." Today, however, a recent *Crier* notice threatened to ratchet up the tension between them and set them to sparring again: The planning commission would meet at city hall on January 29, to approve or disapprove of Cedar Place, and the vote would influence the fate of Grammy's house. Today Anna and Jeff's conflict would simmer with new intensity beneath the surface.

Anna complained, "This is a crummy place to walk. Earnest will get muddy."

"Mud can be washed off," Jeff said.

She remembered the Monday morning when she'd picked up Earnest, splotched with mud, his fur stiff with salt water. "If he gets dirty, you need to take care of it. You can't expect me to bathe him every time."

Jeff's former slightly upturned lips straightened to a horizontal line. "I don't expect anything, Anna. I suggested this park because I wanted Earnest to see a new place. We've been to the other parks a gazillion times."

For today's walk, Jeff had chosen Disappointment Park, so named because the scenery offered nothing to be desired. A few scraggly madrona trees struggled to live around the edge of an abandoned quarry, which was a huge pock in the ground. Little grass grew here, so mud ruled when autumn rains began. No one came for picnics.

Jeff patted his thigh. "Here, Earnest. Let's walk." Without waiting for Anna, Jeff started along the path around the quarry.

Earnest followed, but after a few steps, he stopped. He looked back at Anna, then ahead at Jeff, then back at Anna. His troubled eyes asked, *Aren't you coming? I want us together.*

Anna started out, though Jeff's long strides had already taken him a tennis court's length ahead. For Earnest's sake, she dodged boggy places in the dirt and hurried to catch up. When she reached Jeff, she said, "You could have waited for me. It's no good unless we walk Earnest together."

"I didn't feel like waiting," Jeff said.

"You'd just leave me here?"

"You can take care of yourself."

Yes, I certainly can take care of myself. I don't need you.

Feeling irritated, Anna rested her fist on her hip and dug her heels in the mud. Jeff's walking off and leaving her was rude, but not a big offense. Still, it was a small piece of a larger picture, a microcosm of the macrocosm that had caused her so much grief. He'd left her behind today just as he'd left her behind to work with Mrs. Scroogemore. Both actions boiled down to the same thing: Jeff didn't care about her. He had no regard for her feelings.

Jeff kept walking, but he must have realized that Anna had lagged behind. He turned around and came back with Earnest.

"You're no better than my parents," Anna mumbled.

"What's that supposed to mean?" Jeff asked.

"Oh, never mind."

"Really. Why do you say that?" Jeff looked at her with genuine incomprehension.

"It doesn't matter."

"I don't understand."

"It's just . . ." Anna's sentence faded away, unfinished.

"Please, explain." Jeff was frowning. With impatience? Concern?

Without caring which, Anna blurted out, "One morning I found Grammy dead. I was just ten and I was traumatized. I ran to Mrs. Webster, and she called my parents in Lebanon, but they didn't bother to come back for me." Anna pressed her hand against her heart to protect it from that horrible hurt.

"Mrs. Webster arranged Grammy's burial and enrolled me in boarding school. All that mattered to my parents was filing their next CNN story about the civil war. My mother asked Mrs. Webster to tell me she loved me, but she didn't ask me to come to the phone so she could tell me herself. Her 'love' meant nothing."

Anna remembered sitting on Mrs. Webster's sofa while she'd made that call, and Anna had never felt so sad and alone and insecure. She'd squeezed her hands together and bitten her lip till it bled. For all these years, she'd never told anyone what her parents had done. But she'd never forget it.

Now Anna looked down at the muddy path and wished she'd never mentioned any of this. She had no idea what had gotten into her—except that Jeff had pressured her to talk.

Without meaning to, she'd slipped back into being open with him like in the old days. But never again. She brought her guard back up.

When she raised her head, he was frowning at her again. "I'm sorry," he said.

"Never mind. It doesn't matter."

"That never should have happened. Your parents should have gotten on the next plane to comfort you," Jeff said.

"It was too much trouble. It might have hurt their precious careers."

"No wonder you never talk about them." Jeff reached out as if he were about to put his arm around her, then drew it back. "Anna, I don't understand. Why am I like them?"

Anna widened her eyes, incredulous. "You don't get it? It's so obvious."

"It's not obvious to me."

"They abandoned me. So did you when you agreed with Mrs. Scroogemore to tear down Grammy's house. Like you, they cared far more about their work than me. I'd trusted them, and they betrayed me. You don't see yourself in this picture?"

Jeff didn't answer. He just stood there, his hands in his jeans pockets, his gray muffler wrapped too loosely around his neck to offer warmth. His face was frozen somewhere between puzzlement and anguish. He looked at her as if he were meeting her for the first time.

Earnest picked up Anna's feelings, which prickled from her like thistle thorns, and he pressed against her legs. She reached down and stroked his reassuring neck. She could trust *him*.

But she couldn't trust Jeff, and suddenly she felt vulnerable, as if she were in her own bad dream, standing naked in Disappointment Park and a crowd had gathered around to gawk. All these years, she'd kept her parents' rejection to herself. And now *he* knew.

"I'm going to leave. You can walk Earnest by yourself today. I don't want to be with you," Anna said.

"I wish you wouldn't go," Jeff said.

Only because of Earnest. Jeff doesn't want to miss the chance to make him more secure today.

Anna said, "Earnest will understand if I don't finish the walk. He understands everything." *Unlike you.* She bent down and kissed the top of his head. "Good-bye, Sweetie. See you Monday morning."

Earnest whimpered as she turned around and left. Anna could feel his and Jeff's eyes follow her as she walked toward Vincent. Only when she drove away did she realize that neither she nor Jeff had mentioned the planning commission's meeting. They'd pretended like it wasn't coming in a few weeks, just like, for Earnest's sake, they'd tried to act like they weren't at war with each other. But they were.

The Gamble Island History Museum was located in a red one-room schoolhouse that had been moved from a rural area to downtown. Instrumental in the move had been April Pringle, president of the historical society and once Grammy's friend. Miss Pringle knew more about Gamble's past than any other living person, and that was why Anna chose to talk with her first about the planning commission's meeting. Anna found her shuffling through a drawer of the schoolmarm's desk, which now served as her own.

The classroom's walls were dark rough-hewn boards between which strips of muslin had been tacked to keep out winter drafts. Now from the walls in poster-size black-and-white photos, Gamble's early citizens looked down sternly on students' desks, lined up in tidy rows. The school smelled of dust and age. In the air floated memories of rulers whacking knuckles. The floor creaked under Anna's footsteps as she and Earnest walked to the front of the room.

"Got a minute?" Anna asked.

"Sure, Anna. What's going on?" A wisp of a woman, Miss Pringle pulled back her hair into a severe gray bun. She wore a shirtwaist dress and no-nonsense shoes with rubber soles.

"Have you heard about Naomi Blackmore's application to tear down her historic house?" Anna asked.

"Heard!? Girl, I've been complaining to the city for weeks. The planners wouldn't dare let that go through. The very idea." With indignation, Miss Pringle seemed to spit out the idea and stomp on it.

"The planning commission is meeting about it."

"So I read in the *Crier* . . . Humph."

"Will you come and speak for the house?" Anna asked.

"Nothing could keep me away. I'll get our members over there."

"Perfect."

"You'll need to call the neighbors and the chamber of commerce. You might try some environmental groups. Ducks and grebes nest in that marsh behind the property." Miss Pringle's hands fluttered like wings.

"I'll spread the word," Anna said.

"What is that Naomi Blackmore thinking? Her family's lived in this town for generations. You'd expect her to care about our history."

All Mrs. Scroogemore cares about is money.

"Why, I remember visiting your grandmother in that house when you were a child," Miss Pringle said. "Imagine Gamble losing that treasure. Those people at city hall should have turned down that application the day it reached their desk. They're ignorant about history. The very idea!"

All week after work Anna and Joy had been making Christmas wreaths at Anna's counter. Bits of fir, cedar, and red satin ribbon littered the floor. Now on to straw wreath forms, she and Joy were gluing sand dollars, collected on the beach. Once finished with a floppy bow, the wreaths would bring in a nice profit.

"I ran into Mr. Webster at Norm's Drugs. He says he'll support us at the meeting," Joy said.

"They'll have to listen to him since he lives so close," Anna said.

"I hate to think who Mrs. Scroogemore is lining up to take her side."

"They'll be up against April Pringle. This morning I got her on board."

"She'll show 'em! We'll get 'em!" Joy waved her fist in the air. "Bombs away! I love a good fight."

Joy's enthusiasm traveled across the room to Earnest, lounging on his lily pad. He opened his eyes and unfolded his body. After a yawn and stretch, he padded over to the counter and stationed himself next to the sand-dollar pile.

Every Christmas Earnest waited for the dollars to rain down, pennies from heaven, because he liked to crunch the dollars in his teeth. Anna had to pry them out of his mouth to keep him from swallowing the sharp-edged pieces. Perhaps he enjoyed the salty flavor, or, heaven forbid, he was calcium deficient.

"How are things going for John and Penelope?" Anna asked.

"They just got auctioned off! John's cruel master is going to whip him half to death in a salt mine outside Tunis, and a wicked overlord bought Penelope. Bad news all the way around."

"What if the wicked overlord turns Penelope into a used hag, and John won't want her anymore?" Anna asked.

"Not going to happen! They belong together. Their love is the real thing."

"I'm not sure any love is the real thing." Anna aimed her glue gun at the straw and left a glop.

"How can you say that?"

"I thought Jeff and I loved each other. Look what happened." Anna still felt vulnerable for telling him about her parents. She didn't like him having the power of that knowledge, but then, *so what?*

"Love wasn't the problem with you and Jeff. The problem was that he acted like the Twit," Joy said.

"I dread facing him and Mrs. Scroogemore at city hall."

"I don't. I can hardly wait. Bring 'em on!"

"What if Mrs. Scroogemore hates us forever? She'll never sell us the house," Anna said

"At least we might save it." Joy pressed a sand dollar onto a lump of glue. "And don't worry about Jeff at that meeting. He's earned the opposition we're rounding up. He brought it on himself."

"Yes," Anna said. "He did."

CHAPTER 32

On a cold Saturday morning, Jeff thrummed his fingers on a round claw-footed table in the Unicorn, a Gamble coffee house. It was located in a redbrick building that was covered by a Virginia creeper, whose stems grew in odd directions like dead ends on a city map. The Unicorn was the only place that served food and allowed dogs, and Jeff had brought Earnest along for support. Jeff was about to meet Tiffany, his first NorthwestSingles.com date—and his first date in three years with someone besides Anna.

He rubbed his sweaty palms on his jeans legs and petted Earnest, who'd curled up under the table near the fireplace's flames. *Today isn't really a risk,* Jeff insisted to himself. It would cost him just an hour or two and the price of two pastries and coffees. If he and Tiffany liked each other, fine. If not, they could get up and leave. But, then, that would be awkward, and rejection could humiliate him. *Let's be honest. Today is a risk, a flying leap into the unknown.*

Jeff checked his watch. In ten minutes Tiffany would fling open the door. And who knew? She could be the love of his life. From her online photo, he'd seen she was a pretty blonde. And from her get-to-know-you e-mails, he'd learned she was a photographer—and he'd assumed they were equally creative.

An added plus: She lived on Gamble, so future dating, if it happened, would be easy.

After yesterday Jeff needed something to be easy. Grabowski had called to demand a beefed-up drainage study because of wetlands behind Mrs. Blackmore's property. The request had rankled Jeff because the drainage plan he'd already submitted should have been enough. But what came next maddened him: With overt sadistic pleasure, Grabowski mentioned the planning commission's upcoming meeting, and he snorted, "We really value the commissioners' opinion. It's crucial to our deliberations." In other words, *If the planning commission votes against Cedar Place, you may as well hang it up, buddy—heh! heh!*

When a good-looking blonde opened the door and stepped inside, rubbing her cold hands together, Jeff's heart thumped. *Beginner's luck!* But she wore a white parka and ski hat with a pompom that bounced as she crossed the room. Tiffany would be in a black down coat.

Since half the women on Gamble wore black down coats, Jeff had e-mailed Tiffany to ask how else he'd recognize her. She'd answered that a python would be curled around her neck. *So she has a sense of humor!* Jeff replied that she'd easily spot his Prussian-blue hair. She said he'd hear her coming because of her chronic hiccups. He pointed out that he'd be recovering from unsuccessful plastic surgery and she couldn't miss his bandages. Finally, Jeff and Tiffany had agreed on a red muffler for her and a green one for him so together they'd make Christmas, which was coming soon.

Jeff stared at the door and waited for a red muffler, as Earnest basked innocently in the fireplace warmth. Jeff had not discussed with him the purpose here today—perhaps that had been a mistake when harmony between Earnest and Tiffany would be essential. To prepare for their meeting, all week Jeff had read online about introducing dates and pets. One article had warned that if something went wrong, it could take months to undo. Others had suggested slipping your date a treat to offer in friendship, or letting your date know where your dog liked to be petted. Most important was keeping your dog under control so no atrocity got committed.

Easygoing, friendly Earnest would never commit an atrocity, Jeff believed.

At last, in walked Tiffany in her black down coat and red muffler. She'd clearly posted a younger photo of herself on NorthwestSingles, but she looked pretty good. Before Jeff could ponder the ruse, he stood up in his green muffler and grinned, then warned himself, *Don't try too hard.* He waved to her and pulled out her chair at the table.

The scrape of chair legs on oak brought Earnest out from his hiding place. As Tiffany approached, he took one look at her and planted his paws firmly apart as if he were standing his ground. He pressed his body against Jeff's legs and with a wary expression watched Tiffany advance like an enemy squadron over the crest of a hill. Earnest acted as though he were bracing himself for rocks hurled from a catapult.

"Tiffany. Happy to meet you." Jeff held out his hand.

Hers brushed his palm, more a swipe than a shake. "Nice to meet you too."

"This is Earnest." With pride, Jeff nodded toward his best friend.

Tiffany looked at him as she might have looked at a *Tyrannosaurus rex.* "He's so big."

"He's just your normal Lab."

"He's scary."

"You said on NorthwestSingles that you liked dogs."

"Little fluffy ones. He's a thug."

"Earnest is *not* a thug."

Don't get defensive. Maybe she meant that as a joke, like the python around her neck. Apropos of nothing, Jeff chuckled like an idiot.

Earnest apparently did not think any more highly of Tiffany than she did of him. His hooded eyes seemed to say that looking at her full force might send him into apoplexy. When Jeff lamely pointed out, "He likes to be petted on the chest," Earnest retreated out of Tiffany's reach. His disapproving squint said, *I'd rather singe my tail in the fire than let you touch me, you vile interloper. You have woolly mammoth breath!*

"I don't know what's gotten into him. He usually likes people," Jeff said.

"He doesn't like me," Tiffany said, flat as a tortilla. She sat down and shrugged out of her coat, but left her muffler around her neck. The red wool clashed with her cable-knit sweater, which was the color of a sour, underripe persimmon.

"Give Earnest time. He'll love you." Less than half Jeff's heart was in that declaration, however, because Earnest drew highly trustworthy conclusions about people and he rarely changed his opinion.

Jeff asked Tiffany if she'd like a cup of coffee. She preferred tea. He suggested that they have the Unicorn's specialty, raspberry scones. She was gluten-free, she said, and she didn't like the food here anyway. When Jeff went to the counter for her tea and his coffee, Earnest followed as if he refused to be alone with someone he suspected might be rabid. He seemed to ask, *What would happen if that woman* bit *me?!*

From a blue plastic tray, Jeff set cups on the table and reclaimed his seat. Earnest plopped down as far as he could get from Tiffany. He groaned like he was auditioning for next Halloween's recording of scary sounds. He turned his head away and watched the flames.

Jeff said, "So tell me about your photos. Are they portraits? Nature?"

"Autopsied bodies. Tumors and moles."

"Oh, right. Moles," Jeff said vaguely, feigning interest. "They'd make an unusual artistic statement."

"My pictures are for documentation. I'm a medical photographer at Mountain View Hospital's pathology lab."

So much for creativity. "Do you like the work?"

"Yeah. I really get off on all that blood."

Tiffany's amused expression told Jeff that it was again python-around-the-neck time. But the joke came too close to sarcasm, a cousin of contempt. Jeff forgot to laugh.

Silence crawled on wounded knees across the table. As Jeff rotated his coffee cup for something to do with his hands, he searched his mind for a neutral topic that might stake out common ground. *But maybe there is none.* "Did you grow up in Seattle?"

"Yeah. What about you?"

"Born and bred there," Jeff said. "How'd you get to Gamble?"

"Cheap rent," she said. "You too?"

"No. I visited a friend here, and I liked the forests and small town. In my book, the rural always beats the urban."

"Not for me. I miss the city. I may move back."

As if to encourage Tiffany to do just that, Earnest rose to his feet. He yawned as if his boredom had become intolerable, and to put a little spice in Tiffany's day, he intended to show her his incisors.

"Wow. Look at that dog's teeth." Tiffany shrank back at their ferocity. "Are you *sure* he's safe?"

"Absolutely sure. Earnest would never hurt anybody."

Earnest, however, seemed bent on proving he was more than a muffin. He stepped between Jeff and Tiffany, raised his head, and barked. The bark did not cross the line to vicious, as in, *Prepare to meet your maker because I'm going to shred you to ribbons.* It was more a bark of impatience: *You are a positively soporific and tedious drag. Now shoo. I want Jeff to myself.*

"Earnest, quiet!" Jeff ordered.

Earnest barked at Tiffany again. *We don't want you here. Why don't you go sidle up to an asp?*

"He never barks at people," Jeff said.

"He just barked at me. I'm a 'people.' He must not like my smell."

You, you horrid woman, are what I don't like! Earnest underscored his view by barking again. He reared on his hind legs and set his paws on Tiffany's shoulder so she almost toppled out of her chair.

As Unicorn customers gaped with open mouths, Jeff jumped up and helped Tiffany sit straight again. "I'm sorry. He's always well behaved."

"You've got to be kidding. He's awful." Tiffany got to her feet and yanked her coat off the chair. "This match is not working." One end of her red muffler dragged behind her as she hustled herself—and her tumors and moles—out the door.

Jeff slumped. *Great start to your dating career.* He sat back down and patted Earnest. "I can't be mad at you. You're right."

Earnest rested his head in Jeff's lap as if to say, *Indeed, she was horrid beyond measure.* As Jeff scratched Earnest's triangle ears, Earnest's sad eyes added as forthrightly as anyone ever added anything to a conversation, *She was unworthy.* In other words, Jeff knew, Earnest's sad eyes were saying, *I want Anna.*

Jeff thought about Anna as he sipped his coffee. *Their* first date had started on a morning like this one after she and her gladioli had washed up on his condo's shore. Jeff had taken her to a tyke soccer game, and Anna had cheered right along with the parents: "Good job!" "You can make that goal!" "Keep going!"

Afterward, they'd intended to rent kayaks and look for the otters' lair that everybody knew about in Heron Harbor, but on the way to the marina, Jeff stopped to show Anna his latest house. Only the foundation, subfloor, studs, and roof were finished, but she could see where Jeff had planned the doors, windows, and fireplaces. He walked her through and explained the purpose of each room. Soon they were discussing exterior colors, the master bath's tiles, and the den's furniture arrangement.

"A sofa should go against this wall so your clients can look at Mount Rainier," she said.

Jeff walked across the room and stood under the windows. "It'd be better over here."

"Look how much cozier it would be if you could see the mountain and fireplace at the same time. And you could feel the sun shining through the skylight." Anna pointed to the roof opening where it would be installed.

Jeff had to hand it to her. She was right. But he didn't feel threatened. He liked that he could share his work with her and she would understand.

They went to Plant Parenthood, then stopped at the Chat 'n' Chew for a late lunch, after which they paddled around Heron Harbor and went for dinner at Sawyer's. Since Jeff didn't want the day to end—and Anna seemed to concur—he took her to see the movie *Take Me Home* and for ice cream at the Creamery. When he kissed her on the sidewalk, she tasted like toffee. That had done it. Never before had Jeff been smitten. What more could he ever want than Anna Sullivan?

As Jeff stared at the Unicorn's fire, he admitted that Anna had been a swan, and Tiffany, a mud hen. Anna, gold, and Tiffany, lead. The two women were as far apart as a star and a mole. But he couldn't recross his and Anna's burned bridge, not after she'd compared him to her cold, ambitious parents—and she surely hated him. All he could do was move forward. *Somewhere out there in the ether there has to be another woman.*

CHAPTER 33

On Waterfront Park's rocky beach, Jeff and Anna waited with Earnest for the Christmas boat parade. Each person in the crowd held a lighted red candle and a copy of the carols' lyrics, compliments of the Rotary Club. The moon shone on the dark water, which was ruffled by a cold breeze. Everyone was talking.

Including Jeff. He scolded Anna, "Look how thick Earnest is around the middle. Don't you see he's getting portly?"

Yes, Anna saw, but she didn't need Jeff pointing it out like she was a blindfolded amoeba.

"You're not walking him enough," Jeff said.

"Christmas is my busiest time. I don't have enough hours in the day," Anna defended. "Besides, you know Earnest doesn't like to go out in the rain."

"He doesn't complain about it when *I* take him out."

"Maybe you don't read the signals. Rain makes him unhappy. It shows in his face."

"When I take him jogging, he loves it no matter what the weather is."

In other words, I'm a better dog parent than you are, Jeff was saying.

The gall, Anna thought. She tugged her parka closed against the cold. She was bundled in layers, a thermal onion, but a chill was seeping through. "I walk Earnest every morning unless there's a storm."

"That's not enough exercise. It's a lot harder on Earnest to lose weight than not to gain it in the first place," Jeff nagged. "If you let him get fat, it's a terrible mistake."

You are the terrible mistake. Not to put too fine a point on it, so was agreeing to meet Jeff for the parade. The plan was to turn Earnest over to him for the holiday here instead of at Plant Parenthood. It had seemed like a good idea.

Anna had thought the parade could substitute for their weekly walk with Earnest. If they were singing carols, they wouldn't have to talk. And Earnest had always loved this night. When he'd spotted Jeff walking down the hill to join them, he'd dashed to him, the red bow around his neck dancing as surely as his paws. He'd led Jeff to Anna. *My family is together! Jingle bells! Joy to the world!*

Now, however, Anna gripped her candle and felt little joy. She wished she'd never said she'd come tonight. She felt sad— and not just because Jeff had lectured her about Earnest's weight as if he were a lord and she were a peon. She also felt sad because Christmas rekindled memories of Grammy's death and of lonely holidays at boarding school, and on this Christmas Anna would remember past happy ones with Jeff and Earnest—and she'd be alone again. The prospect made her heart feel like a rag someone was twisting water out of. Just when Anna needed Earnest, he'd be with Jeff.

Who, by the way, was wearing his best cashmere sports coat and gray slacks under the black topcoat he saved for special occasions. Undoubtedly, after the parade he was taking out some attractive, dressed-up woman—maybe that grocery checker. Not that Anna minded. *She* would never dress up for Jeff again. Not if wild horses dragged her to her closet. Not if someone offered her a winning lotto ticket.

When her candle's hot wax dripped on her wrist, she wiped it off to stop the burn. She turned and watched the Christmas Ship, a Seattle tour boat, blasting "Rudolph the Red-Nosed Reindeer" over loud speakers as it came into the dock. Earnest sat between Anna and Jeff and gazed at the ship so intently that he might have expected the passengers to toss him steak and cheese.

When the ship drifted to a stop, a choir in white robes filed out on deck and sang, "Frosty the Snowman," accompanied by a horn, saxophone, and trombone. Then everyone filed back inside, like cuckoos who'd just announced the hour on their clock. Blasting "Santa Baby," the ship started up, circled the harbor, and sailed back to Puget Sound. And the shore got quiet again.

As if by magic, out of the foggy darkness, sail- and powerboats emerged, one by one. They were lit up with clear and stained-glass-colored Christmas lights—strung-up masts, down halyards, along transoms and gunwales, around bows and sterns and hulls. As the boats passed by, their lights' reflections shimmered on the silent water. The Christmas spirit seemed to shine down on the crowd as surely as the silver moon.

Then everyone sang carols. "Deck the Halls." "The First Noel." "The Twelve Days of Christmas." "Silver Bells." And, finally, "We Wish You a Merry Christmas." Jeff boomed out the words in his commanding tenor's voice. Earnest cocked his ears and listened. Anna forced herself to sing for Earnest's sake, but her words came out more as obligatory husks than heartfelt kernels.

We wish you a Merry Christmas.
We wish you a Merry Christmas.
We wish you a Merry Christmas.
And a Happy New Year!

The crowd burst into applause. They blew out their candles, folded their lyrics, and stuffed them into their coat pockets. As everyone began to disperse, up the hill next to Puget Sound Bank, Lloyd McGregor, Gamble's bagpiper and the owner of the Squeaky Wheel bike shop, began playing his usual, "Amazing Grace."

"Here." From around her neck, Anna unlooped Earnest's leash and handed it to Jeff. She told herself, *You will not cry.* "And here are Earnest's Christmas presents." Blinking hard, she pulled a box of small wrapped packages from her tote bag. "I hope he likes his squeaky c-a-r-r-o-t," she spelled, just as she and Jeff spelled b-i-s-c-u-i-t, r-i-d-e, w-a-l-k, c-h-e-e-s-e, and j-o-g to keep secrets from Earnest.

Anna felt too sad to look at Jeff, but then their eyes met. Two puzzled lines were etched above his eyebrows.

"Anna, are you all right?"

"I'm fine."

"Um . . . Do you think . . . Would you like to . . ." Jeff seemed to think better of continuing. He gazed beyond the crowd at nothing in particular.

If I'd like to what? Get a lethal allergy to dog fur and give you Earnest forever? Board a slow and leaky boat to Beijing?

Jeff looked back at her again and took her presents. "Thanks. I'm sure he'll like his c-a-r-r-o-t." He attached Earnest's leash to his collar. "Merry Christmas." Jeff led Earnest up the hill.

With mournful eyes, Earnest looked back at Anna. She watched, feeling lost and miserable and suddenly tired of carrying a grudge. As "Amazing Grace" billowed through the cold night air, Anna thought, *Maybe Jeff was going to ask me to come over on Christmas morning and watch Earnest open his presents. Maybe Jeff was about to try to bridge the gap so we won't hate each other anymore.*

Anna closed her eyes at the unbearable sadness of that

thought. She was standing on the corner of Anger and Grief, and she was not sure in which direction to turn. But then she chose Anger. It was an easier street to travel than Grief. Grief hurt more. It extracted a higher cost. It had more cracks in the concrete.

CHAPTER 34

Late in January, the morning was unusually cold. The sun was barely rising over the mountains, so all Jeff could see was a warm, pink glow. Wisps of clouds hung above the snowy peaks, which the early light turned lavender. Jeff figured it must be going on six o'clock. With clear roads, he'd get to the cabin by eight.

Earnest, never a morning person, was power napping in the backseat. Jeff had startled him out of a dead sleep at 4:00 a.m. Though not pleased at the disruption of his rest, he, a newly recovered Hoover eater, had gobbled down his breakfast and licked his bowl clean. He had staggered back to bed, clearly intending to get in a few more hours of serious snoring.

But Jeff had made him a blanket nest in the car and, with a people cracker, coaxed him outside into the cold. "We're going cross-country skiing!" Jeff had lilted his voice at "skiing" like it was the pinnacle of every dog's desires. Once Earnest had romped through snow, Jeff would have to spell out s-k-i-i-n-g to keep him from going wild at the spoken word.

Now, after working late last night to prepare for next week's planning commission meeting, Jeff himself was almost going wild with anticipation. Judy, his date for the weekend, had driven up earlier with two couples from Starbucks, where she worked in the marketing department. She was at the cabin waiting for Jeff—and for fun.

Jeff had met Judy online. Miles ahead of Tiffany in decency and conversation, she had restored his faith in North westSingles.com. She was nearly as tall as he, and willowy and graceful. For twelve years, she'd studied dance, and her supple body testified to every pirouette and *grand jeté*. Though Judy had been blonde in her online photo, by the time Jeff got to her, she'd gone back to brunette. Her wavy hair cascaded down her back, the better to entwine his fingers in when they made love.

That was his goal for the weekend. Making love! He'd thought of little else but sex since their third date for a drink last week, when Judy had invited him to ski. Though they'd not discussed sleeping arrangements, he assumed that he and Judy would be together—and he was ready. Impatiently cooling their heels in his Dopp kit were five condoms—*well, you never can predict these things.* If Judy brought her own form of birth control, his condoms would be redundant. But he was prepared!

He'd shopped for his contribution to the communal meals thinking only of pleasing her. To get her comfortable with him and loosen inhibitions, he'd bought merlot and chardonnay. Because she'd mentioned that she loved chocolate cake, he'd picked one up at the Sweet Time Bakery. How could he fail with a cake that came from a place named Sweet Time?! Jeff had brought avocados for the salad, olives and dolmas for après-ski hors d'oeuvres, and figs and blueberries for breakfast.

After the catastrophe with Tiffany, the only thing he was not quite ready for was introducing Earnest to Judy. Last week to set the stage, Jeff had explained his and Anna's custody arrangement and asked, "Would it be okay with you if I brought Earnest to the cabin?"

"Sure," Judy said. No hesitation. "I grew up with a black Lab named Dickens. I know I'll love Earnest."

"Your friends won't mind if he's there?"

"How could anybody mind a sweet Lab?"

"My last NorthwestSingles date minded a lot." Jeff explained Earnest's barks at Tiffany as if they were a joke. "Earnest knew the match was wrong." *Ha-ha!*

"He could bark all he wanted, and he wouldn't scare me."

What if Earnest had devised other methods for repelling women? What if he had a secret bloodlust for running off dates?

"Don't worry about your dog, Jeff. There are lots more important things to think about."

Like sex!

Jeff zoomed along the highway toward Judy and her bed.

Till now Jeff had only pecked Judy's cheek in bars as they'd greeted each other or were about to go their separate ways. But when he knocked on the cabin door, she crunched out onto the icy porch, wrapped her arms around his neck, and planted a saucy smackeroo on his mouth. She let him know that there would be no more kisses on the run and she meant business. *Hurrah!*

Euphoric, Jeff introduced her to Earnest, who wagged his tail—*so far so good!* And she introduced them to her friends. Jeff and Judy unpacked his car as Earnest leapt through the snow like an ebullient reindeer. Jeff's hopes for a lust-filled weekend soared.

Except for a long lunch, holding hands in a warming hut, Jeff and Judy skied all day, and Earnest ran along with them, a wheat-colored Alberto Tomba. Back at the cabin, Jeff talked little with her friends because he was so focused on future pleasure. His eyes on Judy, he opened his wine with eager thoughts of loosened inhibitions. He added his olives and dolmas to the hors d'oeuvres tray.

When everyone gathered around the dining table, Earnest climbed underneath to explore the forest of legs. Then he began an ardent game of Pick the Pansy to target who would give him treats. He laid his head in laps, and his beseeching eyes explained that he was a starving orphan who never got anything to eat but moldy gruel. After the Laurence Olivier performance, Earnest feasted on cheese, chips, chunks of meatballs, bits of buttered French bread, an avocado slice, and an olive. He staggered to the living room and conked out by the fireplace.

As Jeff's anticipation heated, at last the dishes got washed, the brandy got drunk, and it was finally—*finally!*—time for bed. Judy used the bathroom first, then disappeared into the bedroom, where under his pillow Jeff had secreted the condoms. He brushed his teeth and stepped into his pajamas, which, if he had anything to say about it, would be shed in the next two minutes. His masculinity in high gear, he opened the bedroom door like he was raising the lid off a box of chocolates—and they were all his!

Earnest plopped down on the rug next to what was about to be Jeff's side of the bed. Nearly panting with expectation, Jeff lifted the covers to climb in. His eagerness seemed to stop time; he felt that the entire universe was waiting for this moment to unfold. Judy was lying there in a filmy pink nightgown with spaghetti straps that he would delight in sliding off her shoulders. She looked relaxed, as if she'd been poured into the sheets. Her lovely breasts were visible, ripe apples to be plucked.

"Hi." Jeff's voice was husky with desire.

"Jeff, you can't really be thinking of letting Earnest stay in here."

Still gripping the covers, Jeff froze. "He always sleeps with me."

"I don't want him watching us."

Oh.

Earnest's presence in the bedroom had never bothered Anna. He'd known when not to climb onto the bed. With impeccable discretion, he'd politely slept on the floor, his eyes firmly closed while waiting for Jeff and Anna to finish. Only later had he stationed himself in his nightly roosting place between them.

But now at this of all times, Jeff did not want to think of Anna. He banished her from his thoughts and slammed his mental door closed. "I'll put Earnest in the living room," he offered.

"Good."

Jeff opened the bedroom door again. "Come on, Earnest. Out."

Earnest looked up. His bristled eyebrows said, *I don't speak English.*

"Come on," Jeff urged.

You must be addressing some other dog in the room besides me.

"I mean it. Go sleep by the fire. It's still warm in there."

Piffle. Stuff and nonsense.

"Earnest," Jeff called in his sternest voice.

"You need to show him who's boss." Judy yawned, like any second she might fall into a deep, immobilizing sleep, and Jeff had better hurry.

He walked back to Earnest and grabbed his collar. Never before had Jeff forcibly dragged his cooperative dog anywhere. It hurt Jeff to do it, but Earnest's recalcitrance left him no choice. "Out. Now."

As Jeff tugged Earnest to the door, he scraped his toenails into the wood between the bedroom's islands of rugs. He wailed, a noise Jeff had never heard from him before. When

Earnest knew he was losing the battle, he took the opposite course, rolled onto his back, and went limp in passive resistance.

Earnest's upturned paws protested, *I need to stay in the bedroom. I'm supposed to protect you.*

Jeff pulled Earnest to the fireplace. "Now, you behave." As he left him in the living room, Jeff looked back.

Earnest's dark and disapproving look said irrefutably, *I am a sensitive dog, and you have bruised my feelings.*

That was not what Jeff wanted to think about as he climbed into bed. He took the delectable Judy into his arms and smelled her fragrant shampoo. Her flesh felt soft beneath his touch. Her breasts pressed into him. Like sipping nectar, he kissed her— long and slow and eager—until the horny desperado in him sprang to life, and he kissed her faster and harder.

Jeff heard a whimper at the door. *No! Please, no.*

Earnest's whimpers insisted, *I want to be with Jeff.*

Jeff broke the kiss. "He'll quiet down in a minute," he mumbled, his lips brushing Judy's neck. He raised his head and added with a wicked smile, "Where were we?" He returned to serious nibbling of her flesh.

Earnest whined again, shrill, high-pitched whines designed to annoy, coerce, and block Jeff's primrose path. *Don't forget me. I'm here! I'm here!*

"He's going to keep everybody awake," Judy said.

Jeff groaned and rolled away.

Scratch, scratch. Earnest's nails on the door.

Judy sat up, and a spaghetti strap drifted down her shoulder. "This isn't working."

Tiffany's exact words before storming out of the Unicorn. Jeff covered his face with his hands.

"Earnest will hurt the paint. He'll ruin the door. We want to get back our rental deposit," Judy said.

"I don't know where else to put him."

"In the car?"

"It's too cold out there. He'd freeze."

"You can't let him scratch all night."

Judy seemed to sprinkle scorn, like vinegar, all over the bed, and there was no dry place left for Jeff to sleep. He threw back the covers, got up, and took his blanket, folded at the foot. If Jeff were a dog, he might have exited the room with his tail plastered between his legs. Lacking a tail, he simply left, emanating dismay and disappointment. *Paradise lost.*

In the living room, Earnest welcomed Jeff with yips and pranced around his legs. *Mission accomplished! We are reunited! I have Jeff!*

"Shhhh." It would take Jeff a while to forgive him. A decade, perhaps.

Jeff curled up into the fetal position because the sofa was too short. He thrashed and tossed all night, while Earnest snored peacefully beside him without a worry in the world. At dawn, Jeff tiptoed around the cabin, packed up his belongings, including his uneaten breakfast figs, and hustled Earnest to the car. As he drove back toward Seattle, he left defeat behind him.

He wondered if Judy and her friends were up yet, and he remembered accidentally leaving under the pillow his damned condoms, those embarrassing, foil-wrapped packages of desire and hope. When Judy stripped the bed, she would find them. She might laugh.

Ahead on the side of the highway stood Humiliation, his thumb raised to hitch a ride. Jeff stopped to pick him up. As Humiliation climbed into the backseat in his trench coat and fedora, he chuckled, *So much for you, Lothario. Eat your heart out.*

CHAPTER 35

⟡

Two alligators were wrestling in Anna's stomach. Tails were slashing, and teeth were snapping, and waves of foam shot in the air. *So much is riding on this planning commission meeting.* For calm, Anna folded her arms around her waist, but the alligators kept at it.

She tried to hide her feelings as Jeff made his presentation behind a podium at the side of the room. In a gray blazer and button-down shirt, he flashed PowerPoint slides about Cedar Place on a screen. His red laser pointer danced on the graphs and drawings like a hyperactive Red Hot, but she looked at them with indifference. She would not let Jeff see on her face that his every word distressed her. She would not allow him that pleasure.

Seated at tables in a "U" on the dais, the planning commissioners seemed rapt by Jeff's ideas. Giving them extra gravitas, which they hardly deserved, in Anna's opinion, were American and Washington State flags set in copper planters of sand on each side of the screen. On the wall, the hands of a clock, big as a bicycle tire, seemed never to move. Anna kept checking the time. So far Jeff's twenty-nine minutes had felt like the entire Jurassic period.

At last, after thirty-two minutes—and Anna had counted

every second—Jeff turned off his laptop. The applause offended her as much as he just had. *Humph. It's just polite applause, really. Nothing more.* Though she, Joy, and Lauren had rounded up supporters, so had Mrs. Scroogemore. Except for Lauren, who had the flu, both sides were here in full force.

As Jeff returned to his seat on the front row—in clear view of Anna's own front-row seat—Joy leaned over and said, "The dirty rat." To avoid him, Anna fixed her eyes on David Connolly, the planning commission's chair.

"Thank you, Jeff Egan, for your insights," said Connolly, a silver fox whom Joy called the Elder Hunk. He had a muscular build and thick gray hair, which sometimes fell devilishly over one of his dark gray eyes. He could have starred as a Western's sheriff, his badge glinting as he drew his gun. *Ka-pow!*

Connolly folded his hands around the base of his microphone, not that a sheriff's voice needed amplifying. "Without further ado, I'm opening this meeting to public comment. I ask you to take no more than three minutes each and be polite. Feelings are running high about Naomi Blackmore's project, and we all need to get along." He nodded toward her on the aisle to his right. "Why don't you start us out, Naomi?"

Mrs. Scroogemore strode confidently to the podium in a pearl-gray Armani suit. She smiled at the clapping crowd and pointed her index finger at favored supporters the way a seasoned politician would.

Joy whispered, "Look at that necklace."

"You'd think the weight of all that gold would make her stoop," Anna said.

With a maroon fingernail, Mrs. Scroogemore hooked an errant strand of highlighted hair behind her ear. She adjusted the microphone, a treacly smile on her lips. Then she pressed her hands through the air, palms down, to signal the crowd to muffle their welcome and let her speak.

"Thank you. Thank you." She tossed her head as if she

were accepting an Oscar. "I'm so glad to be here, and my mother would be pleased. Twenty-two years ago she bought the property on Rainier. She dreamed of developing it, but she died before she had the chance. I swore I'd do it for her, and tonight I'm excited that Jeff has told you about our wonderful plans for Cedar Place." As her supporters applauded, she pointed at them again.

"I'm also excited that *I'm* the person developing my family's property instead of some company that would do it just for profit. *I'm* looking out for our town. My family has lived on Gamble for generations, and I grew up here. I've loved our island all my life. I understand better than any outside investor what we want and need. And I can tell you, we don't need a hard-nosed company forcing a Walmart on us." Her smile was spun sugar, fudge.

"I want our own businesses to thrive. I want our little town to prosper," she continued. "And our kids! Jeff has allotted space for the KiDiMu to move into my building at a reduced rent. I want our children to have the opportunities I had. I believe in the next generation, and I believe in Gamble Island and in all of you. I am certain that Cedar Place will improve our lives, and I can hardly wait to get started giving back to our community all it's given me."

As Mrs. Scroogemore walked back to her seat, she waved at her admirers. Joy snarled, "The mildewed hypocrite. Pardon me while I gag. I'd like to smack her in the chops."

Anna glanced at Jeff, who was also applauding. *How could he?* More important, she asked herself for the one thousand and twenty-ninth time, *How could he have taken on that project? How could it have been more important than the family we used to have?* The questions stoked her stomach's alligators into wrestling another round. *Thrash, thrash.*

"Mr. Chairman? I can't let that woman's words go by without responding." In bicycle shorts and a hoodie with "The Squeaky

Wheel" emblazoned on the back, Lloyd McGregor, Gamble's bagpiper, advanced on the podium like he was leading Scottish troops to war. "Maybe Naomi Blackmore believes she's doing us all a favor by developing her property, but what about the environmental impact?" He raised dark, scornful eyebrows.

"Wetlands adjoin her property, and they deserve protection. In her yard is a hundred-year-old heritage madrona that she intends to bulldoze. Traffic to her new building would cause air and noise pollution downtown. We're at a crossroads here. We can look after our own interests or give in to her greed. It's no different from an outside developer's. It's threatening our environment and the character of our small town."

"You think the parking lot's proposed eight spaces are gonna cause smog, McGregor?" a man shouted.

"Yeah, and you've seen one tree, you've seen 'em all," yelled someone else.

Elder Hunk Connolly's gavel came down with an authoritative crack. "Keep it civil."

Anna looked over at Jeff to see his reaction. For the flap of a hummingbird's wing, their eyes met—before they looked away. Enough of a second passed, however, for Anna to writhe at having been caught. Why had he been looking at her? To gloat? Anna was still pondering the reason when old Mr. Webster walked to the podium.

He smoothed back his few remaining wisps of hair as if he wanted to look his best on national TV. "I've lived two doors down the street from that property for seventy-five years, long before Naomi Blackmore owned it. Money-grubbing developers have tried to ruin my neighborhood time and again, but we've fought them off. Leave us alone. Don't bring in fancy new businesses that will force our small concerns like the Chat 'n' Chew to close. And keep your traffic to yourself. Our kids play in the street. Think of their safety. You may feel we neighbors don't count, but we're important."

Joy shouted, "That's right! We count!"

Anna clapped till her palms turned pink.

Liz Matheron, mother of Tommy, who was Igor the Venus flytrap's friend, hurried to the microphone. She adjusted it shyly, as if she thought it might grab her and pinch her bottom. When she introduced herself as director of the Kids Discovery Museum, she flinched at the sound of her amplified voice.

"I understand Homer Webster's concern about neighborhood children, but not *that* many more cars are going to be coming down his street," she said. "And Naomi Blackmore's generosity to our museum is a huge gift. We'll finally have room to expand our exhibits. We can teach classes. We'll have hands-on demonstrations. Gamble's kids will gain a lot more than they'll lose from Cedar Place."

Before Liz could finish, April Pringle of the historical society wobbled toward the podium on unsteady feet. "Now listen here. You people keep talking about traffic and wetlands and kids, but nobody's bothering to mention the historic house on that property. You can't just pretend it isn't there. Tearing it down would be a tragedy. Why, the very idea!"

Indignant, she pulled the microphone down to her frail lips as Liz returned to her seat. "I'm your elder, and you young people need to stop and think about what you're doing," Miss Pringle said. "That house has been around here longer than any of us. It's part of our community, and we'll miss it if it's gone. It takes us out of our crazy, rushed world back to a slower time, and it's a living memory of the past that we can see and touch."

Miss Pringle grasped the podium's edges and leaned forward, scowling. "You may not think about this, but you're connected to every person who's lived on this island before you, everyone here now, and everyone coming after you. That old house is connected to everybody too, and you're connected to it whether you realize it or not. It just sits there, peaceful, reminding you of how the past and present and future are all part of each other—and you. If you lose that house, you lose an old friend and a witness to this island's history. You tear down that lovely old place at your peril. Naomi Blackmore, build your commercial building somewhere else!"

Anna's hands burned from clapping so hard. "Perfect!"

Joy gave her a high five and nodded toward Jeff. "Too bad he doesn't like to hear the truth."

Anna looked at him, and wouldn't you know that at that exact moment, he looked at her too? Anna practically snapped her neck turning her head away so quickly, but she had seen him long enough to note his frown. *Good.*

At the microphone, Alex Rugoff introduced himself as a recently retired newcomer from Los Angeles, but he said he'd lived here long enough to know what's what. "What about progress? Nobody's talking about moving forward into the future. Building new buildings. Starting new businesses. Keeping up with the times. You've got to admit we're a bit of a backwater. We could use some modernizing." Along with applause, enough boos followed Rugoff to his seat to discourage him from speaking his mind at future public meetings.

To speak her own mind, Anna needed courage, especially when Jeff would watch. Still, for the sake of Grammy and the house, she begged her stomach's alligators to make peace, and took her place at the microphone. She looked around at the faces of her loyal friends and customers, but she did not turn her head toward Jeff or Mrs. Scroogemore. "I want to give a personal view of what Miss Pringle just said about the historic house," she began.

"Many of you know that I lived in it as a child with my grandmother, and now two friends and I rent it for our businesses. We love the house. For us, it's far more than glass and wood and bricks. I know that houses aren't people, but, to me, tearing it down would feel like murder."

Anna held up the Mason jar that Ted Carcionni, the fire marshal, had given her months before. "This is a time capsule that the house's original owner, James Williams, left between two walls." She unscrewed the lid. "Here are square nails, the kind used for construction then. And a bullet. And a crumbling page from an 1880 *Gamble Crier*." With care, Anna held up the paper for the crowd to see. "Everybody was excited about getting Mr. Edison's electric lighting to Gamble someday. One of the residents was starting a steamship ferry to Seattle. The island's first post office opened downtown. Eggs were three cents a dozen then. James Garfield was just elected president."

Between her thumb and index finger, Anna held up a tiny ladder-back chair. "This came from Amy Williams's dollhouse. And this is a clamshell someone drew a little face on." Anna showed that too. "I feel like the Williams family still lives with us because you can feel their presence in the house. It holds their hopes and fears and love and secrets, just like it does for all of us who have lived in it, shopped in it, walked by it, admired it, or taken care of it. It's a part of us.

"Gamble would never be the same without the house, and neither would I. I'm begging the planning commission to vote against Cedar Place. Help us save the house!"

Anna scanned the crowd again before returning to her seat. Mrs. Scroogemore looked like she might explode, and everybody would have to get down on their hands and knees and pick up her angry, pointed shards and her necklace's gold links. When Anna broke down and looked at Jeff, this time he met her eyes with an impassive mask revealing nothing.

Nothing! His expression also seemed to make clear that she was nothing to him. He didn't nod or blink or signal in any way that he was aware of her existence.

For the rest of the meeting, Anna blocked him out with equal disregard. But when she reached the door to step outside, wouldn't you know that Jeff happened to have gotten jostled along with her in the exiting crowd? As a fresh breeze cooled her face, her shoulder bumped against him. Though she'd intended not to speak to him, she was too polite not to come up with a civilized greeting, such as "hello."

But Jeff beat her to it. "The rain has stopped," he said.

"Maybe." *No point conceding anything.* "I think more rain is blowing in."

"You might be right."

As Anna walked ahead, Jeff turned toward the parking lot. Their directions were as different as their views about the house, but that was just the way it was. Neither had said good-bye.

CHAPTER 36

⟨≈⟩

Thanks to the *Gamble Crier*'s article, almost forty mostly gray-haired women showed up for Anna's presentation at the senior center. They sat on folding chairs in front of her and Earnest, who'd come along to encourage her. At the back a younger broad-shouldered man leaned forward, his knees apart, as if he intended to spring out of his seat. As he watched Anna intently, she wondered, *What is he doing here? Where have I seen him before?*

"First you fill a beautiful vase with water, and then you add flower food." Anna showed the audience a silver vase. "I got this at the New to You for three dollars. All it needed was a little polish."

From a glass pitcher, she poured in water and sprinkled in a small green packet's contents. "For Valentine's Day, I got these red and pink roses, pale pink ranunculus, and variegated carnations. See the gorgeous purple streaks in the red petals?"

Anna piled the flowers next to the silver vase, then held up a bunch of geranium leaves. "Look at these furry beauties. They complement the flowers' red and pink tones, and they smell like spearmint." She handed a leaf to a woman in the front row. "Pass it around so everyone can see how delightful it is."

Anna's talk today was part of her plan for growing her business and stepping onto firm financial ground. Though Christmas orders had been good—every wreath and swag had sold—she was trying to rebuild her savings. She also intended to fight back against Thrifty's new flower market. She would not let them defeat her. She would lure away their customers.

She'd invested in brochures and business cards, handed them out, and pinned them on bulletin boards around town. She'd run ads for Plant Parenthood in two church bulletins, the chamber of commerce's newsletter, and the *Gamble Crier*. She'd talked with people who might order flowers—Gamble's mortician, realtors, restaurateurs, church secretaries, and Downtown Business Association members. And she'd given flower-arranging demonstrations at the library, the Cascade Country Club, and now the senior center.

"Once you've got your materials together, you tuck these leaves into the vase for a green background. Be sure you spread them out." Anna fluffed the leaves around, just so. "Because these red roses are largest, I'll put them in first around the vase's lip. See? Like this."

"Anna? Do you cut off the flowers' leaves?" asked the wife of David Connolly, the Elder Hunk. In a blue felt hat, she was sitting next to the man on the last row.

Who was *he?*

"Good question, Sammy. The answer is yes if the leaves are below the water line because they'll rot." With clippers, Anna snipped a leaf to demonstrate. "Now I'll fit some of these smaller flowers here and there above the roses. You don't want to crowd anybody. Flowers need air like we do."

Anna tucked in blossoms till the arrangement was round and full. She held up the vase as the audience applauded. The man at the back smiled and clapped his hands over his head as if he were doing eager upper-body jumping jacks. *What is with him?* Anna had met him, but where? In her shop?

"Now I want to show you something romantic you can do

with petals and small flowers. I'm going to set them in a heart shape on this cookie sheet, but you should put your petals on your dinner table or entry floor—or your valentine's pillow. Anywhere you want to leave a surprise."

From a plastic bag, Anna scooped out violet, rose, tulip, and carnation petals in shades of red, pink, and purple. She formed her heart and carefully tilted the cookie sheet so everyone could see. "Look! One puff of breath and these petals would go flying. They're like love itself—beautiful and delicate and fleeting." How well she'd learned about "fleeting" from Jeff.

So everyone could have a closer look, Anna carried the cookie sheet around the room. As she made her way along the last row, she asked, "Isn't it lovely?"

The man gave her a goofy smile, flashing yellow teeth.

As he fingered his keys like worry beads, Anna had a flash of recognition. He was the unfaithful husband for whom she'd been making a Virtue Special on the day the kitchen caught on fire. Now she knew what he was doing in this audience of senior women: trolling! *What an ego.* How could she be interested in a philanderer like him?

For the last few months, Anna had felt too hurt to consider even the concept of dating, much less an actual date. Given her poor judgment of men, she could end up with Gary Ridgway, Washington's Green River Killer. She couldn't trust herself *or* the men in this world, such as the dishonorable one in front of her. Though she might change her mind and risk again someday, for now she preferred to stay alone.

She did not lean down to show him the heart. She moved on. When she returned to the front of the room, she set the cookie sheet on the table and turned around. The man was gazing at her like a love-struck cocker spaniel.

Anna reached for Earnest. "Want to see how to put a valentine on your dog's forehead?" She stooped down, kissed him between the eyes, and left a lipstick heart.

When the crowd applauded again, Earnest, the eternal ham, stood up as if he were taking a bow. She quickly tied a red bow around his neck. "I thank you all for coming here today. If you have questions, feel free to drop by Plant Parenthood. I'd love to see you."

As the women filed out of the room, many stopped to thank Anna. The man hovered off to the side in the posture of a hungry vulture. Eventually, only he, Anna, and Earnest were left in the room. *Not a pleasant prospect.*

He walked up to her. "Great talk. I enjoyed it."

"Thanks." Anna busied herself picking petals off the table.

He puffed out his chest as if he thought he could shove Johnny Depp out of the way and take his place as *People* magazine's "Sexiest Man Alive." But this man needed to attend to his teeth. Earnest seemed to share that opinion and to worry that something unpalatable might unfold before him. He leaned against Anna's legs.

"Want me to carry this stuff to your car?" the man asked.

"No, thanks. I can handle it."

"I'm strong." He flexed his bicep and chortled, "Stand back, Arnold Schwarzenegger."

Right. Get me out of here. "Really, I'm fine."

"I can take this to your car easy," he insisted.

"I'm sure you could. But no need," Anna said.

Earnest seemed to be losing patience with this hanger-on. He gave him a scornful look that unequivocally urged, *Scram, you perfidious slime.*

"Want to go have a cup of coffee? I bet you could use one after your talk," the man tried again.

"Thanks, but my boyfriend will be here in a minute," Anna lied.

As she stuffed her cookie sheet into a tote bag, the man said, "Um . . . well, okay. Maybe another time." He shrugged and walked out.

Anna breathed clean air again and patted Earnest's head. Thank goodness he was there, the one male she could trust. As he accompanied her to Vincent and watched her load boxes into the back, she remembered that Lauren's valentine poem for her community poetry post was Elizabeth Barrett Browning's sonnet:

> How do I love thee? Let me count the ways.
> I love thee to the depth and breadth and height
> My soul can reach . . .

Anna changed the question: Why do I love thee? She applied it to Earnest and counted her reasons.

1. He had a heart as big as Texas.
2. He was an outstanding cuddler.
3. He didn't have a mean bone in his body.
4. He radiated warmth at night and never hogged the blanket.
5. He was a model citizen and always tried to do the right thing.
6. He was loyal, unlike a certain person she used to know who would go unnamed (but whose initials were J. E.).
7. He loved her unconditionally, also unlike that certain other person. Anna could count on Earnest's unwavering devotion. He'd never betray her.

She slid open Vincent's side door, and Earnest jumped in for the three-block ride to Plant Parenthood. Her protector on guard, he peered out the window.

CHAPTER 37

Jeff scanned the library's meeting room for Anna and Earnest. The library staff had invited them to the reading program's graduation because Earnest had been a crucial volunteer. Jeff spotted them on the front row of molded plastic chairs and gathered strength for an evening of his and Anna's stilted conversation—such as, "The rain has stopped." He walked down the center aisle toward them.

Anna had saved him a place, a surprise. When Earnest saw Jeff, he tugged at his leash to get to him—and Anna let him go. As always, he whined and wagged his tail so it thumped against the knees of people on the aisle, but no one seemed to mind. As he hurried to Jeff, friendly hands reached out to pet him.

"Hey, Earnest!" Jeff said.

Earnest danced around Jeff's legs and whimpered what he always did: *You're here! You're here!*

Jeff led him back to Anna and sat down next to her. "Hello," he said. If enthusiasm had a heartbeat, his would have measured as a flatliner.

"Hi," she said.

Silence. Here we go again.

"Four score and seven years ago," Jeff half joked to fill the empty verbal space.

Anna almost smiled. *Amazing. Another surprise.*

"Three blind mice. See how they run," she answered.

"So how's it going?"

"Fine."

"Busy?"

"Very. You?"

"Very." *So that about covers things.*

The green Martian flicking his antennae in the corner and being ignored was the planning commission's vote. Any day now Jeff and Anna would learn their decision, and Jeff was sure that she was waiting for it with breath as bated as his was. He'd bet she lay in bed at night, gnashing her teeth and telepathically begging the commission to disapprove of Cedar Place. Of course, he was doing the same thing, only begging for approval. Many times a day, he beamed his wish toward city hall: *Vote for my project!*

For a moment, Jeff resented his and Anna's collision course all over again, but then he thought that now was not the time to dwell on it. This evening was about Earnest and his contribution to the reading program.

For the last four years, the library board's chairman had been none other than old Mr. Webster, Anna's neighbor and now, after his curmudgeonly comments at the planning commission meeting, Jeff's foe. Refusing to be a petty carrier of grudges, however, Jeff tucked his pique into his pocket. He nodded cordially at Mr. Webster as he stepped up to the front of the room.

Mr. Webster had dressed up for tonight's graduation by hiding his hallmark long underwear beneath a plaid wool shirt. He'd combed back his flyaway white wisps of hair, and his ruddy face shone from a recent scrubbing. He set a cardboard box on the table that stood under a bulletin board, and turned around to face the audience.

"We're here to present certificates to everyone who took

part in our last reading program," he began. "I've heard what a great class you kids have been. You're reading above your grade level now, and I understand that Earnest encouraged you to read aloud. I want to congratulate you for your hard work."

A murmur went through the audience. Parents wrapped their arms around their second graders' shoulders. Having heard his name, Earnest raised his head and moved his ears forward, his sign that he knew he was being discussed.

"Okay. First is Billy Carcionni. Come up here." With all the formality Mr. Webster could scrape out of himself, he held out a certificate. "Your dad's our fire marshal, Billy. You've got a lot to live up to."

As Billy approached in his Cub Scout uniform, his mother said, "Ted couldn't be here tonight. He's on duty." Her camera flashed as Billy shook Mr. Webster's hand.

"Now Katherine Franklin," Mr. Webster called.

Jeff leaned back in his chair and straightened out his legs. He folded his arms across his chest. The parade of students coming up to Mr. Webster pleased Jeff—everybody winning, verbal pats on the back, goals achieved.

Jeff's father had never shown up for evenings like this, and often his mother had missed them for work. But if Jeff had a kid, he'd crawl over broken glass to get to these events and be a good dad. He'd take his child for ice cream to celebrate finishing the reading program. He'd frame a photo of his child shaking Mr. Webster's hand, and keep the picture on his desk. He'd attach the certificate to the refrigerator door with silver star-shaped magnets.

Having his own family was a pleasant prospect. He'd wanted it with Anna. It seemed like ten years ago.

Though Jeff was facing Mr. Webster, he could watch Anna out of the corner of his eye. She sat there like she'd been whittled out of oak, and she was squinting as she did when she was sitting on a powder keg of feelings. Surely on this graduation night, she wasn't obsessing about her grandmother's house, but maybe she was. Or maybe, like him, these children made her think about the family she wanted and didn't have.

He and Anna had talked about their hypothetical family. They'd agreed that they'd gladly work themselves to nubs being conscientious parents. They'd lead scout troops and drive car pools. She'd bake thousands of cookies, and he'd shepherd kids on dozens of hikes. On Christmas Eves, they'd stay up all night assembling rocking horses and jungle gyms. Jeff and Anna would hug their kids so often that they'd wear holes in their skin.

Compelling thoughts, but pointless, Jeff concluded with a pang. *That hypothetical family is not going to happen. Not with Anna, anyway.*

After Peony Yee came up in her ruffled pink dress to receive the last certificate, Mr. Webster took a picture frame out of his cardboard box. "Now we're going to honor our team's hardest-working member. I'd like to call Earnest up here. For four months he's shown up every Monday afternoon and devoted himself to you kids. He knew just when to encourage you and when to let you flounder till you could encourage yourselves."

Jeff looked at Anna just as she looked at him. For a moment, all hard feelings seemed to wash away through a storm drain and get swallowed by the sea. Anna handed the leash to Jeff so he could lead Earnest to his award. Jeff took her gesture as generous, thoughtful.

At the front of the room, he, Anna, and Earnest faced the graduating class and their parents. Mr. Webster turned the picture frame around so everyone could see. "On the top it says, 'Public Library, City of Gamble, State of Washington,' and Earnest's name is inscribed below." He lowered the frame to Earnest's eyes. "That's your name right there." Mr. Webster pointed to it.

He read, "Be it hereby known, because of your demonstration of loyalty and dedication, meriting our great trust and respect, we are pleased to award you this citation with sincere gratitude for your generous service to the Gamble Public Library and its reading program. Signed Mary McGregor, Librarian, February 10, 2014."

Earnest acted as if the citation were just another people cracker. He was glad, but he didn't make a fuss. However, Jeff's heart swelled like it might thump out of his chest. "In sincere appreciation . . . meriting trust and respect . . . loyalty and dedication." *Those were heady words.*

Jeff grinned till his cheeks hurt. He and Anna bent down and hugged Earnest together as the audience rose for a standing ovation.

"Good job, Earnest. We're proud of you." Jeff patted his back.

Anna kissed his forehead and left another lipstick print, but Jeff didn't mind.

"I'm speaking for all of us when I thank Earnest for what he's done here," Mr. Webster said. "I know you kids want to thank him yourselves, so why don't you come up here and pet him?"

All talking at once, a mob of children descended on Jeff, Anna, and Earnest. When the students jostled them, Anna nearly lost her balance. Jeff reached around her shoulder to steady her. It felt so good to hold her that he left his arm there. To his amazement, she leaned against him just like in the old days.

Earnest, with dignity, accepted the pets of small hands and the thanks of his many young friends. When he looked up at Jeff and Anna, he must have noted their unexpected closeness. His eyes lit up. His ears rose, attentive. His wagging tail said, *Wow! My people are together!*

CHAPTER 38

"Bad news." Jeff handed Brian Cooper a letter from David Connolly, the planning commission's chairman. Connolly had just rankled Jeff as much as Mad Dog Horowitz had. In the mailroom, Jeff's first thought had been to bring the letter to his boss for guidance and commiseration. "Damn them. It's not fair," Jeff said.

"Life isn't fair," Brian reminded him.

"I've worked my ass off on that project. Their decision is a slap in my face."

"Hard work doesn't always mean success. You know as well as I do that projects get derailed for all kinds of crazy reasons," Brian said.

"The reasons in that letter are *ridiculous*."

"Calm down, boy." As Brian read the letter, he pushed his wire-framed bifocals higher up the bridge of his bulbous nose. He whispered a few bulleted paragraph headings to himself. "Hummm. Size . . . Traffic . . . Heritage tree." When he finished the second page, he gave the letter back to Jeff. "Sounds like they're looking for nits to pick."

"Same nits that got picked at the commission's meeting. Anna knows half the town, and she persuaded all her friends to come and speak. The whole thing was practically rigged." Jeff's jaw was stiff enough to shovel sand.

"I take it you and Anna haven't gotten back together."

"Never." Jeff dug his fingernails into his palm. "I could argue against every word in that letter."

"Then do. You don't have to sit there and take their decrees."

"What if you can't fight city hall?"

"You're not fighting city hall. This is only the planning commission's opinion. They don't have the last say," Brian said.

"My planner told me the commission influences his decision. The sadistic bastard."

"Plenty of them in the business. The power goes to their heads." Brian took a sip of coffee from his mug bearing a Frank Lloyd Wright logo.

"I'm not sure what to do," Jeff said.

"Simple. Call your planner. State your case before the commission has a chance to sway him." Brian set his mug on a red ceramic coaster. "Remember, it's not over till the fat lady sings."

Jeff punched numbers on his phone, fumbled, and started over. Not helping was, first, the bandage on his index finger, which he'd cut last weekend on Earnest's dog food can. And, second, Jeff's anger. When wasps were buzzing in his heart, it was not a good time to make this call.

He hung up, buried his face in his hands to block out the world, and breathed slowly to the pit of his stomach. After ten breaths, the wasps had calmed down. *You can't let that smug gorilla get to you. Keep your cool,* Jeff told himself.

This time he dialed more smoothly. To his surprise, Grabowski answered and spared Jeff the indignity of leaving a groveling message that asked for a return call.

"I've been looking over the planning commission's letter. I want to talk with you about it," Jeff said.

"Shoot."

As in, fire away and state your case, or shoot somebody? Both might fit. "Point by point?"

Grabowski seemed to snicker, though Jeff couldn't tell for sure. "Point by point is as good a way to proceed as any," he said. "I've read the letter. It mentions some of the issues I warned you about when you filed your application."

"You didn't say Cedar Place would be too big, but the commission did." Jeff took another calming breath. "The design follows the code to the letter, and I've allowed more space than required for the sidewalk and parking. The building's not any bigger than the library, post office, or Thrifty Market. Nobody argued about them."

"The commission is talking more about aesthetics. They probably think Cedar Place would be a Gas-X building. You know that ad. People puffed up like someone's pumped air into them." Grabowski chortled. *Har! Har! Har!*

Jeff wished he could reach through the phone and grab him by his flea-infested beard. "The building is well proportioned," Jeff said. "And that brings me to the second point. I designed it in the Pacific Northwest architectural style so it will fit in downtown. Nobody can say it'll change the character when it's no different from lots of the houses that are already there."

"Except it's bigger. The commission's more concerned about size than style. They don't want some building dwarfing everything around it."

"Nobody thinks the library, post office, and Thrifty Market are dwarfing other buildings."

"So you said. Anything else?"

The abruptness of that question let Jeff know that Grabowski wasn't interested in arguments. He was closing his door.

Jeff stuck a mental foot in it. "Yes, something else. The traffic," he insisted. "How can a few shops cause smog and traffic jams. We could have gone for a big-box store that *really* would have a made a difference."

"Traffic depends on your perspective. If you're a neighbor, a few more cars impact your life. So does demolishing a historic house and cutting down a heritage tree if you're used to seeing them every day. The change would unsettle neighbors," Grabowski said.

"The house needs a lot of work, and Mrs. Blackmore has no plans to fix it. Surely the neighbors would rather live around a nice new building than a mess," Jeff said.

"Tell that to the historical society."

There is no persuading this oaf. "How much weight do you give the planning commission's vote?"

"We certainly consider it." Grabowski laughed again. "We'll continue to study your proposal. We'll get back to you." He seemed to tap dance into the wings and leave Jeff blinking at an empty stage. A click let Jeff know that Grabowski had hung up.

Jeff slammed down his own phone. Grabowski's words could not have been less definite, but his tone told Jeff everything he needed to know. It had served him a heaping entrée of frustration and a side dish of anxiety, seasoned with a pinch of fear. If Jeff were going to serve Grabowski something in return, it would be stir-fried fury.

For a moment, Jeff imagined walking away from the project, telling Mrs. Blackmore sayonara and moving on. But then the fighter in him came out slugging. In life, you had to struggle for what you wanted. That was an unwritten law. Another was that obstacles always cropped up and tested your mettle.

As a child, Jeff had learned how to dodge the obstacles presented by his father. In college, Jeff had fought for his degree. And now it was time again to call on his determination. If Grabowski turned down the permit, there were always ways to appeal.

CHAPTER 39

At the end of the day, Joy arrived in Plant Parenthood with champagne and celebratory chocolate-chip cookies. Lauren followed, bearing Camembert, crackers, and pears. Joy wore black skinny jeans, a red turtleneck, and a scarf on which was printed "Hallelujah!" in ten languages. In a pale yellow dress, Lauren looked like a long-stemmed daffodil, heralding spring.

"Victory! Let's drink to those saints on the planning commission!" Joy jiggled out the champagne's cork, and with a resounding pop, it flew toward the ceiling. "Best sound known to man." As she filled three New to You glasses, Lauren unwrapped the Camembert and crackers and set them on a flowered china plate.

The prospect of cheese roused Earnest from his lily pad. He charged, panting, across the room, his eyes shining with unbridled lust. They pinned down Lauren and made clear his sybaritic intention: *Gimme! Gimme! I want cheese! At any moment I will wilt from hunger.*

Lauren cut him a sliver, which he vacuumed from her palm. *More! I will perish without nourishment. You will miss me if I'm gone.*

"Earnest knows no shame." Lauren handed him another piece. "Come over here, Anna. Protect me from your dog."

"Your champagne's waiting for you, Anna." Joy raised her own glass. "Here's to the commission, our kindly benefactors." She took a hearty gulp.

"I'll be there in a minute." Anna was wielding a plumber's friend over her sink's drain. *Cha-chook. Cha-chook.* "Leaves got plugged up in here. I've got to get them out myself. Mrs. Scroogemore isn't going to help."

"Anybody heard from the vampire lady? I thought for sure she'd evict us by now," Joy said.

"As long as she's making money, why would she want to get rid of us?" Lauren asked.

"Spite," Joy said. "She looked plenty mad at that meeting."

"Money matters more to her than pride." Lauren sliced more Camembert and set it on crackers. She avoided Earnest's eyes, which skewered her with cheese desire.

Anna pumped the plumber's friend again, then moved the rubber dome away and squinted down the drain. The rotted leaves refused to cooperate and get unstuck. "You know, this drain could be a metaphor for our lives right now. We're blocked."

"I don't know about you, but I'm flowing pretty well." Joy raised her glass again.

"I mean our way forward is blocked. Our future. We have fabulous news from the planning commission, but we don't know what's going to happen," Anna said.

"You want to try any harder to put a damper on tonight?" Joy asked.

"Sorry," Anna said. "But it bothers me. We're in limbo. We can't make plans."

"Who can?" Lauren moved on to slicing pears. "Nobody knows the future. We're all groping through life half blind."

"Look at John and Penelope. What plans can they make? For all they know they'll be slaves forever," Joy said.

"So how do they keep going if their future seems so bleak?" Anna asked.

"They have hope," Joy said. "They'd probably die if they couldn't cling to thoughts of freedom."

"So what hope are we supposed to cling to?" Anna asked.

"I hope Bradley Cooper is waiting in my bed," Joy said.

"I mean about this house."

"Easy. I hope Mrs. Scroogemore goes on a moonlit swim with a school of piranhas." Joy shook her bag of cookies onto one of Lauren's plates.

"I hope we can stay here long enough to figure out our next step," Lauren said.

Anna resumed her assault on the clogged vegetation. *Cha-chook! Cha-chook!* "Once Grammy said your soul turns black if you don't have hope."

"Heaven forbid I have a black soul," Joy said.

"Maybe we should go ahead and keep hoping this house is ours someday," Lauren suggested.

"That's a long shot when Mrs. Scroogemore hates us," Joy said.

"If you think your hope is a long shot, you'll kill it. We can't be negative." Lauren turned her back on Earnest and sank her teeth into a piece of cheese.

"Okay. So I'll be positive. I'm thinking miracle. I refuse to give up hope that we get this house," Anna said.

Cha-chook! Cha-chook! The lump of rotting leaves loosened in the darkness. Anna turned on the water and washed them down the drain.

Gamble's old timers met every morning for coffee at the Chat 'n' Chew Café. Each wobbly chair and table in the large sunny room was a different style, and white curtains embroidered with a zigzag design covered the lower half of the old wavy-glass windows. On a blackboard behind the counter, Peggy LeClerc, the grandmotherly owner, wrote her daily soup and salad menu in lime-green chalk. Oilcloths—of polka dots, checks, and stripes—covered the tables, each of which held a pressed glass vase of plastic carnations and ferns.

Anna sipped her chamomile tea and asked Peggy, "Ever thought of having real flowers in here?"

"These have worked fine for years," Peggy said.

"Fresh roses and asparagus ferns would perk things up."

"Maybe, but they'd droop pretty quick. You can't keep flowers fresh forever."

"You could replace them every week."

"That'd cost an arm and a leg."

"Not necessarily." Anna twirled her teaspoon between her thumb and index finger. "You've got nine tables. A rose and fern on each one would cost maybe twenty-five dollars a week."

"Whew!" Peggy whistled. "Some filthy rich Arab sheik could afford that. Not me."

"How about twenty-two dollars? Every Monday I could put something beautiful in these vases. Your customers would like it. Let me try once and see how it goes."

Peggy slipped her fingertips under her hairnet's elastic band to keep it from digging into her forehead. "You know I'd buy the Brooklyn Bridge from you. I've liked you since you were a child."

"So that's a yes?"

"Well . . ." Peggy hesitated. "A trial, yes."

"I'll bring you beautiful roses on Monday as soon as I get back from Seattle!" When Anna finished her tea, she hugged Peggy and left.

Walking back to Plant Parenthood in the chilly afternoon, Anna realized she was sweating. She'd never tried to sell Peggy anything but Girl Scout cookies in fourth grade, and soliciting business from her this afternoon had been hard. Even when a sale was small and to a good friend like her, it took courage to ask. Still, Anna had taken another step in her plan to reach out for new orders. She'd mark today a success.

Anna wanted to tell someone her good news, but Earnest, who'd normally hear it, was waiting for her in the shop. If she and Jeff were still together, she'd call him from her cell right now and talk with him. He'd accused her once of being a financial flake. Would he be glad she was expanding her business?

Why was she asking herself that question? How did he keep weaseling into her thoughts? To block Jeff from her mind, she moved on to a more worthwhile question: What color of roses should she pick up for Peggy on Monday? Malibu Pink, Yellow Stardust, Latin Lady Red? Or High and Orange Magic? Polar Star White? Maybe each table could have a different rose. *Yes. That's the answer.*

As Anna turned onto Rainier, she realized that pondering the roses' colors hadn't worked. Jeff was sneaking into her thoughts again. Today there seemed to be no keeping him out.

She wondered if she secretly *wanted* to call him. That arresting thought brought her to a stop.

Since Anna had learned of the planning commission's decision, she'd worried about Jeff. Their rejection of his work had surely distressed him. He was probably angry. Surely he was hurt. Jeff could be sensitive, and that made him good at his job. It was also one reason why Anna had loved him.

As she walked down the block toward the house, she considered whether she might have been too quick to judge Jeff. Maybe she should have heard him out. Maybe she'd been too harsh. Everything had happened so quickly on the day the kitchen caught on fire. She'd been shocked. She hadn't stopped to see his side, and then everything started changing, and there was no going back.

Would I ever want to go back? She was asking herself that question as she opened Plant Parenthood's door and Earnest bounded over to greet her. After she told him about Peggy's order, Anna remembered that Jeff had tried to take him away from her. Just as she'd not considered his side about his project, he'd never considered *her* side about Earnest or the house. If she hadn't hired Mad Dog Horowitz, Jeff could have stopped here one day and taken Earnest, and she might never have seen him again.

No. Anna would not worry about Jeff. As far as the planning commission was concerned, he could take care of himself. He'd said that very thing about her when he'd walked off and left her at Disappointment Park. He hadn't cared about her. So why should she care about him? *Better to think about rose colors.*

CHAPTER 40

In March, Gamble Island seemed to waken from a long deep sleep. Fruit trees bloomed their heads off, and daffodils, planted years ago by a Johnny Appleseed of bulbs, winked yellow along the country roads. Spring was in the air, a new start, fresh and clean. The days grew longer. The gray skies seemed to get tired of irritating everyone and often gave way to blue.

Usually, Jeff liked this time of year. He took Earnest for forest romps and set him free to chase raccoons' scents and hunt blackberry bushes for future picking. But this year was different. Though Jeff continued the adventures, he was chronically distracted, waiting, waiting, waiting for Grabowski's decision. The movie of Jeff's life dragged in slow motion.

Still, every day he went to work and put on an act that all was well and "worry" did not belong in his vocabulary. But he *was* worried, and the longer he waited for news, the harder it became to fight paranoia. Grabowski might have agreed with the planning commission and perhaps was letting Jeff's file languish on his desk to torture him. At night Jeff stewed over that possibility and counted grievances like sheep. One, Grabowski's mental cruelty. Two, Grabowski's sadism. Three, Grabowski's arrogance, based on nothing. Four . . .

At work Jeff checked his mail dozens of times each day. He

joked, only to himself, that he was wearing a path in the carpet from his office to the mailroom. He snatched every white business envelope from his box and devoured the return address. But always the envelope was a false alarm. That was why on March 17, St. Patrick's Day, Jeff could scarcely believe his eyes when he found a letter from the Department of Planning, City Hall, Gamble Island, Washington.

In his hands, the letter felt heavy with importance, denser than iridium. However, Jeff did not rip into the envelope in the mailroom. Whatever news Grabowski was about to lay on him Jeff wanted to receive alone. He walked back to his office, closed the door.

He'd also needed privacy in his high-school senior year when an envelope had arrived from the University of Washington. Without opening the flap, he could tell that it contained a paltry single page. If he'd been accepted, he believed, the envelope would have bulged with brochures about dorms and registration—or with confetti, which had spilled into the lap of a friend when she'd opened an acceptance letter. Jeff's envelope looked anorexic. His dreams seemed to shrivel in his hands.

Jeff took the letter to his room, stared at the sealed flap, and prepared himself for the rejection that the admission officer might be doling out: *We've had many fine applicants like yourself, and it's been difficult selecting the next class—and, sorry, pal, you won't be in it.* Finally, in a formal and civilized fashion, Jeff sliced the envelope with the letter opener his uncle had given him for Christmas, and shook open the page. He read. His clouds of worry parted, and light shone down on him. The university had accepted him—and changed his life.

Just as the letter now in Jeff's hands would change his life no matter what Grabowski had decided. Jeff had spent huge professional capital on this project, and his reputation at the firm was riding on seeing it through. It was the largest job he'd ever taken on and headed up alone. If Grabowski turned it down, cleaning up the wreckage of defeat would take months. Jeff would draw a Monopoly Chance card: "Do not collect the raise you had your heart set on. Give up thoughts of passing go."

But then, if Grabowski approved Jeff's proposal . . .

At his desk, he studied the envelope on which his future depended—his salary, his status at the firm, and his professional reputation. Jeff was desperate to open the letter, but, if he were honest, he was also scared.

Hardly breathing, he worked his index finger between the envelope's body and its flap. He pulled out the letter, a single page, like the University of Washington's, and quickly skimmed the words. When he finished, he set his glasses on his desk and pressed his fingertips on his eyelids with relief. The sadistic bastard had not been quite so sadistic after all. Cedar Place would be built. With luck, Jeff's design might win an award from Seattle's chapter of the American Institute of Architects, as Brian Cooper hoped.

Jeff might have whooped and run to tell his colleagues the good news, but he only stared at the letter. In the past, he'd have taken off the rest of the day and hurried to tell Anna. Now he couldn't, not just because she would wither at the sight of him, but also because his victory meant her defeat. She would be devastated, and for that he was truly sorry. In a finger snap, Grabowski's letter had dissolved his anger at her.

Maybe he could call her and try to mend their frayed connection. Somehow he could find a way to make peace. He could sit her down and explain how much he'd wanted the project to mean to her, how hard he'd worked for a win-win conclusion. If only Anna had listened to reason, everything would have been different.

"Mrs. Blackmore, I have good news. We got the permits." Jeff gripped the phone.

Only she could growl with glee. "We beat those people! I thought I'd have to pay lawyers hundreds of thousands to fight them. I'd never have given up."

"You don't have to fight anymore. It's over. We can move forward." Jeff heard a yoga video playing in the background.

"What's the next step?" she asked.

"I pick up the permits and talk with the planners. Then we tear down the house."

"Fantastic!" Mrs. Blackmore sounded breathless, as if her feet were dangling over her head in yoga's scorpion position. "How soon can we start?"

Jeff thought for a second. "I'd say in about three weeks if your contractor can line up his demolition team that soon."

"I'll light a fire under him. Can we pick an exact day to begin?"

Jeff flipped through his calendar. "Three weeks is April seventh. How does that sound?"

"Excellent. We've waited long enough."

"What about your tenants?" Jeff asked.

"Don't worry about them. I'll send them an eviction letter tomorrow. I'll tell them to move out by the seventh or we'll knock down the house around them." Mrs. Blackmore's laugh rang with the resonance of tin.

Her laugh was another sheep of grievance Jeff could count at night. One, Mrs. Blackmore's cackle. Two, Grabowski's sadistic *har-har-har*. Three, Anna's disappointment. Four, Jeff's inability to protect her from it.

CHAPTER 41

Everywhere Anna looked was a reminder of what she was about to lose. Grammy's beautiful house. The flower beds, whose weeds, to her, had been a personal offense. Anna's former vegetable garden, where Grammy had taught her to sow seeds, fertilize, and mulch. In two weeks, to Anna's crushing disappointment, a bulldozer would scrape the entire property to the bone. Eventually, her childhood vegetable garden would be paved over for Jeff's parking lot.

Every time Anna thought about Mrs. Scroogemore's eviction letter and the planners' decision to demolish Grammy's house, she felt like they'd ripped out her heart and flung it into the bulldozer's path as well. In the last week, as she'd packed vases, ribbons, and wraps, she'd fought back tears, and grief had harried her. She was David with no slingshot to fight Goliath. She could never stop the giants who held the power: Mrs. Scroogemore, the planners, Jeff. There was nothing to do but try to accept the unfairness and move on, as devastating as that would be. With pain, Anna told herself, *I give up.*

If she couldn't save the house, however, she intended at least to save some of Grammy's plants. Anna wanted cuttings of her roses, rhodies, and camellias, and she needed to dig up dahlias, peonies, and asters that had descended from Grammy's. Even if Mrs. Scroogemore had Anna arrested for stealing plants, she would keep potting them and lining them up in her condo's backyard till she found them a permanent home.

As Earnest gnawed his ball and watched over her in his sphinx position, Anna poured soil from a bag into one of the plastic pots she'd salvaged from Gamble Nursery. She snipped a six-inch stem off the gnarled New Dawn rose bush, cut off the stem's bottom leaves, and pushed it into the soil. After firming it with her fingertips, she watered the cutting and fit a Mason jar over it. "Grow into a big bush, you lovely rose," she encouraged. "I'd like to save your mother bush, but it would take two men to dig her up."

The New Dawn rose was a special, old-fashioned climber that Anna and Grammy had ordered from a catalog and planted as a scrawny stem one chilly afternoon. The rose grew to a giant, which, if not pruned back each year, would have overgrown its trellis and covered a whole side of the house. The flowers were white with hints of pink, and in the summer, bees and butter-flies swarmed around them as if they'd been personally summoned.

Once Grammy had found a chrysalis attached to the trellis's slat, and she dropped the hard brown case onto Anna's palm. Grammy told her that in spring, when the weather warmed, a butterfly would emerge, a magical surprise. "You can look at this now and think there's nothing going on inside. But just wait! A creature is growing into what she's meant to be. When she's ready, she'll fight her way out. She'll meet her destiny."

"Does she have to fight very hard?" Anna asked.

"Pretty hard. If she doesn't, she won't be strong enough to survive. She'll die."

"That's not fair."

"Tell that to a chicken or a sparrow. Birds have to peck their way out of their shell," Grammy said. "We all have our shells and cocoons of adversity to struggle against. They make us strong. Fighting is a fact of life."

Anna brought the chrysalis to her bedroom and placed it on the windowsill. All winter she checked to see if the butterfly had presented herself, and, finally, one spring day Anna came home from school, and there she was, a tiger swallowtail, sitting on the curtain rod, airing her yellow-and-black-striped wings. She seemed to know how gorgeous she was. She was poised on the rod as if she were announcing her presence to the world.

Below in pieces on the windowsill was her chrysalis and former home. No longer of use, it was a discarded sign of her battle waged and won. Yet no one would have looked at her and thought she'd faced hardship and fought like a tiger for the strength to live on earth. When Anna opened the window, the butterfly flapped her delicate wings, and with grace, she swooped across the lawn.

Now buoyed by the memory, Anna cut another stem from the New Dawn rose and snipped off the leaves for a second future bush—and a thought came to her on wings as silent as the butterfly's had been. Maybe Anna's own fight wasn't over. Maybe she, Lauren, and Joy had too easily accepted defeat. Maybe they could still do more to save the house. Those "maybes" stayed in Anna's mind as she filled another pot with soil and planted the stem. *Fighting is a fact of life.*

Earnest, apparently tired of being a sphinx, rose on his paws, and with a resounding *ptooey,* spit out his ball at Anna's feet. He loved the ball so much that she and Jeff often passed it back and forth when they traded him for visits. Earnest had worn down its once-bright orange fuzz to slimy gray felt, which stayed vile no matter how much Anna scrubbed it.

Earnest fixed her with desperate eyes that begged, *Exercise is crucial for my body. If you don't throw my ball again, I will grow feeble and arthritic. I could be irreparably damaged. Really. Forever.*

With iron determination, Earnest's longing eyes bent Anna to his will. She put down her scissors and threw the ball across the yard. He ran after it and picked it up in his mouth, then pranced back to her and plopped it at her feet. *Kerplunk.*

His gaze urged, *Oh, please. I'm a retriever. You must help me be true to my nature. Fetching is my job.*

Anna threw again. As the ball flew across the grass, she thought, *He never gives up.*

And then she thought, *Neither should I.* She needed to fight her way out of her own chrysalis of hurt and betrayal. She needed to keep trying to save Grammy's house. If she didn't, she'd be sorry. And, worse, she'd always wonder what might have been.

CHAPTER 42

———⊗———

Gamble's mayor, Alexander Maksimov, looked as old and frag-
ile as his Polar fleece jacket, which he must have worn every
day since fleece had been invented in 1979. The sleeves were
pilling, and the collar had shredded around the seams. Someone who was either blind or lacking half his fingers had sewn
patches on the elbows.

Anna glanced at the Seattle Seahawks lined up in his poster.
She cleared her throat. She explained that the city planners had
granted Mrs. Blackmore's permits, and bulldozers would arrive
on April 7 to demolish the house. "We need to stop her. It's a
historic Gamble landmark. Losing it would be a travesty. Can
you help?"

Mayor Maksimov rubbed an arthritic finger over his chin.
Whoever had sewn on his patches must also have shaved him,
because the stubble on one side of his jaw was longer than on
the other. "I can't personally do anything, Anna. I try to stay
out of skirmishes, even though I'd like to get into them sometimes. And I definitely try not to cross the Planning Department."

"What about the city council? Could they help?"

"I can only think of a single time that the council stepped
in to alter a planner's verdict. In the end it didn't work."

"Can't somebody do *something?*"

Mayor Maksimov rested his hands on his swivel chair's arms. His gaze went to a red Ford passing by the window. "I suppose the council could vote to appeal Naomi Blackmore's demolition permit to our hearing examiner. I could put it on the agenda for our next meeting."

"Oh, please, would you?" Anna leaned forward on the edge of her seat.

"Yes, but I can't guarantee the outcome. A vote like that could be complicated when the town's already stirred up about the project."

"At least the house might have a chance."

"Not necessarily." Mayor Maksimov wagged his finger at no one in particular. "If the council does vote to appeal, the examiner could rule in favor of Naomi. Then your only recourse would be to go to court."

"We couldn't afford the legal fees." Mad Dog Horowitz had taught Anna more about them than she wanted to know. "When's the next meeting?"

"Next Thursday, the twenty-seventh."

"If the council votes yes, we'd have time to stop the demolition while the examiner decides," Anna said, excitement stirring inside her.

"That's true, but don't get your hopes up. The Planning Department rules the roost in this town."

Not exactly encouraging news. But not enough to stop the fight.

Anna had only a week before the meeting to organize supporters.

Now that the days were longer, it was light after six o'clock. Rain was pouring onto Anna's beach-ball-striped umbrella and splashing on her yellow galoshes. Though she was bundled up in an Irish wool sweater and yellow slicker, she was shivering. Earnest seemed not to mind the damp and cold. He pressed against her legs and watched people pass by on the sidewalk outside Thrifty Market.

On Anna's clipboard was a petition urging the city council to appeal Mrs. Blackmore's demolition permit. So far Anna had gotten over three hundred signatures, a major accomplishment considering the short few days she'd had to canvass the town. But her success had taken a toll. She'd caught a cold, and at the end of each day she dragged home and went to bed. Still, determination and the pressure of time's passing drove her forward.

All weekend Anna, Lauren, and Joy had called friends to corral them to the city council meeting on Thursday, three days away. The plan was to gather a crowd in Thrifty's parking lot and march in a show of force to city hall. The house's supporters could speak to the council, just as they had to the planning commission. But then, Cedar Place's supporters could also speak. The house had become a lightning rod for opposing groups. The most anyone could hope for was that the crowd would be polite.

Anna and Lauren had also made posters announcing the meeting, and pinned them to community bulletin boards outside Thrifty Market, Sweet Time Bakery, the ferry building, police station, and post office. Joy had put on her lowest-cut sweater, and, like her heroine Penelope, she'd loosened her hair so it fell, free and sexy, to her shoulders. Then she'd paid a call on the *Gamble Crier*'s single, thirty-something male editor. She'd placed her elbows on his desk, leaned forward, and let him feast his eyes as she begged him to write another editorial on the house. The heat of her persuasion melted his resistance. His support would appear in the *Crier* tomorrow.

"Sir, may I talk with you a minute?" Anna asked another thirty-something male. Dressed in a power suit, wing-tip shoes, and a navy overcoat, he was likely returning from work in Seattle.

"Only a minute. I'm in a rush," he said.

"I'll hurry." Anna smiled. "I'm wondering if you'd sign this petition." She held out her clipboard.

He waved it away, unwilling to take time to read. "What's it for?"

"We're asking the city council to appeal a permit that the Planning Department granted."

"What permit?"

"To demolish the old Victorian house on Rainier. Maybe you've heard about it."

"I certainly have." He looked down at Anna as if playing tiddlywinks might be a better use of her time. "I'm a friend of Naomi Blackmore. Does she know about your petition?"

Gulp. "I don't know." Anna reached down for the consoling top of Earnest's head.

"Surely you *do* know she won't be happy about it," he said.

"I expect so."

"Are you one of those women who opposed her building? She's told me about you. You've been a real pain."

Anna mustered her grit. She would not back down. "We're trying to save the house. It's important."

"Give it up. If Naomi has to, she'll fight all the way to the Supreme Court."

Before Anna could reply, the man walked away, trailing the smell of an acidic aftershave.

Phooey on you. "Thanks for your time, sir."

Grammy had said that fighting was a fact of life.

CHAPTER 43

Jeff walked off the ferry a satisfied man. It was a pleasant evening, and at work he'd had a productive conference with Mrs. Blackmore's contractor, who'd start Cedar Place in less than two weeks. The permit process was behind Jeff, and the project was moving forward at last. He'd run the gantlet, and now Cedar Place shimmered in his future. He'd prevailed!

Jeff joined the other commuters on the long ramp to the terminal. All the feet on the worn green carpet made muffled thunder, which faded at the exit as Jeff stepped outside to fresh, clean air. The sky was clear. At Thrifty Market he'd pick up a steak to celebrate Cedar Place's imminent groundbreaking. All was right with the world.

Across the street, Joy and five women whom Jeff did not know were shouting at the passengers and waving homemade signs. For a second, he wondered if he'd missed mention in the *Crier* of an upcoming election for the city council or school board. Local politics always brought out citizens and heated up the town.

But then he read Joy's sign, and his heart keeled over, paralyzed. He couldn't believe his eyes. Written in brash red letters was: SAVE GAMBLE'S MOST IMPORTANT HISTORIC HOUSE!

The other women's signs also thumbed their noses at him: "ONCE HISTORY IS DESTROYED, IT'S GONE FOREVER!" "SAY NO TO CEDAR PLACE!" "SAVE OUR PAST!" "COME TO THE CITY COUNCIL MEETING THURSDAY NIGHT @ SEVEN."

Jeff stopped and stared as commuters flowed around him to the street. *What the hell?* He'd bet a year's paychecks that Anna was behind every word in those signs and she'd wrangled the city council into hearing more pleas about Mrs. Blackmore's house. Jeff's deal was done, and he had the permits to prove it. Why couldn't Anna just accept it and give up? Did she have to keep stirring her damned pot of opposition? He'd been a fool to feel sorry for her or to think that at last they might make peace.

Jeff turned and hurried, disgusted, through the parking lot to avoid Joy and her friends. Eager to get home, make a few calls, and find out what was going on, he sprinted up the hill, turned onto Rainier, and headed to his apartment. As his annoyance propelled him down the street, in the distance he saw bright lights and a crowd in front of Mrs. Blackmore's house. He got closer. TV cameras were aimed at the porch, and the lights were shining on Anna.

She was standing with Earnest behind a small grove of microphones, which let Jeff know she'd contacted media not just on the island, but also in Seattle. She held a sign that urged, "HISTORY TRUMPS GREED!" Under the lights' glare, her eyes seemed flinty, and Earnest's fur looked bleached. Her hair's tufts spiked like barracuda teeth.

"I'm trying to save my grandmother's historic house and her hundred-year-old madrona tree," Anna told the reporters. "We can't let developers destroy our island's heritage. History can't be replaced. Thursday night is our last chance to speak our minds and save a Gamble landmark."

How absurd. A decrepit house is not *a landmark.*

Anna pointed to the madrona. A woman in a dark green running suit was lounging on a wooden platform high up in the branches, from which hung yellow balloons and a banner: "SAVE THIS TREE!" She waved at the crowd as if she were wearing a tiara and throwing doubloons from a dragon float in the Mardi Gras parade. Her confident smile rankled Jeff as much as Anna had.

"That's Madeline," Anna said. "She's going to sit up there till the city council votes to appeal this house's demolition permit to Gamble's Hearing Examiner. And she'll stay till he cancels it and rescues this house once and for all. Madeline's committed. We've got volunteers to watch after her for as long as it takes."

Someone shouted, "You go, girl! You rock!" Then people chanted, "Save the house! Save the tree! Save the house! Save the tree!"

As Jeff pushed his way out of the crowd, the chant changed to "No mini mall! No mini mall!"

How ridiculous! It's not *a mini mall. It's a small commercial building.*

By the time Jeff got to Thrifty Market's newspaper stand, he was breathless. He couldn't put distance quickly enough between him and Anna's circus. He fished two quarters from his pocket, slipped them into the slot of the *Crier*'s collection box, and pulled up the window for a copy. By the light coming through Thrifty's plate-glass window, he opened the paper and flipped through the pages to an op-ed headline: "City Council to Vote on Appealing Controversial Permit."

The editorial began, "When a town loses its history, it loses its soul. . . ."

Jeff blanched. Once again he knew where that biased jerk of an editor stood. *Surely I haven't come this far only to be blocked another time.* But Anna and the editor might drum up enough ill will to make that happen. They could get hundreds of people to a meeting that could ruin Jeff's career.

He shouldn't have counted his chickens and let down his guard. He should have remembered Yogi Berra: "It ain't over till it's over." *Damn Anna. Damn the editor. Damn Madeline, the tree hugger. Damn those women and their signs at the ferry dock. Damn the TV crews. Damn the house.*

CHAPTER 44

Despite the rain, more than a hundred of the house's supporters gathered in Thrifty Market's parking lot. Bumping umbrellas, they greeted each other in jeans, rain hats, and hoodies. Under Thrifty's green-and-white-striped awning, April Pringle and Lloyd McGregor, minus his bagpipes, talked and waved their hands. As excitement rippled through the crowd, someone shouted, "Save the tree! Save the house!"

If only, Anna thought.

The city council's vote tonight might as well be the peak of a crescendo in Beethoven's "Battle Symphony," which old Mr. Webster played too loudly on his ancient stereo. Months of worry and effort had built to this moment, and every day of those months was etched in the tension on Anna's face. All afternoon while Joy had made last-minute calls to round up allies, Anna and Earnest had handed out flyers about the meeting, and Lauren had painted signs for the crowd to carry down the block to city hall.

"It's now or never." Joy stamped her feet in the chill. "We should get going in about twenty minutes."

"I have six flyers left. Anybody need one?" Anna asked.

"Put them on windshields. Lots to choose from." Lauren

swept her hand through the air to indicate the parking lot. "There's still time to get people to join us."

Anna glanced around at cars to target. "Look who's here." She pointed two rows down to Jeff's blue Honda.

"Slap one of those babies on him. Stick it to him," Joy said. "Leave it facedown so he can't miss it when he climbs behind the steering wheel."

"That would be mean," Lauren pointed out.

"He's earned mean," Joy said.

"It would be throwing gasoline on fire," Lauren warned.

"Whose side are you on?" As Joy pushed damp hair back from her face, her dark roots showed.

Anna hesitated. "Jeff doesn't need a reminder about the meeting."

"Your flyer wouldn't *remind* him. It'd notify him that enemies are waiting for him at city hall," Joy said.

Anna shook her head with indecision. "I don't know . . ."

"Do it! Go get him! Or I will." Joy waved her fist.

If Jeff hadn't been Gamble's Benedict Arnold, we wouldn't be here in the first place, Anna thought. "I guess you're right."

While Joy and Lauren handed out signs, Anna and Earnest walked to Jeff's car. Earnest seemed to sense that something disagreeable was about to happen because he pressed back his ears and let her know, *I prefer harmony and peace.*

Normally, Anna would have agreed with him, but not after a day of strong tea, adrenaline, and gearing up to plead for the house. She lifted Jeff's windshield wiper and set the flyer facedown on the glass. Just as she was replacing the wiper, footsteps approached from behind—and Earnest whined and tugged his leash.

Anna didn't have to look to know that Jeff had caught her in an underhanded act. But it was hardly criminal; she felt justified, and she refused to slink away, embarrassed. She turned around as Earnest threw himself at Jeff. *You're here! You're here!* said each fervent tail swish.

"Hey, Earnest." Careful not to drop his grocery bag, Jeff stooped down and greeted him.

Then looking solemn, he straightened up and stared at Anna intently enough to singe her skin. "May I ask what you're doing?"

"Um . . . Well, I was . . ."

Across the parking lot, the crowd began to wave signs and chant, *Save the tree! Save the house!* Joy yelled, "Yahoo!"

"You were . . . what?" Jeff asked, not giving Anna an inch of slack.

"You don't have to treat me like I'm three." Anna slipped on self-righteousness like a porcupine pelt. "I was leaving you a flyer about tonight's meeting."

"Obviously I know about it. I don't need your flyer," Jeff said. "You were being sneaky and passive aggressive."

No one had ever accused her of that! Anna bristled her quills. "And *you* are being insensitive. You can't expect me to sit around and watch you destroy Grammy's house. No way will I not try to stop you."

"No way will I not do the job I was hired for. I do have a job, if you remember. I work," Jeff said.

"You don't have to be sarcastic." Anna folded her arms across her chest. "And just for the record, I could never forget that you work." She said "work" as if skunks were spraying from the letters. "Your work ruined everything."

"*Wait* a minute . . ." Jeff narrowed his eyes.

"*You* wait," Anna interrupted, fueled by the evening's tension. It felt good to speak her mind. "You knew how much I cared about Grammy's house, but you arranged to tear it down without a thought of me. Cedar Place was more important to you than I was. You wanted everyone to admire you. You thought you'd prove you weren't like your father, but you won't prove a thing except that you think only about yourself."

Jeff looked like his lungs were collapsing and there was no more oxygen left in the parking lot for him to breathe. Lines that Anna had never seen before appeared around his squint, which seemed to be about both self-protection and disapproval of her. Rain spattered his glasses.

"You're the one thinking about *yourself*," he snapped. "You think a house can make up for your parents' abandoning you, and it'll keep you tied to your grandmother's love. But it won't. The past is gone, and a house isn't going to bring it back. You threw us away for *that*."

Earnest's grief-stricken eyes went back and forth between the two people he loved most. He couldn't help but pick up their anger. He whimpered, *Stop! Stop!*

"Look what you've done to him." Jeff's words seemed bitten off rebar. "You've upset him. Hell, you've upset his whole life. Because of you, he lost his family."

"Because of *me?!* What about because of you? You're in total denial."

"And you're blind and stubborn," Jeff shot back. "Have you ever considered for a single second that Mrs. Blackmore wanted to build a big-box chain store? I persuaded her to go for a building that would fit in downtown, and I designed special spaces for you and Joy and Lauren's shops. You wouldn't listen to what I was trying to do. All you cared about was chasing the past, but life goes on."

Anna stepped back, withered by Jeff's anger. She needed space.

"Your grandmother's dead," he continued. "You can't get her back, but you could have had me, and I loved you. Brian Cooper promised me a raise for Cedar Place. I wanted it so we could get married. What a joke."

Wails came from deep inside Earnest. *Stop fighting! Oh, please, stop. I can't bear it.*

Jeff squatted down and cradled Earnest's head against his chest. He smoothed back Earnest's ears and kissed his forehead. "I'm sorry, Buddy. I really am. I promise you'll never have to hear those words again."

The crowd chanted, *Save the tree! Save the house!*

Anna wanted to say that the last thing she ever meant to do was upset Earnest, but she was too shocked to speak. Regret seemed to swallow her in one large gulp—regret about her beloved dog and maybe about other things as well—she'd have to sort them out when she could think straight.

From across the lot, Joy shouted, "Come on, Anna. We're about to leave."

With effort, Anna stuffed all her feelings back inside.

Jeff kissed Earnest again. "Take care of yourself, Buddy. I'll pick you up tomorrow and make this up to you. I'll buy you some cheese. We'll go for a hike."

Without a word to Anna, Jeff stood up, yanked the flyer off his windshield, and wadded it into a sodden ball. He tossed it in with his groceries, set the bag in his backseat, and locked the car. As Jeff turned around and stormed toward city hall, Earnest yanked his leash and tried to follow.

Anna pulled him back. "Come on, Sweetheart. We have to go." She led him toward the crowd.

Clearly torn, Earnest looked at her, then at Jeff's retreating back, like he was trying to decide which of his people needed him more. His eyes darkened with confusion. Anyone could tell that his loyalties were split, and he was unsure what to do—and the uncertainty caused him visible pain. He slumped as if he were an electric dog and someone had unplugged him from his socket. His ears and tail drooped.

Earnest's paws followed Anna, but his eyes followed Jeff to the sidewalk as he started across Rainier. Earnest was so focused on Jeff that he hardly seemed to notice all the noisy people. When Anna bent down to pick up the sign that Joy had left for her, she accidentally loosened her grip on Earnest's leash. For the first time ever, he jerked it out of her hand and ran.

"Wait, Earnest!! Wait!" She tore after him.

Save the tree! Save the house!

Anna chased Earnest to the curb as his leash dragged behind him.

"Earnest, come back here!"

On countless occasions, Earnest, the world's most responsible dog, had felt his duty was to keep Anna safe, and he had pulled her back from jaywalking. He'd always looked both ways before crossing a street. But now he was so intent on reaching Jeff that he did not consider his own well-being. Without looking, he dashed into Rainier as Jeff stepped up on the opposite curb.

Time seemed to pass in slow motion. There were a million points when the action could have stopped and Earnest could have paused or turned around. He could have slowed his charge to Jeff by only a second, and it might have made all the difference.

But he kept running. Anna saw his paws skim over the asphalt. With every step, his ID tag clinked against his collar's buckle, and his ears flopped against his head. Their tinge of biscuit beige outlined the triangle shape. The rain had dampened the fur on Earnest's back so it was darker than usual, more honey than wheat.

As Earnest reached the center of Rainier, Anna heard a screech of brakes and a hideous thump. She screamed and ran to him. Jeff turned around and ran to him too. In the glare of a pickup's headlights, Earnest was lying on the asphalt in a pool of blood.

CHAPTER 45

————— ⤫ —————

Jeff scooped Earnest off the asphalt and carried him, bleeding, to the car. He set him on the backseat as Anna slid over next to him from the other side. When Jeff climbed into the driver's seat, each of Earnest's whimpers shaved a strip off Jeff's heart. He had to get help before it was too late.

When he pulled out of Thrifty's parking lot, he glanced in the rearview mirror. Tears were streaming down Anna's face. As she tried to comfort Earnest, Jeff heard him lick her hands to try to comfort *her.* How could he be concerned for Anna when *he* was obviously hurt? He must have felt the same concern for Jeff when he'd run into the street.

Jeff blinked back his own tears at Earnest's selflessness. Jeff could hardly keep driving. He clutched the steering wheel till his knuckles turned white. *Just get to the clinic,* he told himself. *If you break down, you can't do Earnest any good.*

Everything in Dr. Nilsen's waiting room seemed unsettled. Huddling at the bottom of the aquarium, the clownfish looked sullen and barely fanned their fins. The kissing gouramis weren't puckering up, and the angelfish looked like they were tired of trying to live up to their name. The scraggly plant at the receptionist's counter was wilting. Her silent phone seemed to brood about not being asked to ring after closing time.

Sitting next to Anna on a Naugahyde sofa, Jeff jiggled his foot, thrummed his fingers on his knee, and stared into space. The drive here had flattened him emotionally, but he'd expected to feel better once he got Earnest into Dr. Nilsen's capable hands. *Wrong.* Now Jeff was more shattered than in the car. He felt like he was lost on Uranus, and his rocket back to Earth had broken down.

He now saw in blazing Technicolor the toll on Earnest of his and Anna's fight, and he felt chastened to the core. If Earnest did not survive, Jeff would never, in ten lifetimes, shake his guilt for distressing him so much that he'd tried to cross the street to comfort Jeff tonight. He could be reincarnated in ten different countries in the next three hundred years, and in each new body, he would feel horrible remorse if he came upon a dog. His remorse would be unshakable, eternal. He could not escape it. Ever.

Anna looked like she felt the same. As she sniffled and swiped her cheeks with a crumpled tissue from the bottom of her purse, Jeff bet she'd give anything to relive the last hour so Earnest would not have gotten hurt and they wouldn't have to be here. Sharing the regret should have brought them closer together, but they stared into space, in their own worlds, as if he spoke Chinese and she spoke Romanian—and if they tried to talk, they wouldn't understand each other.

What would Jeff say anyway when piggybacked onto his remorse was horror at Earnest's injuries and fear that he might die. His blood was smeared all over Jeff's sports coat, pants, shirt, and hands. He might as well have just laid down a scalpel in an operating theater.

So far he hadn't gone to the restroom and cleaned himself up because Dr. Nilsen might come out to let them know Earnest's prognosis—and Jeff would be gone. He also felt a superstitious

nagging that washing off Earnest's blood would be like washing *him* down the drain. Sticky hands were far easier to live
with than that disquieting image.

Please, please don't die, Buddy.

"Want a cup of Dr. Nilsen's coffee?" Jeff asked Anna.

"No, but thanks for asking," she said.

"Mind if I get one?"

"You don't have to ask *me*."

"I'm worried about crossing the room and leaving you
here. You don't look so good."

"Yes . . . well . . ." Anna contorted her fingers into an anatom-
ically challenging position. Weeping had smeared her mascara.
Her face was puffy, but the rest of her seemed to have withered
and shrunk. Her hair stuck out in tufts, which suggested that a
tornado may have sucked her into its vortex and spit her out
on a freeway in rush-hour traffic.

"I'll be okay if you cross the room. Go get your coffee," she
said.

"You're sure you don't want any?"

"All I want is for Earnest to be okay."

"Me too."

"I know." Tears trailed down Anna's cheeks again.

We're falling all over each other, trying to get along, Jeff thought
as he stretched out his legs, crossed his ankles, and sipped his
coffee. Earnest's injuries had shown Jeff—and surely her, too—
that their grievances against each other meant nothing compared to their love for him. Earnest mattered most. They'd do
anything for him. Like they also used to feel they'd do for each
other.

Jeff would take a while to sift through Anna's accusations
tonight. For now, he was willing to admit she was right about
one thing: Proving that he was not irresponsible like his father

partly fed Jeff's drive for success. But he would never agree that his job had been more important to him than Anna had been, or that he'd thought only of himself when he'd taken on Cedar Place. He'd hoped for it to help, not hinder her. His intentions had been honorable.

On the other hand, he'd admit that not telling her about the project from the start had been a mistake. And he should have better understood the importance of Mrs. Blackmore's house to Anna. Any little kid whose parents had abandoned her to pursue their ambitions would have latched on extra hard to a caring grandmother—and to the house they shared. And when the little kid grew up, she was bound to be touchy about the ambition of someone she loved—especially if it made her feel abandoned again, a hurt repeated.

Jeff couldn't blame Anna for her feelings. He blamed himself for not being more sensitive to them. He was very, very sorry. About Anna, Earnest, everything. The whole damned mess.

Jeff wrapped his arms around himself to hold in his regret. *Anna is right. When it comes to importance, love ranks right up there with water and air.* Jeff would quit his job and beg on the streets if only Earnest would be okay—and if only they could all go back to the peaceful life they'd had.

Dr. Nilsen had stayed after hours to take care of Earnest. The long day showed in his shoulders' slump and the sag around his eyes. Lacking his usual energy, he plodded into the reception room. He pulled an empty chair from the row along the wall and sat facing Jeff and Anna. He said, "I know you're upset. But don't worry. Earnest's going to be all right."

Jeff's eyes met Anna's. Their collective relief seemed to fill the room and press against the walls. He let out a slow no-longer-tortured breath and said, "That's fantastic news."

"He's stable. We've cleaned him up and given him pain meds." Dr. Nilsen leaned forward and rested his wrists on his knees. "So here's the plan. . . . Tonight I want to x-ray Earnest's chest to see if he's got extra air in his lungs. That'll tell us if the car ruptured his diaphragm. The car also skidded him on the pavement so he's got road rash and some bad lacerations. I'll have to stitch up one on his thigh right away."

Dr. Nilsen paused and looked at Anna. "Are you all right?"

Jeff turned to her. Her face was as white as drafting paper.

"Don't faint on me. I can only take care of one patient at a time," Dr. Nilsen said.

"Do you want some water?" Jeff asked her.

"I'm just wobbly. It's hard to hear about stitches in Earnest. I'd rather they were in me," Anna said.

To shore her up, Jeff took her hand. It was cold and stiff, but it was the most familiar hand in the world to him besides his own. She did not pull away or seem to mind Earnest's blood on Jeff's skin. Something between him and Anna seemed to shift. Months of wasted anger piled up at their feet like discarded calendar pages.

"Do you mind hearing about a broken leg, Anna?" Dr. Nilsen asked.

She shook her head.

"I'm pretty sure Earnest's left femur is fractured. I have to x-ray it too. Our surgeon will be here tomorrow morning, and he can put in a metal plate."

"Will Earnest have a cast?" Jeff asked.

"No, but maybe bandages, depending on the surgeon's incision. Earnest will have to be confined for four to six weeks. You'll be able to take him out to do his business a few times a day, but otherwise you'll have to restrict him."

"How?" Anna asked.

"In your kitchen or a crate. The surgeon can talk with you

about all that." Dr. Nilsen cupped his hand around his stethoscope's chestpiece. "So are we all in agreement here? You want me to go ahead?"

"Absolutely," Jeff said at the same time that Anna said, "Of course."

"You two need to go home. Earnest knows you're out here, and he keeps looking for you. He might relax if you were gone," Dr. Nilsen said.

"Can we tell him good-bye?" Anna asked.

"If you only stay a minute."

Dr. Nilsen led them through an exam room to the back of the clinic. When Jeff stepped into the surgery, his pulse seemed to stop, as if his heart had decided it ached too much to pump any more blood. Earnest was lying on Dr. Nilsen's steel table, looking moth-eaten around the edges. His fur was rumpled, and his eyes, exhausted. But he raised his head and tried to get up—in Jeff's opinion, a valiant act. A technician with a gap between her front teeth held Earnest down.

For Earnest's sake, Jeff forced himself to act nonchalant. He coaxed his reluctant lips to smile and pretended that his buddy was fine and Jeff was used to seeing him with cuts and broken bones. But Anna's sharp intake of breath showed that she could not fake aplomb as well as Jeff. He pressed his hand against her back and steered her to the steel table.

Jeff stroked Earnest's ears, then cradled his chin in his hands. "Oh, Buddy. I'm so sorry," he whispered. *Sorry you're hurt. Sorry for the misery we've caused you tonight—and for months.*

"I'm sorry too." Anna leaned down from the table's other side and kissed Earnest on top of his head. Anyone would have thought that her and Jeff's apologies to Earnest were also meant for each other.

"We can't stay, Sweetie. We have to go home so you can rest." Anna's voice wobbled like the rest of her.

"Dr. Nilsen's going to take good care of you," Jeff said. "In the morning the surgeon will fix your leg, and then you can come home. Soon you'll be good as new."

As Anna kissed Earnest again and Jeff leaned over and stroked his muzzle, he rested his head on the table and seemed to relax. Perhaps he sensed that his people were understanding each other again and a match had been struck in their relationship's dark, unhappy room. He thumped his tail on the table, a weak and nearly silent gesture, but it was the best he could manage.

Jeff urged himself, *Hold it together.*

CHAPTER 46

By the time Jeff drove Anna home, it was nearly ten o'clock. As usual on their island at night, they rarely passed another car, and nothing was open but Thrifty Market and Sawyer's. Peace seemed to float like feathers through the air. Marauding raccoons were the closest anybody got to crime. Jeff turned onto the condo's street, a couple of blocks from city hall.

If the city council were still meeting, Anna could get there for the vote. But it was not so important to her as it had been hours before. Though she still wanted to save the house, tonight her worry for Earnest had tempered her zeal. The fight still crouched in her shadows, waiting to spring—but she was not sure she'd welcome it again.

"I wonder if Dr. Nilsen is stitching up Earnest's worst cut," she said.

"He'd get to it right away," Jeff said.

"I hope Earnest's diaphragm isn't ruptured."

"We'll know tomorrow. I imagine they'd repair it at the same time they set his leg."

"It hurts to think about." Anna mentally begged Earnest's pain medication to do its job. "Do you think he'll be all right?"

"Dr. Nilsen said he would."

"I mean in the long run. What if he limps forever?"

"We'll have to wait and see."

Anna didn't want to wait. She wanted Earnest to be chasing gulls on the beach or charging after his stick that very minute. She didn't want months of watching to see if his hobbles turned into normal steps. She rubbed her thumb over stitches in the Honda's upholstery and thought about the stitches that would be in Earnest's leg.

"I keep telling myself that Earnest ran into the street of his own accord," Anna said. "But we were fighting, and he was worried, and he wanted to get to you. I feel like it's our fault he got hurt."

Jeff's exhale sounded weary. He pulled up in front of the condo and turned off the ignition and lights. "Anna, we have plenty to beat ourselves up about. I've been doing it too. But Earnest would be the first to forgive us. You know how he is. He lets things go in two seconds."

"I know." Earnest rid himself of grudges like he shook off water droplets after swims. Anyone could tell that he did not believe in sitting on slights till they hatched into resentments. Anna thought, *Earnest lets things go—like maybe I should too.*

In the few hours since she and Jeff had finally been honest with each other, she'd admitted to herself that she'd judged him too harshly. He'd meant well with Cedar Place. And though she hadn't exactly liked being called "blind" and "stubborn," he might be right about her clinging to the past. She'd have to think about it.

Meanwhile, she was so tired of being mad at Jeff. The anger had dragged them both down too long. Maybe slates never got wiped completely clean, but it was time to shed her bad feelings. The question was: How? As usual when Anna needed guidance, her thoughts went to Grammy, though Jeff might accuse her again of clinging to the past.

Once Anna's third-grade teacher had planned a field trip to the Seattle Zoo. Anna would see elephants and polar bears and a two-headed snake! Tigers would roar, and monkeys would swing from ropes. A Komodo dragon would flick its forked tongue. For weeks Anna talked of little else, and she hardly slept the night before. But the next morning she woke with fever and a sore throat—and blazing disappointment.

Grammy wrapped her up in an afghan of crocheted hearts, and put her, inconsolable, to bed. "When something terrible happens, it's an opportunity. It's your job to turn it into something good," Grammy said.

That afternoon she brought Anna paper, colored pencils, homemade cinnamon rolls, and tea, which Grammy sometimes spiked at night with rum. Together, she and Anna drew red-and-black-striped pterodactyls and green fire-spitting winged serpents. They invented their own mythical creatures—a lion with a crow's beak, an elephant with fins. Anna would never have met these fantastic beings at the zoo, Grammy pointed out. Anna's unfortunate classmates would never know them.

Just as Grammy had turned disappointment into a memorable afternoon, maybe Anna was supposed to transform her anger at Jeff into something good. Maybe that something should be forgiving him.

Anna could never kiss Jeff and make up like people did in movies. Too much water had flowed under their bridge, and nobody knew yet about the house's future. Still, she could follow Earnest's example of letting go of grudges. She could hand back her anger to the god of war and move on.

Anna tugged at her parka's sleeve to have something to do with her hands. "Jeff, I'm tired of fighting."

He turned his silhouette so they were face-to-face. "Me too."

"I'm sorry about all the misunderstanding."

"No need to be sorry. I can see how you felt the way you did," he said.

"I was too quick to judge."

"So was I. I'm sorry too," Jeff said.

His words were balm. "Well, we've got that straight," Anna said.

For the first time in months, Jeff smiled—wholehearted and sincere. Anna smiled back the same.

"We should be there tomorrow when they set Earnest's leg," she said.

"I'll call Dr. Nilsen in the morning and find out what time."

"Maybe we can see him for a minute before they give him anesthetic."

On the quietest of tiptoes, peace returned to Jeff and Anna.

When the phone rang near midnight, Anna's eyes sprang open, though she hadn't been asleep. Her stomach hurtled to the floor. She did not want to answer because Dr. Nilsen's night technician might be calling to say that Earnest had taken a turn for the worse. Or Jeff might already have heard the news and want her to rush to tell Earnest good-bye.

Quivery, Anna rolled on her back and reached for the receiver.

"How's Earnest?" Joy asked.

"Oh, it's you. Thank goodness," Anna said.

"Always nice to be appreciated."

"I was scared you were someone from Dr. Nilsen's clinic."

"I figured Earnest was there." A tenor crooned on Joy's radio.

"Earnest has a broken leg," Anna said.

"That poor boy. Smoke inhalation and now this. He's had a hell of a last few months," Joy said. "News traveled fast tonight. You wouldn't believe how many people asked about him at the meeting."

The meeting. Anna, Joy, and Lauren could have won a victory, or the council could have ended the women's last stand with a tomahawk to their gizzards. Part of Anna wanted to know which, but another part wasn't ready to hear. She dreaded more conflict when her psychological well was dry.

"The meeting went on and on. I just got home a little while ago," Joy said. "You should have seen the fireworks at city hall. Standing room only. Reporters. People stomping around. It was quite a scene."

"I'm sorry I missed it."

"You didn't miss the vote. The council postponed their decision so they could deliberate more in a private session. I don't know when they'll meet, but Mrs. Scroogemore can't tear down the house yet. We've thwarted her at least for a while," Joy said.

"That's good."

"I vote we keep a few things in our shops and hang on till everything's decided. She'd never pay a sheriff to serve us an eviction notice."

"Okay." Anna meant to sound resolute, but her word came out anemic.

Joy paused, as if the anemia were registering on her. "What's the matter?"

"It's been a long night."

"That poor dog," Joy said again. "We can talk tomorrow."

"I'll be late. A surgeon's setting Earnest's leg in the morning." Anna rested the back of her wrist on her forehead.

"Jeff going to be with you?"

"Yes. We're actually getting along."

Joy chuckled. "Wonders never cease."

"I'll tell you about it tomorrow," Anna said.

"Sorry I woke you. Go back to sleep."

Anna didn't sleep. There were too many unknowns—too many feelings to process and things to worry about. Missing the comfort of Earnest's snores and his body pressed against her, she lay there for hours, blinking in the dark.

CHAPTER 47

⸺❧⸺

"I'll pay the bill," Jeff offered.

"I can do it," Anna said.

"No, really. I'll do it." *Here we go again, falling all over our-selves to get along.* Anna had reactivated Jeff's urge to provide. He wasn't sure how that had happened, but he wanted to look after her.

"Why don't we split the bill?" Anna handed her credit card to Dr. Nilsen's Saturday receptionist.

"You're sure you've got enough money?" Jeff asked.

"We agreed to share Earnest's expenses, remember?"

Jeff did not want to remember. He never again wanted to think of the mediation, when Mad Dog Horowitz had infuri-ated him, and he and Anna had agreed to divide the costs of Earnest's care. Fortunately, Jeff's skin no longer prickled with disgust at thoughts about that day. It seemed like long ago. Back when the big bang happened or dinosaurs ruled the earth.

Jeff looped a beach towel around Earnest's middle and shored him up to keep weight off his leg. Anna coaxed him along the gravel path toward Vincent, waiting in the parking lot with plenty of sprawling room for Earnest in the backseat. Ecstatic to be free from the clinic, he hobbled along in his dreaded plastic cone, and he stopped to sniff messages left by Dr. Nilsen's other patients. Some were so interesting that Earnest acted like he wanted to inhale the gravel.

Jeff and Anna carefully hoisted him into Vincent. Though the day was cool, Jeff left the window partly open because Earnest liked to sniff the wind. He liked it to blow back his triangle ears as he half-closed his eyes in ecstasy.

Jeff thought, *We have a lot to make up to him.*

Jeff had never had a problem with the exterior stairs to his apartment. Usually, he bolted up them two at a time. Today, however, he studied them through Earnest's eyes, and scaling them looked more forbidding than clumping across Mount Everest's ice fields with broken crampons and a backpack of bricks.

"This isn't going to work. Even if I hold up Earnest with a beach towel, he could never climb those stairs on a broken leg," Jeff said.

"But it's Saturday. You get Earnest for the weekend," Anna said.

"It's impossible. He has to go out three or four times a day."

"Maybe he should stay in the condo," Anna said. "It'd be easy for us to get him to the backyard."

She said "us." Did she mean she wanted Jeff to care for Earnest *with* her? It sounded like it. And sharing the load would be better than each of them tending Earnest alone.

"Good idea," Jeff said.

From the backseat, Earnest watched them intently. The puzzled ridges in his forehead asked, *What's the deal? What's going on between you* now?

Jeff might have answered, *More than I ever imagined.* He headed toward the condo.

* ★ *

Jeff glanced around the condo. It looked like the home of a disorderly chimp. Plants were lined up on all the windowsills and counters and in the kitchen corners. Cardboard boxes, their contents spilling from the top, were piled on each other and strewn through every room.

These former contents of Plant Parenthood were stark reminders that Anna had begun dismantling her shop and that her grandmother's house was poised for destruction, depending on the city council's vote. But Jeff chose not to mention the mess because he didn't want to ruin his and Anna's détente. She seemed to have made the same decision, because she did not mention the mess, either.

But the house's future was out there, waiting, a shark's fin circling their boat. Also waiting was another blowup between Jeff and Anna. It was just a matter of time.

In the condo's living room, Earnest plopped down on his bed as if he were king of a small nation, such as Liechtenstein, and Anna and Jeff were peons whose sole purpose was to attend to his slightest whim. If he'd had a signet ring, he'd have presented it for kisses. If he'd spoken words, for his dinner he'd have requested vichyssoise, savory Parmesan puffs, pheasant under glass, roasted venison with blushing pears, and people-cracker blackberry crumble.

Earnest did not complain about his confinement. With dignity, he visually surveyed his palace and waited patiently for his pills, disguised in hot dogs or Brie. He graciously accepted cows' hooves. With the finest cooperation, he allowed Anna to work the beach towel under him, and Jeff to carry him to the backyard. Outside, with majesty, he raised his leg.

When evening came, Jeff went to Say Cheese and brought back a pizza, which he and Anna ate at the kitchen table. They laughed—and caved—when Earnest's eyes commanded bites. After dinner, by mutual agreement, Anna got a comforter and pillow, and they made Jeff a bed on the sofa (which he chose not to point out was too short). By mutual agreement, Jeff, because he was stronger, would usher Earnest out alone at night for bathroom breaks. Also by mutual agreement, till Earnest was able to walk without support, Anna would stay with him on weekday mornings, and Jeff on weekday afternoons.

Later, Jeff felt odd sleeping on what used to be his and Anna's sofa in what had once been his and Anna's condo. It was like leaving his house wearing two left shoes. But as he listened to Anna's breathing from the bedroom, he looked out at the silver crescent moon, in the shape of an occupied hammock, and he decided that sleeping here again so close to her and Earnest also felt, well, really good.

In the morning Anna pulled mysterious containers from the refrigerator and shuffled around the kitchen in her fuzzy pink slippers and fleece robe. One by one, she cracked five eggs and dropped them in a glass bowl. She added milk and whisked them around, then poured them into a skillet and snipped in chives from a pot on the deck.

Jeff and Anna used to make their Sunday breakfast together, but now he sat, cross-legged on the floor. His role fell somewhere between a guest and Earnest's personal attendant. "I never had to get up once last night. Earnest didn't stir," Jeff said.

"He's still pretty drugged." Anna sprinkled salt and pepper on the eggs.

"I think he was being considerate. He didn't want to wake us."

"Typical. Doesn't surprise me." Anna put two slices of bread into the toaster and pushed down its lever. "You want jam?"

"Yes, thanks," Jeff said. "You're making the same breakfast we always had on Sunday morning."

"Habit, I guess."

"Do you have eggs and toast on Sundays by yourself?" Jeff asked.

"No. Too much trouble. Oatmeal's usually it."

A small chafing-dish flame warmed Jeff's heart. Because she was making him a special breakfast? Because she'd not carried on their Sunday ritual after he'd gone? Either way, he was glad.

"Here you go." Anna set their breakfast plates on the blue straw placemats that she and Jeff had bought at Hall's Imports.

He got up, pulled out what had been her usual chair, and helped her sit. Then he took what had been his usual place across the table. He pinched off his usual corner of toast and handed it to Earnest, who took it with his usual snap of teeth. *Nothing's changed. Well, nothing and everything.*

"Remember the day we adopted Earnest? How he tried so hard to get us to bring him home?" Jeff asked.

"He was adorable."

"Still is. He picked us out as much as we did him," Jeff said.

"Remember the Fourth of July when we were waiting on the curb for the parade, and he was sleeping behind us in his flasher position?" Anna asked.

"Yes, and people thought he was panhandling and left a dollar on his stomach," Jeff said.

"If he'd been wearing his plastic cone, they'd have felt sorrier for him and given him a five." Anna laughed with Jeff.

An A-plus observer of human emotion, Earnest watched. Far back inside his cone, the corners of his mouth turned up in Labrador retriever mirth.

Jeff scooted back his chair. "I'm going to get more coffee," he said before he remembered that he was in *her* place and the coffee wasn't theirs. "Sorry. May I have another cup?"

"You know where the pot is."

He set his cup on the few inches of counter space not taken up by plants. He poured. "Want some too?"

"Please."

When he leaned down to pick up Anna's cup, he rested his hand on her shoulder.

CHAPTER 48

Anna shook out the blue down comforter, which Jeff had left in a heap on the sofa before rushing to the ferry. His familiar masculine smell lingered in the cotton, along with a whiff of his shaving soap. She hugged the comforter and thought, *Nothing stays the same for five minutes. Life is one never-ending change.*

The most monumental recent one was her change of heart toward Jeff. This morning she'd given back his condo key. She'd never have believed that she'd feel grateful he was staying here, but now she welcomed his presence. Her attitude shift astonished her.

You'd better enjoy it while you can, she thought as she folded the comforter and set it on the sofa again. Soon, one way or another, a decision would be made about the house, and everything would change again. If Jeff didn't get to build Cedar Place, he'd be angry with her. If the house got demolished, she'd be angry with him.

Anna again remembered when she and Grammy had been driving through fog after the Huskies game, and Anna had kept wiping the windshield and craning her neck to see ahead. Grammy had said that the past was gone, and the future hadn't happened yet, so enjoying the present was all there was. But how could Anna enjoy the present with Jeff when a threatening future loomed over them? No matter who won about the house, she and Jeff would be at odds again.

It was easy to predict that their relationship would end with a spear-tipped exclamation point. Anna felt as if she and Jeff were riding through Central Park behind six white horses in Cinderella's glass coach, and up ahead they'd hit a concrete wall. It was hardly a happy-ever-after ending. Yet there was no alternative.

As Anna washed the dishes, she stared out the window at hyacinths and tulips in a bed across the street. Earnest napped in a rectangle of sunlight from the window above the sink. When she ran hot water over Jeff's mug, she kept thinking about time. Her future was a problem, and her present could fall apart at any minute. So what about her past, which Jeff had accused her of clinging to?

He and Grammy had insisted that the past was over, but was that always true? Anna sometimes felt that it was a living thing that clung to *her*. It followed her around, insisted on being her dancing partner, and then stepped on her toes.

Such as all the times she'd remembered finding Grammy dead, and a lightning bolt of panic zigzagged through her in the present the same as it had on that terrible morning. Or all the times when she'd thought of spending holidays at boarding school with whatever teacher was assigned to girls not going home—and she'd felt lonely, as if at that very moment it was Christmas all over again. So how could she say the past was past if it was still a part of her, a ball and chain of memory?

Anna took a clean dishtowel from the drawer and dried her and Jeff's granola bowls. She stooped down for Earnest's dish to wash next. He was snoring softly and impersonating a sack of potatoes, and he seemed happy despite the plastic cone.

As Earnest's chest rose and fell, he also seemed indifferent to his stitches and injured leg. *It is amazing how he rolls with life's punches,* Anna thought. As she watched him sleep, she remembered finding him at Second Chance Shelter. And it suddenly struck her that in one day he'd lost his home and the person he loved most—just as in one morning twenty-five years earlier, Anna had lost her home and Grammy.

Perhaps Earnest had felt as sad and hurt as Anna had, but no one would have guessed that he'd ever been troubled. He'd seemed to accept his fate. From the moment he'd plopped his paw into Jeff's hand at the kennel, as far as Anna could tell, Earnest had never looked back with longing or resentment.

Like all dogs, he lived in the present. What's done is done, he seemed to feel, and he greeted the future with joy. Change, whichever way the wind blew, seemed to pose no problem for him. He embraced it. He trusted. Even when a truck hit him, he moved on.

As Anna bent down and petted his shoulder gently, so as not to disturb him, she thought that she should be more like him. Enjoying the now. Trusting fate. Reconciling with hardship. Not being so stubborn, as Jeff had said.

Maybe Anna's parents had hurt her, but that wasn't all that filled her past. Along the way, she'd gotten plenty of love—from Grammy, teachers, friends, Earnest, and even Jeff for three years—and she could sip from a nearly full glass. And maybe life was not just an endless change, as she had thought, but also a jumble of pluses and minuses. Both the good and the bad had strengthened her, nudged her along her path, and gotten her where she was meant to be. And that place was the here and now. In her kitchen with the best dog on the planet.

Earnest rolled over and bonked his cone on a chair leg. He yawned and resumed his nap. All this time, he'd been setting an example for Anna, but only now did she see it.

Anna spritzed cleanser in the bathroom sink. If the rest of the condo looked like a hoarder's nest of plants and boxes, at least she could keep this one room clean. She scrubbed the porcelain and faucets and sloshed around water. A few of Jeff's whiskers from his morning shave washed down the drain.

On the glass shelf above the faucets, he'd left his Dopp kit, unzipped. In such a precarious place, it was asking for an accidental poke to send its contents flying to the floor. Though she had no idea how long Jeff would stay here, Anna set the kit in the drawer where he used to keep it, safely out of the way.

Strange. She'd never filled the drawer with her own belongings. For months it had sat empty, though Anna could have used the extra space. The drawer seemed like a living thing, with its own opinions and expectations. And what those came down to, the drawer might say if it could talk, was that it had been waiting for Jeff to come back.

CHAPTER 49

On the midday ferry, a few men read newspapers, and a woman with Nordstrom shopping bags watched gulls dive-bomb for fish. A mother whispered to her son as they returned from what Jeff guessed had been an orthodontist appointment. In the quiet, he missed his commuter friends' raucous card games and political discussions on their usual five-thirty ferry.

Nearly two weeks after Earnest's accident, however, Jeff still had to get back by noon so Anna could go to the bare-bones operation at her shop. As odd as a midday ferry felt, he'd willingly swim Puget Sound at midnight to live up to his part of their deal, because he wanted her to be happy.

At the condo they'd slipped into an amicable routine, and to his amazement, without discussion, they'd smoothed their wrinkles of past umbrage. They'd also evaded mention of the future council vote. But it was always there, about to cause another rift between them. Because of the future, Jeff had accepted his place on Anna's sofa as her temporary roommate—without pushing for more.

He'd be glad if the council delayed the vote for a decade. But as he leaned his head against the ferry's window, his cell rang, and the caller ID said "City of Gamble." As he answered, he said good-bye to his and Anna's pleasurable days of ignoring the vote, and hello to their inevitable split.

"Jeff Egan," he said as if he were still at work.

"I thought you'd like to know the council voted not to send your permit to the hearing examiner," Grabowski said.

"Fine." Jeff's word came out more as a sourdough lump than a Joy-to-the-World frosted sugar cookie. A month ago he'd have been ecstatic, but now all he could think of was how unhappy Anna would be.

"The council knew Naomi Blackmore had lawyers lined up and ready to go. Nobody wanted to waste money on a legal fight when she had a right to develop commercial property in a commercial zone," Grabowski said.

At last he acknowledges the zoning laws. Jeff had traveled a long and torturous route to what should have been that easy goal. "So what next?"

"Proceed as planned. You have a green light. You can start the demolition whenever you want."

"Okay."

"Our building inspector will be keeping an eye on you." *Taunt, taunt.*

On his deathbed, Grabowski would gather strength to be a jerk. "I'm sure the inspector and I will get along. My plans are up to code," Jeff said.

For the rest of the trip across the Sound, he stared out the window at distant Olympic Mountains. *Funny about success,* he thought. *You struggle to get ahead in life, but it doesn't mean much if you have no one to share it with. And when the person you'd like to share it with will hate you for it.*

Jeff was about to call Mrs. Blackmore and tell her the news, but he decided to send an e-mail. He wasn't in the mood to hear her crow about a victory that made him feel sorry.

He pressed his phone's e-mail icon and typed with two thumbs:

To: Naomi Blackmore
Re: Cedar Place
Council gave go ahead. No hearing. Will call tomorrow to discuss schedule.

And to break Anna's heart.

When Jeff walked off the ferry, he felt drained. The spring day should have warmed him, but then the weather was probably a teaser and rain would soon roll in. Nevertheless, he held up his face to the sun as he walked toward Rainier. In ten minutes he'd be at the condo to spell Anna and see Earnest, who was now gleeful about his cone liberation.

This time, as Jeff had learned from past mistakes, he would break the news to Anna himself so she wouldn't hear it from someone else. He owed her that, though he had no idea what to say or how to make her feel better. He'd been racking his brain for a way out of the mess, but nothing had come to him. Because he had to follow through and do his job, he was trapped. The council's vote marked the end of his and Anna's new friendship, and there was nothing he could do about it.

Jeff approached the intersection of Rainier and Witt's End, so named because George Witt's house, perched above the beach, was the last one on the road. Everybody laughed about that name, and tourists took selfies in front of the street sign. Next to it was another sign, yellow and black, block print: NO TURNAROUND. Once you'd started down the road, that was it.

★ ★ ★

Farther along Rainier, Jeff came to a Jones & Mulligan Realty sign that had not been up when he'd walked to the ferry that morning. From the Plexiglas box attached to the post, he pulled out a copy of the realtor's brochure. The lot was for sale. A quarter acre. Flat. One lone apple tree grew at the back in a clump of weeds next to an alley.

The lot was on the edge of the commercial district, far enough from the heart of town to keep the price affordable, but close enough that no one would think twice about walking an extra two blocks. *Hmmm. Interesting.* Jeff would keep it in mind.

He folded the brochure and slipped it into his pocket. He had to hurry. Jeff would give Earnest raw carrots and zucchini for lunch.

CHAPTER 50

Perched on stools around Plant Parenthood's counter, Anna, Joy, and Lauren arranged tiny Easter bouquets of violets and lily of the valley in vases made of eggshells, which Anna had hollowed out and dyed soft pastels. With all but her barest essentials moved to the condo, her shop was nearly empty. There was nothing left to carry home at the end of the day but the stools and a few more boxes. That would be it.

"So what are we going to do?" Because Joy had been comforting herself with cookies since the council's vote, her face looked plumper.

"There's nothing more we *can* do. It's over," Anna said.

"Isn't there somebody we can strangle?" Joy asked.

"That wouldn't help anything," Lauren said.

"It would help *me*. I'd feel better if I could strangle Mrs. Scroogemore," Joy grumbled.

"Anger doesn't do any good. It's not worth it," Anna said. Look what it had done to her and Jeff, and how hard it had made life for Earnest.

Lauren, in a long flowered skirt and velveteen matador's jacket, sorted through violets. "This fight's worn me out."

"I've still got plenty of venom to spread around," Joy said.

"Save it for John and Penelope. They're going to need it if they have to fight their way back to England," Anna said.

"He hasn't escaped from the salt mine yet, and then he has to find her. It's going to take a while," Joy said.

"You haven't written much lately." Lauren set her elbows on the counter and rested her chin on her palms.

"As you both know, we've had other things going—not that preparing for the council meeting did us any good," Joy said.

"We gave it our best shot. We can't ask more from ourselves than that," Lauren said.

"But we lost," Joy said.

"Lost" seemed to echo around the room and bounce off the walls.

That was how Anna felt: lost. Later today she would put daffodils and tulips in Easter bunny vases for April Pringle and Peggy LeClerc, and chocolate eggs into a bird's nest she'd found in the woods for Tommy, who'd given Igor a new home. The gifts would mark the end of Anna's floral career in Grammy's house. Her work and history here would be over.

Also over was her peaceful interlude with Jeff, who'd tried hard to cushion the blow of the council's vote. He'd moved back to his apartment supposedly because Earnest could now be left at home alone—but Jeff had probably also thought that the sight of him was salt in Anna's wound. Now the condo felt like it was missing something, and Earnest had gone into a funk. Easter was supposed to be about rebirth, but in Anna's air hung death by stoicism.

She pulled tiny heart-shaped leaves off a violet's stem. "This morning I looked on craigslist for another place to rent. There's nothing."

"Something has to come up sometime. We'll find a way to stay together," Lauren said.

"I wish we could find another old house," Anna said.

Joy worked a lily of the valley into her bouquet. "Damned Mrs. Scroogemore. And Jeff."

"He meant well. I believe that now," Anna said. "He tried to get us into a warehouse, but it won't be vacant for a few more months."

"He's still right up there with the Twit, as far as I'm concerned," Joy said.

"No, the Twit was cruel. Jeff may have hurt me, but he didn't intend to." Anna fluffed up her tiny bouquet and started a new one in another eggshell.

As Anna climbed upstairs, she felt as if she were dragging her heart behind her on a string. Tattered, bruised, and heavy with sadness, her heart bumped on each step. When she reached the turret, she closed the door and wished that Earnest were here, but he had to stay confined in the condo kitchen for another week. She'd brought home his faux oriental rug and her white wicker rocker, so the turret was as spare as a monk's cell.

With a sigh, she sat on the floor and leaned against the wall. The peace she always felt here evaded her. *Dear house,* she said in her mind, *I've lost you. A bulldozer is going to destroy you in a few days, and there's no more I can do. I've tried hard to save you, but I've let you down.*

I'm just bricks and boards, the house replied. *You can picture me in your memory. That'll be enough.*

Grammy and I won't be connected anymore, Anna replied.

Piffle! Grammy jumped into the conversation. *Girl, I'm not going anywhere. Don't you know that love is eternal? We'll always love each other. Stop being glum.*

I've lost my shop. I can't find a place to rent, Anna said.

Just wait. Good things come with time, Grammy said. *Hope for the best and expect even more.*

Right, Anna thought with suspicion. But then, she remembered the love in her nearly full glass. It was a good thing that had come with time. Also, Earnest was healing, and she and Jeff didn't hate each other anymore.

Go out there and meet your beautiful life like that butterfly did. Remember? Grammy asked.

Anna closed her eyes and pictured the butterfly's empty chrysalis on the windowsill and the flap of her glorious wings as she'd crossed the lawn. Instead of begrudging her fight to free herself, she'd gone out to greet her fate. It had been waiting for her, full of hope.

Grammy urged, *Don't hold back! Let go! Enjoy!*

Till what would have been closing time if Anna still had her shop, she pulled her knees to her chest, looked out at Gamble's roofs, and thought about Grammy, the house, and the butterfly. Its joyful swoop across the lawn had been a kind of Easter—a pupa's rebirth in a new form. Slowly, it occurred to Anna that maybe rebirth was going on every minute, everywhere, and, like fights, it was a fact of life. Phoenixes rose, reborn, from ash heaps. In a burst of renewal, daffodils rose from the earth every spring. New ideas sprang from old tired ones. Maybe Anna herself could rise above the spirit-crushing disappointment of losing the house, and, as Grammy had suggested, go out to meet her own beautiful life.

That's my girl, Grammy intruded in Anna's mind.

As Anna smiled to herself, Joy shouted from downstairs. "Anna, you've been gone so long. Are you alive up there?"

Yes, Anna was alive. Very alive. She untied her heart from the string she'd been dragging it by, and she put it in her chest again. With a lighter step, she went downstairs. She had bouquets to finish. There would always be more bouquets. They, too, were a fact of life.

CHAPTER 51

———— ✦ ————

Jeff had never been to Naomi Blackmore's house. As she hung his raincoat in her entry closet and he glanced down the hall to her living room, he couldn't say he'd ever want to come back.

He'd have expected a modicum of taste from a wealthy woman, and he had to hand it to her: She'd not painted her walls hot pink. But as he followed her into the living room, he cringed at the moose head over her fireplace, the deer antlers in her chandelier, the cheetah skin on her thick white carpet, and the grizzly's claws holding up the copper ashtray on her coffee table. Her trophies belonged in a hunting lodge, not coupled with floral chintz slipcovers and ruffled pillows.

It's a good thing she's never met Earnest, or his head might be up there with the moose. Jeff noted that the moose looked like Mick Jagger.

Jeff was not squeamish, but he'd never seen the point of killing innocent wildlife for sport. When Mrs. Blackmore picked up her gold cigarette case from the mantel, it occurred to Jeff that maybe *she* belonged on the wall, and the moose should be lighting up a cigarette and blowing smoke around the room. If life were fair, the moose would be nibbling grass around the gazebo on her lawn, which rolled down to the beach. But life wasn't fair, as Jeff well knew. Animals and people got screwed every day, though he did believe that life usually met their needs.

"Are you the hunter?" he asked.

"You bet. Bagged them all over the world," Mrs. Blackmore said. "Now we hunt from a helicopter. Makes it easier."

"Indeed."

"I'll show you my zebra when you leave. He's in the den."

"Can't wait," Jeff said through lying teeth. He'd do whatever it took to butter her up before he sprang his question on her, the purpose of his visit.

He spotted a gold lighter on her coffee table and got up from the sofa. "Here, let me do that for you." Shamelessly gallant, he held the flame to her cigarette as she puffed—and he held his breath to stave off a coughing fit.

"How did you celebrate the city council's vote?" he asked.

"Dinner with friends at my club. They couldn't believe those ridiculous girls trying to stop my project. Who do they think they are?"

"They are ridiculous," Jeff agreed, amiable as a favorite uncle. "I thought of a way you can get back at them."

"Oh?" The downturned ends of Mrs. Blackmore's mouth turned up.

"I've heard they wanted to buy your house. You could sell it to them for a dollar and let them move it somewhere," Jeff said.

"Why would I ever do something like that for those damned girls?"

"Because you'd saddle them with a house that's falling apart. They'd spend years trying to keep it together. Think of all their hard work!" Jeff forced a conspiratorial grin.

"Here's even better. Think of saving yourself the demolition cost! Eventually those women will have to admit the house is hopeless, and they'll have to pay to tear it down themselves. Add it all up. The price of moving the house, trying to renovate it, and finally demolishing it." Jeff held up three fingers. "You'd be condemning those women to huge expenses and years of trouble."

Mrs. Blackmore's face brightened. "You're brilliant, Jeff!"

"Have you ever seen *The Money Pit*? It's old, but you can get it on Netflix," he said.

"Yes, *The Money Pit*! That's what those girls will have. How thrilling!" When Mrs. Blackmore clasped her hands together, her long platinum nails would have given the grizzly's claws a run for their money.

"So you like my idea?" Jeff asked.

"It's fantastic! Nothing like retribution."

"Absolutely! Retribution!" Jeff agreed. *And* she *is the recipient!*

He told himself to tone down his relish. If she realized how sly a fox he was being, she'd shoot him and hang him up with the moose.

CHAPTER 52

The afternoon sun shone down like it was smiling light, and in the apple tree, birds belted out songs. Squirrels, nimble as Mikhail Baryshnikov, leapt across the roof of Grammy's house. A breeze whispered from the harbor and cooled Jeff and Anna's foreheads as they dug in the new garden—and as Earnest lay beside them in his library lion position.

In the last weeks, he'd witnessed major changes. Movers had jacked up the house, set it on a trailer, and driven it down Rainier to a new address. Volunteers had cleared the lot and carved out paths and flowerbeds. Inside the house, Anna, Joy, and Lauren had been cleaning and organizing their new shops. And everyone had been happy, especially Earnest's two most special people, for whom he'd clearly rejoiced to see living together again in the condo.

Now as he sunned himself, the intense expression on his face suggested that he was busy thinking. Perhaps he was pondering his life before the recent changes, sorting through memories, and deciding which to discard or keep. He might have tossed out smoke inhalation, Mad Dog Horowitz, Tiffany the tumor princess, the drafting table leg, the damnable pickup truck that hit him, and that satanic plastic cone. But Earnest would definitely save in his heart forever steak, blackberries,

Parmesan cheese, people crackers, and Granny Smith apples. He'd keep power naps, peewee soccer games, the Christmas boat parade, the library's reading program, his wizard hat on gotcha days, and his vile but beloved ball.

As a highly sensitive and intelligent dog, Earnest could separate wheat from chaff, and he would treasure what pleased him. Especially Anna and Jeff. He would never forget Anna's lipstick hearts on his forehead and Jeff's tireless tugs on Monty, Earnest's once-stuffed rabbit.

Anna and Jeff lugged the last flagstone that had been piled in the yard and set it in its proper place at the bottom of the front porch steps. Laying their new path from the street to the house had been like fitting together pieces of a jigsaw puzzle, and the stones now depended on each other for a harmonious effect. If one were removed, the empty spot would jar the whole—just as taking Anna, Jeff, or Earnest from the family they'd become again would ruin it for all of them. When they rarely mentioned their months apart, they called it their "winter break" and changed the subject.

Now Anna and Jeff would finish the path by filling dirt between the stones and planting creeping mint—and then customers could find their way to the front door without slogging through mud. April Pringle had persuaded the Gamble Island Rhododendron Society to plant free rhodies, camellias, and azaleas in beds around the house, and Mr. Webster had donated a small madrona tree to replace the heritage one that had been lost. Once Anna and Jeff had time to seed the lawn and put in Grammy's plants that Anna had saved, the new yard, though smaller than the one they'd left, would be as beautiful.

Jeff stood up, offered Anna his hand, and pulled her to her feet. He put his arm around her shoulders and led her down the path to Lauren's poetry post and the picket fence, which they'd moved here with the house. When they turned around to look at it, Anna couldn't help but smile. The fight to save it had receded to a wisp of memory. The house standing on the lot Jeff found had erased the conflict.

The house looked dignified and proud, a dowager who'd seen plenty in her time, including a recent war between two perfectly good people, and a move from the property she'd graced for one-hundred-and-thirty-five years. She'd survived it all, and now she'd finally found an excellent resting place. Though a little of her paint was peeling and a few of her steps were uneven, she commanded respect.

Her gingerbread was intact, and her front porch offered respite from a busy world. Her old wavy-glass windows reminded that world of an earlier age. Anna had planted lobelia, nasturtiums, and geraniums in the window boxes so the house boasted color, like jewels. The lion's puzzled face embossed on her front doorknob suggested that the world was a perplexing place, but the bear's-tongue doorbell reminded everyone to laugh.

"The house looks good, don't you think?" Jeff asked.

"She got through the move like a trooper," Anna said.

"I like our flagstones better than the concrete sidewalk that went to her before. It fits her better," Jeff said.

Anna could tell from his use of "her" that he got it. Grammy's house was not an "it"—she was a "she." Though made of wood and glass and bricks, she was like a living thing with a body and soul. For many more years, she would offer shelter as Grammy had. Grammy would live on in her, and from her turret windows, she'd wink at the world.

From the street, Anna could see through an upstairs window into Lauren's hair styling studio and used bookstore, which in a couple of weeks would reopen, along with Plant Parenthood and Joy's Gift Shop. Lauren was rolling buttery yellow paint on a wall, and Joy was brushing antique white onto the interior trim. Soon nobody would suspect there had ever been a fire.

Jeff had shocked Anna, Lauren, and Joy with news of Mrs. Scroogemore's offer to sell them the house for a dollar. He'd insisted on meeting her to pay it himself so Joy wouldn't have a chance to strangle her, and he'd told the three women that they each owed him thirty-three-and-a-third cents. His co-coach and attorney, Alan Biggs, had drawn up the papers for the sale pro bono, and Anna, Lauren, and Joy had pitched in their savings to buy the lot.

After Jeff arranged for the house mover, Joy quit comparing him to the Twit, and in *Wild Savage Love* she named a helpful British sailor "Geoffrey" after Jeff. Anna said that getting the house went way beyond too-good-to-be-true. It traveled to the realm of beyond-your-wildest-dreams.

What also went beyond Anna's wildest dreams was the love that had been poured into the house the last few weeks. Besides April Pringle, Mr. Webster, and Alan Biggs's help, others in the community had offered support. On work Saturdays, like today, Peggy LeClerc brought over complimentary sandwiches for lunch from the Chat 'n' Chew, and one afternoon Ted Carcionni stopped by with a new shiny red fire extinguisher. David Connolly, the Elder Hunk, arranged for a ten percent discount on renovation supplies at Chuck's Hardware, and that had lowered the materials' cost when Jeff had rewired the house. Dr. Nilsen presented Earnest with a doghouse won in an auction raffle, and he and Jeff set it on a brick foundation by the back door.

On moving day, Lloyd McGregor had stationed himself and his bagpipes in front of the lot, and, as the house arrived, had played "Amazing Grace." The move really was an amazing grace, Mayor Maksimov pointed out to Anna. "Gamble was divided about this house, but now everybody's happy. The people hell-bent on progress will have Cedar Place, and you and your friends saved history. No one will forget the past."

Now Anna embraced the past, present, and future. She'd

decided that they were equally important because they were all part of the eternal flow of time. The good and bad of the past had formed her, and in the present she experienced the now. The future—well, Anna intended to swoop toward it like the butterfly had swooped across the lawn to greet her destiny. As the past, present, and future flowed into each other and blended together, Anna would hope for the best and expect even more.

At the end of their new stone path, Jeff took Anna into his arms and kissed her. In their past was happiness and misery, about like everybody else on earth, and in their present was a real, as opposed to a floral, smooch. In their future would be a wedding and children, to whom they'd resolved to be conscientious parents. And, of course, in their past, present, *and* future was Earnest.

He could not sit by and watch the two people he loved most in a clinch like that without expressing his opinion, which, like many dogs, had to do with joy. He rose to his paws, and, on his healing leg, he barely limped around Anna and Jeff, like he was drawing a magic circle that they could never step out of again. In that circle was the present moment, which Earnest seemed to know—as well as Grammy ever had—was a gift everyone was meant to enjoy. And in his circle, with that gift of the present moment, lived love.

ACKNOWLEDGMENTS

I could never have written *Earnest* without the kindness and support of special people, to whom I owe sincere thanks.

First, my agent, Cullen Stanley, and my editor, Michaela Hamilton, stood behind me from conception to completion. Their presence made all the difference in my work. Steven Zacharius, my publisher, buoyed my spirit each time we met. Kristine Mills Noble again designed a beautiful cover. With grace, Karen Auerbach oversaw promotion, and Paula Reedy, production. Vida Engstrand's and Alexandra Nicolajsen's hard work and dedication were huge gifts.

When I needed expertise, generous people answered my calls for help. Kirkham Johns escorted me through the world of mediation. Jane Allan shared her knowledge of city planning. Fritz Jorg answered my questions about insurance, Luke Carpenter explained fighting fires, and Bill McClain was my soccer consultant. Janice Hill and Rachel Strohlmeyer, DVM, opened their big hearts and talked with me about Earnest's vet care. And Diane O'Connell contributed editorial wisdom that strengthened the story.

Almost everyone I consulted was a dog lover, but most especially my neighbors, Paul and Peggy Zuckerman, who talked with me about Maggie, their yellow Lab. Much of her now resides in Earnest, such as his lust for blackberries and his propensity to sprawl on his back in his flasher position. Paul's devotion to Maggie is everywhere in the book.

Other friends were there for me in one wonderful way or another: Jimmy Wolf, Debby Harrison, Linda Anthony, Wendy

Hubbert, Marielle Snyder, Patty Johns, Natalia Ilyin, Kathy Renner, Gisele Fitch, Suzanne Kerr, Julie Valentine, Alexandra Kovatz, Darryl Beckman, Clell Bryant, and David Sackeroff. I can't imagine writing—or living—without them.

Finally, I am blessed with family who shored me up while I wrote *Earnest*. My niece and dear friend, Lonnie Matheron, was my personal poet laureate and the contributor to Lauren's poetry post. Bridget, my loyal German shepherd, kept me company in my office and provided constant support. And, most of all, John, my beloved husband, kept me going through months of work. I always say that I could never write a word without him, and that's the truth.

EARNEST

Kristin von Kreisler

ABOUT THIS GUIDE

The following discussion questions are included
to enhance your group's reading of *Earnest*.

DISCUSSION QUESTIONS

1. Are Earnest, Anna, and Jeff all earnest? Do you think they equally show sincere conviction and try to do the right thing? What stands in their way? How do they overcome it?

2. What part does time play in the story? Why is the present so important? And why does history matter? What influence does the past have on Anna, Jeff, and Earnest? How might it impact their future?

3. Does the house seem like a character in the story? Does it have a life of its own? Does it change and develop? How does the house remind you that the past, present, and future are all part of each other, as April Pringle says?

4. What lessons does the butterfly teach? How do they apply to Anna, Jeff, and Earnest?

5. As individuals, do Anna, Jeff, and Earnest handle hardship well? How does it make them grow?

6. Why is Gamble central to the story? Does the name have special meaning? Does the small town affect Anna and Jeff? Is the community important?

7. How do Anna and Jeff respond to the various holidays? Do their responses reveal their character?

8. Did you mind that Jeff signed up on Northwest Singles.com? Is he right or wrong to want to date again? Are you glad when he gets thwarted? Why or why not?

9. Did you find yourself taking sides with Anna or Jeff? Did your sympathies change as the story unfolded? Did you feel they were equally to blame for the breakup, or was one more responsible than the other?

10. How did you feel about Mad Dog Horowitz, Lincoln Purcell, and the mediation? Did you think that Anna or Jeff should have gotten custody of Earnest, or should they have shared him?

11. What role do flowers play in the story—both in Plant Parenthood and in the house's garden? How is the New Dawn rose's name and history significant?

12. At the end of the story, are Jeff and Anna very different people from how they were at the beginning? How have they changed? What specific factors brought about the change? Did Earnest change too?

Kristin von Kreisler will be happy to meet with your reading group by Skype, or in person if you're in the Seattle area. Contact her at www.kristinvonkreisler.com